Praise for

Nooks & Crannies

★ "Original, engaging, and funny."
—*School Library Journal*, starred review

★ "A compelling puzzle, vividly drawn characters, and a clever and capable young detective."
—*Booklist*, starred review

★"Well thought-out and deftly executed."
–*Publishers Weekly*, starred review

"Readers will delight in the unexpected twists and turns at every junction."
—*BookPage*

"[A] swell mystery."
—*Kirkus Reviews*

Praise for

The Actual & Truthful Adventures of Becky Thatcher

★ "A delightfully clever debut."
— *Publishers Weekly*, starred review

"Delightful."
—*Kirkus Reviews*

"The deliciously impetuous, devilishly clever, and uncommonly brave Becky Thatcher is now one of my all-time favorite heroines, and I'm desperate to follow her on more adventures. Captivating, exciting, and great barrels-full of fun, this is a book to adore."
— Anne Ursu, author of *The Real Boy* and *Breadcrumbs*

"Lawson provides an ingenious tale purporting to reveal Twain's characters for who they really were."
—*Center for Fiction*

Also by Jessica Lawson

The Actual & Truthful Adventures of Becky Thatcher

Waiting for Augusta

Jessica Lawson

Illustrated by Natalie Andrewson

Simon & Schuster Books for Young Readers
New York London Toronto Sydney New Delhi

SIMON & SCHUSTER BOOKS FOR YOUNG READERS
An imprint of Simon & Schuster Children's Publishing Division
1230 Avenue of the Americas, New York, New York 10020

Also available in a Simon & Schuster Books for Young Readers hardcover edition
Book design by Lucy Ruth Cummins
The text for this book was set in Bembo Std.
Manufactured in the United States of America
0416 OFF
First Simon & Schuster Books for Young Readers paperback edition May 2016
10 9 8 7 6 5 4 3 2 1
The Library of Congress has cataloged the hardcover edition as follows:
Nooks & crannies / Jessica Lawson.
pages cm
Summary: Eleven-year-old Tabitha Crum, whose parents were just about to abandon her, is invited to the country estate of a wealthy countess along with five other children and told that one of them will become her heir.
ISBN 978-1-4814-1921-5 (hc)
[1. Inheritance and succession—Fiction. 2. Aristocracy (Social class)—Fiction. 3. Identity—Fiction. 4. Twins—Fiction. 5. Great Britain—History—Edward VII, 1901-1910—Fiction. 6. Mystery and detective stories.] I. Title. II. Title: Nooks and crannies.
PZ7.L438267Noo 2015
[Fic]—dc23
2014023223
ISBN 978-1-4814-1922-2 (pbk)
ISBN 978-1-4814-1923-9 (eBook)

For Christopher Mallory Lawson,

who loves old houses

There are only three motives for all crimes, Tibbs: money, power, and love. Sometimes those things get muddled together, of course, and you could argue that hunger is a bloody good motivator as well, but one might lump that in with love of self or love of others or love of food, and—well, never mind all that. Pass the pickled radishes.

—Inspector Percival Pensive,
The Case of the Gilded Guardian

The Times

EXCLUSIVE REVEAL OF WINDERMERE SIX

Thanks to an anonymous source, the *Times* is pleased to share an exclusive list of the six children who were transported yesterday evening to Hollingsworth Hall, the magnificent and secluded home of Camilla Lenore DeMoss, the Countess of Windermere. They are, in no particular order:

OLIVER APPLEBY

Heir to the Appleby Jewelry fortune, this young chap is known to be an excellent student who also excels at rowing and cricket.

VIOLA DALE

The Dales are well known throughout London for their dedication to social reform and relief for those in distress. Young Viola has been a presence on the charitable event circuit since the age of two.

FRANCES WELLINGTON

Miss Wellington's parents are internationally known art collectors who have an impeccable eye for up-and-coming talent in sculpture and painting. They also delve into gems of historical value. Frances is privately tutored, and her deliciously expensive introduction to London society is already being buzzed about.

BARNABY TRUNDLE

Young Barnaby attends school in South London. His father works in the textile industry. One of his teachers says Barnaby is "occasionally quick-tempered with other boys in his form."

EDWARD HERRINGBONE

The Herringbones are close acquaintances with the aforementioned Dales, their own admirable interests lying mainly in reducing poverty by increasing educational opportunities. Edward has been called "an indubitable library of a boy" by one of his teaching masters at St. Stephen's.

TABITHA CRUM

Miss Crum's father is employed by the Wilting Bank of South London. A neighbor of the family says that the lucky child "talks to herself" and calls the Crums "socially famished."

The *Times* will be following this story with all due fortitude, and will be devoutly providing England with further reports as trustworthy divulgences become available.

Nooks & Crannies

1

Remember, my dear Mr. Tibbs, that mysterious circumstances frequently begin with an arrival: Unexpected letters or visitors or poisoned meat pasties are often indications that one will soon be forced into mental and/or physical strain.

—Inspector Percival Pensive,
The Case of the Petulant Postman

Just past three o'clock in the afternoon, when schools across London were releasing much-adored children by the bucketful, Tabitha Crum was ushered into the cold as well. She tarried at the edge of St. John's gate, threading an arm through the bars and observing the world for a moment, ignoring the jostling of boys and girls who seemed in such a hurry to return to the places they belonged. "Today," she whispered to a small lump in her satchel pocket, "we find ourselves in a curious situation, sir." Slipping an envelope from her bag, she lightly tapped it against the obtrusion. "Off we go."

The cobblestone streets in the village of Wilting were made

eerie and muted by thick November fog, and clip-clopping carriage horses snorted up and down the road, emerging and disappearing into the mist. *Almost like ghosts,* Tabitha mused. She clutched and rubbed the pretty envelope, letting one fingernail linger along the seam. The hand-delivery messenger had passed two letters to the teacher, glaring severely and emphasizing three times that they were *not* to be opened, but given to the parents of the children. What she and beastly Barnaby Trundle had done to deserve the elegant envelopes was unknown. The only certainty was that the glue was of a stubbornly good quality and Tabitha's nails were of a woefully short length.

"It's as though they've sealed it together with spite," Tabitha muttered to the pocket lump, earning an offended glance from a passing elderly lady. Whether it was the muttering, the remark itself, her outgrown uniform, her worn grayish schoolbag that resembled a mangy rabbit, or a combination, Tabitha couldn't be sure. Perhaps the woman was offended by children as a whole, rather like her mum and dad.

Licking chapped lips as she passed the corner bakery with its beckoning aromas, Tabitha felt a stirring in her belly unrelated to having eaten only broken crackers and cheese rind for lunch. Ludicrous or not, it was impossible to ignore the tiniest possibility that the envelope might contain . . . a small bit of light. Hands shaking from chill and an unfamiliar amount of prospect, she lifted the paper to her nose and took a long sniff. It smelled faintly of flowers.

A summons from Scotland Yard to become an Inspector-In-Training.

An invitation from King Edward to attend and gamble on a horse race.

Notification from a long-lost relative who actually wants me and wouldn't view me as an imposition.

"What's that, Pemberley?" Tabitha whispered to the lump, which was now squirming and fretting about. Mouse whiskers poked out, followed by a mouse face. "I don't know how you manage to read my mind, but I suppose that's what best friends do. And yes, those are all unlikely scenarios, but it's nicer to imagine such things than to rip into the paper and find an advertisement for tooth powder or elocution lessons, isn't it?"

Not caring to dwell on the possibility of such disappointing contents, Tabitha was grateful when a distracting bellow sounded behind her. Oddly enough, the bellower seemed to be calling her name from the street. Before she could turn, a familiar bicyclist veered close to the curb and sprayed Tabitha with filthy water left by a midday storm.

"Your invitation is bound to be a mistake. There's no way she'll let *you* in!" yelled a horrid voice.

Wafting alongside the insult were the scents of burned toast and rotting cinnamon. There was only one boy at St. John's who wore such pungent odors. Sure enough, she turned to see Barnaby Trundle pedaling a slow circle in the road.

"Best to stay home, Drabby Tabby! I've heard the place is haunted and the spirits are hungry for filthy, ratty girls like you." Barnaby stuck his tongue out as far as it could go.

Tabitha wiped a muddy water streak from her face and flushed, both at the insult and the realization that he had opened his envelope and she had no idea what he was referring to. She thought of exactly seven things that she would like to do to her classmate, one involving a rather nasty collision with a refuse wagon.

Barnaby took one hand off the handlebars to send her a mocking wave before smoothing his reddish locks and disappearing around a corner.

Squeak!

Tabitha pulled Pemberley from the satchel pocket. "Nice and dry, are you? It was clever to tuck yourself away like that." She nodded seriously. "And yes, Pemberley, you're right. I should have defended us."

Squeak?

"Oh, I don't know, something like, 'Believe me, Barnaby Trundle, I won't be staying home. I rather think *you* should, though. I've heard most spirits have a fondness for repulsive boys with no manners and an excess of their father's hair crème. And an obscene amount of completely unnecessary aftershave. Any ghosts will smell *you* out in a minute.'" She let Pemberley sniff her hand for crumbs, run up her sleeve, and burrow under her shirt collar. "It's a shame I'm not just a bit bolder, isn't it? One day you and I shall make good on a bit of mischief."

Even soaked and unavenged as she was, a flutter of excitement warmed its way up Tabitha's back and neck, tickling the tips of her ears. *So, he's opened his.* And according to Barnaby, her envelope was a mistake. Based on the boy's despicable nature, his claim must mean that the contents were sure to be something quite good. *(Well done, Inspector Crum.)*

Tabitha put a pencil in her mouth as she walked along. Instead of reading through reports at the Scotland Yard office of the Metropolitan Police Service, Inspector Percival Pensive always did his deducing in a corner booth of his favorite pub, puffing a pipe or chewing pensively on his pocket watch chain. Neither pipe nor pocket watch was practical for an inspector of her youth and means, and so Tabitha made do with pencils. "Now, Pemberley," she whispered, "what could it be? Let's review the clues. Barnaby said to stay home, so that would make it an invitation to go somewhere. . . ."

Squeak.

"Yes, yes, a place owned by a woman . . . haunted, he said, though that bit was clearly rubbish." It would be easy enough to find out more. There was a moment, one brief moment, where the act of disobedience hung in the air like a buttered crumpet, waiting to be fetched and gobbled up. Tabitha's hand lifted as though of its own accord, and her free fingers rose to meet the envelope's edge. Carefully, deliciously, she held her breath and began a tiny tear at the corner.

And stopped.

She dropped both hands, holding the note to her side as she continued toward her home. *Tabitha Crum,* she scolded herself, *they'll never grow to love you if you can't even follow a clear and simple rule, especially one that was emphasized three times and accentuated with a glare.* A second voice, that of her mother, snuck in to repeat the answer to a much younger Tabitha's question. *You want us to love you, is that right? Love, Tabitha Crum, is to be earned, not given away to just anyone like a festering case of fleas.*

She'd been seven when her mother had made the comparison of love and irritable itching. Tabitha remembered the statement quite well because it was the same year children at school had suddenly gotten it in their heads that she had a case of head lice. That had been a difficult time and nobody had gotten close to Tabitha since. Of course, with the addition of a pet mouse over the last year, her lack of friendship could perhaps be further explained by the misapprehension that she spoke to herself. Pemberley was a most excellent consultant in all matters, but he tended to stay out of sight, so Tabitha could somewhat understand the slanderous comments.

Or it might have been the unfortunate, uneven, unattractive, blunt-scissored haircut her mother was so fond of giving her.

Or it could have been the simple truth that making friends can be an awkward and a difficult thing when it's a one-sided endeavor and you've a pet mouse and you've been painted as odd and quiet and shy, when really you're just a bit misunderstood.

In any case, nobody at St. John's seemed lacking for companionship except her. But Tabitha reminded herself that there were far worse things than not having friends. In fact, she often made a game of listing far worse things:

- eating the contents of a sneeze
- creatures crawling into her ear holes

- losing a body part (Though that one was debatable, depending on the part. An ear or small toe might be worth a friend or two.)

While Tabitha stopped to stare at fresh scones piled in the window of Puddles Tea & Confectionery and speculated whether the envelope's contents would outdo last year's Christmas box of used tights, two passing men knocked her to the ground, as though she wasn't worth moving for.

"Two more are floating around somewhere!" one of them said, stabbing a finger at his newspaper and not noticing her in the slightest. "It's simply *unfathomable*. After all this time? That place has got to be like heaven above! Gilded soaking tubs and secret rooms filled with money and the like. And to ask *children*, of all people. I say, Rupert, life is simply beyond unfair. . . ."

Tabitha picked herself up, slightly rattled. She sighed at the careless bumpers and at the memory of Barnaby Trundle's last words. Under normal, unsprayed circumstances she wasn't filthy, but she was skinny and knobby-kneed and wearing a uniform far too small for someone who'd grown several inches in the last six months. And apparently those elements combined to make her the sort of person who was prone to being callously clipped down without notice or apology.

"Oh, Pemberley," she said aloud, rounding the final corner before reaching her home and tugging on the end bits of her hair, wishing *it* would grow several inches, "if only life were like a book, and I could choose precisely what part I played." She ignored the puzzled glance from her neighbor, Mrs. Dullingham, who was leaning out of her door to fetch a grocery delivery. "If only the envelope contained a—"

And at precisely half past three, Tabitha stopped musing and walking, having spotted a curious sight outside her modest brown brick home: her father's briefcase, her parents' traveling trunks, and a jewelry case crowded together at the front entrance.

None of her things were among the pile.

2

The trouble with disagreeable people, Tibbs,
is that the majority of them seem to be either
one's direct relations or part of one's daily job.
Present company excluded, of course.
—Inspector Percival Pensive,
The Case of the Haughty Housemaid

Tabitha opened the door. "Hullo," she called. "I'm home." Mr. Tickles was the only one immediately visible, and he didn't bother to acknowledge her entrance or presence with so much as a meow or yawn. Even so, Tabitha found him to be the most agreeable member of the household. He was lazy and well fed enough to cuddle in her lap on occasion, and though he sometimes seemed to smirk in the manner of a favored sibling, Mr. Tickles left Pemberley alone and had a lovely purr.

She sidestepped a box full of new blue-and-white-swirled teacups and saucers. As far as Tabitha knew, the whole of her mum's existence was divided between eavesdropping on wealthy women at shops, buying things at shops in front of wealthy women, returning things to shops when the wealthy women were not around, and taking finishing classes. *There's nothing more desperately wretched than being stuck firmly in the middle class,* she often told Tabitha.

Peeking into the kitchen, she saw that her mother had done the weekly food shopping: ingredients for Tabitha to make a standard (and very boring) hash, wilty vegetables, a round of cheese, tinned ham, and a small settlement of cheap candies. Tabitha snatched a licorice whip from the pile for Pemberley's sweet tooth and placed her satchel in the wooden bin labeled TABITHA'S THINGS—DON'T GO LEAVING THEM ANYWHERE ELSE OR YOU'LL GET DISH DUTY. Mrs. Crum didn't allow clutter in the first-floor living area, on the off chance an important guest might drop by. It was a pointless note, as she had little to clutter with and she did the washing up every evening regardless of her things. And the only one who Tabitha had ever seen drop by was Mrs. Dullingham, who was looking to borrow an egg or two.

"Hullo? Mum? Daddy? Are you both well? Why are all of your things piled at the—"

"Tabitha!" Mrs. Crum screeched from upstairs. "Get up here and don't you touch those teacups, for goodness' sake! That Sapphire Delight pattern is the height of fashion! I heard Mrs. Davies-Hildebrande herself say so just the other day."

"Yes, Mother." Making sure Pemberley was firmly under her collar flap, Tabitha climbed the narrow set of wooden stairs and stood in the bedroom's doorway, watching her parents. She stared at the unusual packing going on, momentarily disregarding the envelope.

Her mother stood in front of a mirrored bureau, plucking items from another jewelry case. Some pieces were thrown on the floor in disgust and others were stuffed into a deep-blue bag of velveteen. Shoes and hosiery were flung everywhere, and pieces of white paper lay strewn across a small desk in the corner, spilling over to the floor.

Mr. Crum scowled. "What is she doing home already? Was she sick again?"

"I'm never sick, Daddy," said Tabitha. *And if I am, Mum makes me go to school anyway.*

"Oh?" Mr. Crum raised a thick eyebrow. "Then why don't you eat the liverwurst I leave on your plate each Sunday?"

Tabitha considered the question. "That's Mr. Tickles you give the liverwurst to, Daddy. Not me."

"Ungrateful, either way," he muttered back. Mr. Crum stopped struggling with a suitcase's fasteners and studied Tabitha. "Your mother and I have something to discuss with you. *Do* move your spindly little legs and get in here. We're in a bit of a hurry." He yanked on his pocket watch. "The hansom cab should be here at four o'clock."

"Are we going somewhere?" The winter break wasn't for another three weeks. Tabitha bent to examine a fallen pin. "This is pretty."

Mrs. Crum bumped Tabitha to the floor with her hip. "What have you got there? What are you taking?" Her angry eyes relaxed when she saw the small brass bird in Tabitha's hand. In a rare moment of charity, instead of administering a shrewish lecture, she nodded her head and patted Tabitha's shoulder.

"You can keep that ugly thing," Mrs. Crum said. "I'd completely forgotten I still had it. The only thing I remember is that the bird is called a bittern. It's bad luck to carry bitterness around, that's what I say, but I daresay it suits you. Pins are so out of fashion these days—all the store ladies say so." She moved back across the room, trying on a feathered hat. "And *you're* not going anywhere," her mother said, peering out the window. "Your father and I have decided to travel. We've been terribly full of stress lately, and a holiday will be just what we need. You'll be staying at Augustus Home. It's been arranged."

"Augustus Home? But that's an orphanage." It was, in fact, the orphanage directly across from her school, St. John's. Drab and grayish-brownish and full of peculiar-shaped windows, the Home leaned to one side and loomed into the street. "How long will you be gone?"

"A year. There's been a misunderstanding at the bank. We're getting a bit of distance."

"A year!"

Mr. Crum jerked toward her so quickly that his toupee shifted. It was time to reapply his hair glue. "Yes, a *year*. Maybe longer. I told your mother you were old enough to stay home alone. You must be nine or ten by now."

"Nearly twelve, Daddy. What about Mr. Tickles?" For a moment, Tabitha hoped that he would be coming with her to the Home.

Mr. Crum stepped over to the window, peering out. "Mr.

Tickles is coming with us, of course. Listen to me. Your mother has insisted we leave you with someone, and the only place that would have you is Augustus Home. They need extra kitchen help during the days and evenings. We told them you would do nicely."

"Day and evening work? But what about school?" she asked, jumping out of her mother's way.

Bending over with a grunt, Mrs. Crum seized the final scarf from her bottom dresser drawer. "You've been taken out. As of today, actually. Oh, Tabitha, please don't look at me that way. It's for the best. You'll build character at the orphanage, and I've arranged for you to have every third Thursday off from duties. *You're welcome* for that. Besides, nobody likes a spoiled child. Lady Worthington-Silva was quoted as saying that just the other day. Apparently some horrid urchin tried to beg money from her."

Despite Tabitha's best efforts, a surge of something hot and painful flowed from her chest to her stomach to her toes and back up. She blinked furiously and took a step toward her mother. "I don't understand." She shut her eyes tightly for a moment, trying to halt any naughty tears of shock from spilling out. Emotion of any kind upset her parents, and at home she had trained herself to be *un*spoken rather than *out*spoken, but it was hard not to protest this. Everyone would know she'd been abandoned, which was many times worse than simply being a daughter of unloving, neglectful parents.

Being permanently rejected by those who were supposed to hold her dear was, in fact, on her list of *far worse things*, though she may not have admitted that particular item to herself.

"What have I done?"

"Oh, *stop*. The orphanage is the perfect place for you. We won't have to pay a thing," Mr. Crum bragged. "That's after *three* letters on your mother's part, so do try to be grateful."

Mrs. Crum patted her hair in agreement. "Speaking of letters, I need to write one to cancel my finishing class. Shame, really, as we were supposed to do the 'Dining with Dukes' unit next week. What's that envelope in your hand, Tabitha?"

Tabitha had nearly forgotten about the letter. Deflated, she placed the envelope on the bed's edge. "From school. They gave it to two of us and said for you to open it."

Mr. Crum snorted. "Been kicked out for insolence, have you? That's convenient. No need to open it, with you already taken out. Beat them to the punch, didn't we?"

"I haven't been kicked out, Daddy," Tabitha said. She let her finger trace the swans on the envelope's flap. "The seal's quite nice."

The envelope remained untouched.

"And Barnaby Trundle seemed to think it could be something fancy," she added. "He got one too."

Mrs. Crum reddened. "Oh! You *know* how I hate Mrs. Trundle! Horrible woman. She had the nerve to say I certainly filled my dress out well at that dreadful school function last year. And not a single family with connections or money was there, so it was a total waste of time." She grabbed the envelope from Tabitha, feeling the paper. Her eyes widened at the wax. "I've seen that seal recently. A lake scene and swans." She squinted and frowned. "Turn on another oil lamp, for God's sake, Tabitha! We're not in the Dark Ages anymore. I swear, it's a wonder you even remember to keep them filled. Really, I don't know where our money goes, but we ought to have at least a few electric lights by now. It's nearly 1907."

Mr. Crum took out his watch, as if to check the year. "What's in the bloody envelope, then? We're on a deadline."

Carefully, with a bleat of anticipation as the seal broke neatly at the seam, Mrs. Crum lifted and unfolded a single sheet of pale-yellow stationery. "Oh!" She fanned herself while reading the contents. "Oh!"

"Don't say 'oh' like an idiot, just tell us what it is. If we owe money for something, she'll work to pay it off." Mr. Crum shook a fist in Tabitha's direction.

"Shut up, Mortimer. Just shut up and listen to this. I knew it! I absolutely knew something like this would happen to me." She continued fanning. "It's an invitation! I saw the same seal in the *Times* this morning."

Bustling over to an armchair imprinted with her substantial seat impression, Mrs. Crum reached over the side and came up waving the newspaper with her free hand. "It's right in here, darling. Six envelopes have been sent out across London. It's supposed to be some sort of secret, but of course someone's spilled it to the papers. It's from the Countess of Windermere, Camilla DeMoss, the richest philanthropist in England! King Edward himself gave her a title, you know." Perspiring with excitement,

Mrs. Crum tossed the paper toward her husband, striking Tabitha squarely on the nose.

All blood drained from Mr. Crum's already pasty face. "Camilla DeMoss? Countess of where?" He ignored the newspaper and Tabitha's face rubbing, snatching the invitation from his wife with sweaty urgency and reading it aloud:

To the Parents of Miss Crum:

Miss Tabitha Crum is hereby invited to a weekend at the estate of Camilla Lenore DeMoss, Countess of Windermere, to commence Friday, November 30. Transportation to Hollingsworth Hall, Windermere, Lake District, will be provided from the Hotel McAvoy, Kirby, at three o'clock in the afternoon. Formal attire is requested, but not mandatory. Enclosed are funds for train fare and any other expense you may encounter.

Parents are invited to dinner and a tour of Hollingsworth Hall on Friday and will then take lodging at nearby Clavendor Cottage. They will be called to attend luncheon on Sunday. No response is required, as all children/parents are fully expected to attend. I look forward to your presence and trust that it will be a profitable weekend for all. Your discretion is advised, assumed, and appreciated.

Camilla Lenore DeMoss, Countess of Windermere

"Profitable? Profitable?" Mr. Crum's lips quivered as he mouthed the second-to-last line to himself. His fingers drummed against his chin, as though counting imaginary bills. "Gives money away like candy, she does. What can it mean?" He whirled to face his daughter. "How do you know her?" he demanded, advancing toward Tabitha, shaking the note with such intensity that she stumbled backward, her thin frame slamming into the dresser.

"For God's sake, give her some space," Mrs. Crum said. "She'll break the dresser. And you're being ridiculous. She hasn't got any friends, let alone countess connections." Her eyes began to glaze over with the promise of high society. "Oh, Mortimer, Hollingsworth Hall! Imagine, me, with a countess! Perhaps . . . perhaps I can pick her brain on how to get a title." Mrs. Crum nibbled her upper lip and gazed at the wall, seeing extravagant parties and important people and illustrious power. "Agatha Crum, *Countess of London*. Agatha Crum, *Countess of Rome*. Agatha Crum, *Countess of Paris, all other large cities, and the seacoast of Spain*."

Tabitha picked up the envelope and took out a thin wad of bank notes. "I suppose I'll need a proper dress, if I'm to go," she said softly.

"Nonsense," Mr. Crum sneered, snatching the bills and spreading them out. "It says 'formal attire not mandatory.' Right there, it says. You'll wear what you have. The money will be for our trouble. Besides," he said with a gleam in his flinty eyes, "it may go better for you if she thinks we're fairly poor."

"I thought we *were* fairly poor," Tabitha said. "And that's why I sleep in the attic."

"Ignorant, that's what you are." Mrs. Crum sniffed. "We're not poor. You sleep in the attic because it keeps you submissive and humble, and Mrs. Lanolin-Griffiths says humility and a submissive nature are what top bachelors look for in a wife. Once again, *you're welcome*. Now go pack. We don't have luggage for you, just use a pillowcase or something. No, wait. That might look callous on our part." Pursing her lips tightly, Mrs. Crum surveyed the open closet. "There's an old carpetbag buried in there somewhere, I believe. Mortimer, it's that dreadful brown-and-yellow disaster you bought for me years ago."

Mr. Crum grunted. "You were right, darling. Ugly as a shaved cat. Foul enough to be an excellent match for Tabitha."

"Yes, that's the one." Mrs. Crum smoothed her thin, gray-brown hair. "Mortimer, we shall need to inquire about the train immediately. Let's stay at the Hotel McAvoy this evening." She nodded at the bills in Mr. Crum's hands. "After all, we've got the money for it."

Tabitha frowned and tapped at the back of her neck four times. *Stop squirming, please,* she told Pemberley. "But the invitation says it's to start tomorrow afternoon. Won't tomorrow morning be quite early enough to leave?"

"Nobody wants your opinion on anything," Mr. Crum snapped. "Your mother's right. We'll take the night train north this evening. We can delay our own little trip, I daresay." He nodded, agreeing with himself. "Nothing will be seen as amiss until

Monday. Perhaps," he said, taking Mrs. Crum's hand, "perhaps we're finally due for a windfall."

"Oh, Mortimer! Do you really think so?"

He pounded the dresser twice, rattling the empty drawers. "I don't see why not! We've practically been invited to see royalty. And there's no sense in staying here when there's a game afoot. Best to get a jump on the competition. Now, if I could only learn what her angle is." Mr. Crum stared at the ceiling, neck tilted as though he was searching for the Countess's angle among the cracks. Then he stalked out the bedroom door, reopening it quickly. "And Agatha, dear," he called to his wife, "we'd better bring the *papers*." He tapped the side of his nose several times. "Don't want to leave any loose ends about if we don't come back to the house. Just shove them anywhere." He pounded down the steps.

Mrs. Crum hastily formed a single stack of the scattered papers, which she rolled and shoved deeply into the nearest place of confinement, which happened to be the carpetbag that Tabitha would be using. "Hurry up, go gather your things or we'll leave without you. You might as well take everything you have, as we'll be sending you to the Home right after the weekend."

Pausing to regrip the carpetbag's handle, Tabitha slipped the fallen newspaper under her free arm and left her parents' room, tucking Mr. Crum's interesting words about "loose ends" and things being "seen as amiss" into a corner of her mind.

Her crawl space was an odd assembly of slanting ceilings, an uneven floor, and one tiny square window. The only luxury present was half an inch of honey candle perched on a jam jar lid next to Tabitha's sleeping mattress, which was made of old sofa padding. The candle flame offered no warmth but lent a lingering scent of sweetness to her personal area that saved it from feeling unbearably cold in spirit.

Tabitha lifted Pemberley to the window ledge and set him beside a small pile of paper scraps and chewed pencils. He scampered to his bed, a cleansed tin of Pemberley's Miracle Mustache Tonic that she'd plucked from Mr. Crum's trash long ago.

"So it appears we've been dropped, my dear sir," she told the mouse. "We are on our own. Or will be, after this weekend."

Pemberley paused in his search for spare nibbles and squeaked twice.

"Good riddance, you say? Oh, Pemberley, you're awful." Waving an index finger in his small face, she gave him a corner of cracker that she'd tucked into her sock at lunchtime. "But I don't blame you one bit. Not after what happened to your dear mum and brothers. Or sisters. Your family, that is. But I'm your family now, so never fear." She dropped a delicate kiss on his mousy back. "You, sir, are the Timothy Tibbs to my Inspector Pensive. We shall be just fine together for always."

The tiny mouse had shown up in the attic corner one year before, nestled among several brothers (or sisters, Tabitha wasn't sure which) where the wooden floor planks had eroded to form a shallow place. They were all squeaking from painfully shrunken stomachs. When no mother mouse came to remedy the problem, Tabitha suspected that Mr. Crum's latest victim in

the kitchen trap was the parent of the little ones.

Despite her best efforts, all but one of the mice died within two days. Pemberley clung stubbornly to life. He had been so tiny that she fed him milk with a small paintbrush she swiped from St. John's art supply closet. He was smart enough that Tabitha was able to teach him simple tricks with old cheese and cracker ends, and soon Pemberley could twirl, hide, beg, and even hug her thumb on command, though he often did that of his own volition. A book she'd fetched from the public library stated that a healthy mouse could live up to three years. One very lucky fellow had lived to be seven.

Tabitha had hoped that Pemberley would remain in the world until she'd grown enough to leave her parents. And now, with the news of her move to Augustus Home, he had done just that. "I'll pack quickly, Pemberley," she told him, "and then we'll leave these cozy quarters for a year."

It was not cozy quarters in the attic, but she would never share that with Pemberley. He was a fragile fellow, having experienced loss so early in life. She hated to burden him with unproductive thoughts, including her suspicion that they might be spending quite a bit longer than a year in Augustus Home.

Tabitha folded a secondhand sweater that most likely had belonged to a boy and browsed through the rest of her clothing, making a pile of things to take with her. It was a small pile. "What else shall we take? Ah, yes." She added knitting needles attached to a skein of yarn, a partial scarf, and the one Inspector Pensive novel she owned.

It was only the previous summer that she'd discovered the Inspector, a serendipitous introduction made while spending glorious days at the library. Mr. and Mrs. Crum didn't keep track of school holidays, and Tabitha had simply continued leaving the house at eight and returning at four, despite the fact that students had been given a lengthy break from classes. She'd been allowed to keep a rather banged-up copy of *The Case of the Duplicitous Duke's Doorway* after dusting and keeping the shelves tidy for several weeks.

She rubbed her new bittern pin, kissed it on the beak, and added it to the carpet bag. "Now, what will become of you, Miss Crum?" she asked herself.

Four insistent bangs sounded on the attic door. "Get down here *now* and take out the garbage. I won't leave the house smelling filthy!"

"Fetching refuse." She sighed. "That's what's to become of me for the moment. Coming, Mum!" she called. Gently pressing Pemberley back underneath her collar, Tabitha climbed down the attic ladder to fetch the rubbish. Even pieces of garbage had a home, she observed. A place they belonged with other thrown-away bits.

Tabitha had no place at all.

"None of that, Pemberley," she whispered. "We're lucky to be having a bit of an adventure before getting thrown to the wolves, and I won't have us pitying ourselves. I simply won't have it." And she meant it. If there was one thing that kept Tabitha Crum going during the days and brought her comfort throughout nights, it was a flicker of hope that she kept burning despite her misfortunes. It was a small hope, really.

It was the hope that life could and deserved to be better for her. It was a hope that one day, wherever that version of her life was, it would present itself in a way that allowed her to leap and cling and claim it so adamantly that it could never let her go or push her away.

"Come now, Pemberley," she added, finishing the round of bins and wiping a curl of potato peeling from her leg, "you're so busy dwelling on this orphanage business that you've forgotten about the mystery ahead! As Father said, perhaps a game is afoot. And I have quite as much curiosity about these other children as I do about the countess herself."

Once again she wondered what she and Barnaby Trundle could possibly have in common that would warrant twin invitations to Hollingsworth Hall. Perhaps Barnaby was right. Perhaps it was all a big mistake.

But she rather hoped not.

3

"Physical drills are nonsense, Tibbs," said Pensive, waving a hand at his partner. "Mental acuity provides the lion's share of an Inspector's strength, thus making daily observations *my* particular version of organized exercise. Feel free to keep swinging your arms in those ridiculous patterns, though. Quite entertaining."

—Inspector Percival Pensive,
The Case of the Backhanding Butcher

Tabitha nibbled her toast and stared at her mother's disappearing mountain of food with an attentiveness that wobbled between disgust and fascination. The Hotel McAvoy's dining room was generous with portions, and Mrs. Crum's enormous plate had been delivered with three eggs, four sausages, fried mushrooms, black pudding, baked beans, fried bread, and several slices of tomato.

"Ah," said Mrs. Crum with a delicate belch. "I do love a light entry into the day. The pudding is delicious."

"Much better than Tabitha's cooking," Mr. Crum agreed. "Wipe that vacant cow expression from your face immediately, Tabitha, and go somewhere for a few hours while we visit with the other parents."

"You'll change before we're picked up this afternoon," Mrs. Crum said, thrusting a piece of paper into her daughter's hand. "Take this. Your father was clever enough to bribe the front desk man for information."

Tabitha ignored the empty feeling in her belly and studied the piece of paper, smudged with Mr. Crum's breakfast.

Oliver Appleby: Extremely rich, well dressed, highest education, probably spoiled

Barnaby Trundle: Modest wealth, charming hair compared to Tabitha, horrible mother

Frances Wellington: Very rich, well connected, highest etiquette levels

Viola Dale: Charity supporter, consorts with the poor (possibly diseased from contact)

Edward Herringbone: Intelligent, most likely a bore

"*Five* other children," Mr. Crum said, shaking his head. "Completely foul of the countess to have invited so many, if you ask me."

"Very rude," Mrs. Crum agreed, pushing Tabitha from her chair. "Get up and make yourself scarce. We need to get Mr. Tickles settled with his caretaker. Come back to the room at two o'clock." She shooed Tabitha away, waving the back of her hands like one might do to repel a starving kitten.

Undaunted by the gesture, Tabitha left the dining room and examined the Hotel McAvoy foyer. A lone chair was tucked away into a curtained corner near the furnace irons, and Tabitha nestled into the space. Quick as a whip, she reached into the back of her tights for the newspaper she'd taken from her parents the day before. She hadn't read it on the train because the Crums, Mrs. Crum in particular, disliked the sight of her soaking up pages of articles or Pensive novels. *Remember, men don't like readers, they like pretty,* Mrs. Crum was fond of saying.

The lobby was empty enough for Tabitha to take Pemberley from her sweater pocket. He scurried into her lap and nibbled at the toast crumbs there.

"Do listen, Sir Pemberley, and feel free to take notes." Tabitha scanned the *Times* until she came across the right headline.

Squeak.

"What's that? You can't take notes? Well then, no notes, but you must listen *most* carefully." She cleared her throat and read aloud to Pemberley in her best whispered Inspector voice:

RENOWNED (AND VERY RICH) RECLUSE OPENS HOME TO CHOSEN FEW

In a baffling display of what surely must be charity, Camilla Lenore DeMoss, the Countess of Windermere, has issued six invitations around London, summoning a small group of children to spend the weekend with her in her Lake District manor. According to our source, the children's parents will be housed on property in Clavendor Cottage. This will mark the first occasion that anyone has been a formally invited guest at the magnificent Hollingsworth Hall estate since the Countess acquired the property.

While her donations to various causes are well documented, little is known of the Countess's personal nature and appearance, as she switches staff every six months and has had all employees sign strict confidentiality papers since King Edward gave her a title in 1895. She has been described to the *Times* in the following ways by a variety of those claiming to have witnessed her magnanimous presence: tall, rather average, quite petite, always dressed in the height of London fashion, matronly, dowdy, certainly approaching seventy, not past the age of forty-and-five, wonderfully verbose and kind, horribly taciturn and strict. The only consensus lies in rumored eccentricity in habits and in vague whispers of a large amount of unfortunate death in her past. Her husband and brother-in-law are said to have died tragically before she and her sister moved into Hollingsworth Hall in 1880. Several years later her only son disappeared amid reports of a violent family argument. Her sister expired shortly thereafter, leaving her with an even larger amount of disposable income. Details on the manner of those deaths and her son's disappearance remain sparse and conflicting.

Despite the lack of solid fact regarding the lady herself, countless organizations and individuals praise the Countess of Windermere as the greatest type of philanthropist—one who keeps her generosity consistent and without conditions. The *Times* will do its utmost to report the mysterious happenings that take place at Hollingsworth

Hall this coming weekend. The whole of England is no doubt holding its breath to learn more about this very titled, very secretive, and very rich woman.

Tabitha tapped her chin. "Well, Pemberley. That gives us little to nothing in terms of expectations. A mysterious lady, indeed. What on earth could she want with us? And what shall we do with ourselves other than wonder about it?"

The hours passed quickly enough in the hotel. Tabitha moved pieces on the foyer's chess set for a bit and then perched on a long bench next to an umbrella stand and swung her legs, making a game of figuring out the stories behind each person present. A young woman with a long coat over an aproned dress had just delivered a box wrapped in beautiful white ribbon, dropping it on the front desk along with a note and a curtsy.

"See there," Tabitha whispered to Pemberley. "The front desk man is a spy for a famous French chef, hoping to steal the pastry recipes of the shop down the street. And the lovely shop girl who just delivered a box of—what is most certainly—pastries is his secret accomplice. The note she passed to him while blushing has a recipe for the perfect croissant."

As she peered around the room for a fresh prospect, Tabitha's eyes settled on the mahogany telephone booth, which was occupied by the back of a man's brown jacket and matching brown hat. The man's shoes shuffled back and forth along the booth floor in an odd manner, as though he were dancing in place, and he shook his head vehemently at something the person on the

TELEPHONE

other line had said. The man's voice was muffled by people coming in and out of the front door, but Tabitha caught an insistent, slightly animated tone.

"Hmm, Pemberley. Perhaps Mr. Jacket and Hat has finally tracked his long-lost love to a manor house here in the Lake District and is demanding to speak with her."

Pemberley gave a satisfied squeak at the supposition.

Tabitha didn't often fantasize about such mushiness, but long-lost thises and thats were popular among the good-night tales she made up for Pemberley. Soldiers with amnesia and their sweethearts, orphans and parents, lost puppies and owners all reunited into tidy little happily ever afters. Her mouse, Tabitha reasoned, was sensitive about the early loss of his parents and siblings, and was comforted by such stories.

Pemberley let out another squeak and scuffled against the lining of her sweater pocket.

"Hush now, Pemberley," Tabitha warned. "Let's listen a bit more." She casually moved to a long bench closer to the telephone booth, hoping to hear snippets of Jacket & Hat's conversation. She was slightly surprised when the voice didn't match the elegant clothing. The man sounded like he came right out of the rough streets and alleys of East London. Not that character could be judged by a voice, she reminded herself. Barnaby Trundle, for instance, had a perfectly respectable voice that he often used in a most unrespectable manner.

"—all arrived, they have—all six children. Yes, I called the *Times* and you were right about passing along the names as well, luv, they've agreed to transfer payment to the hotel."

Tabitha inhaled softly. Was the man talking about her and the others? He must be.

"Now that you mention it, they do seem a bit nervous. No, nobody seems to know why they've been invited. Yes, I've 'eard a few of them mention the possibility of coming into money, but it's all speculation. Best to assume the invitation was vague on that front, right?" He jerked his head around, and Tabitha ducked behind a curtain before his face could turn her way.

"Wha'? No, no, I'll get back in plenty o' time. Right, luv, I can't wait either. We'll do it up right and be married in style once we get this final bit done. Brilliant stroke of luck. It'll be tied ends for us. Cheers, luv." He hung up and patted a suitcase next to him. "But if it don't turn out, luv," he murmured to himself, "I'm afraid I'll have to leave you to the mess."

He stepped out of the booth and Tabitha remained hidden, not daring to peek. Masking herself behind thick velvet, she heard the man drop his suitcase at the front desk, indicating that they should hold it for him.

"When will you be back?" the attendant asked.

"Hard to say. Sooner rather than later, I hope. Haven't had a proper holiday in fifteen years."

But who was the man? A newly engaged newspaper man looking for gossip to sell to finance a wedding? That must be it, she decided. The countess having guests was sure to be quite a big deal, and nobody had gotten an interview yet. But if the money didn't come through, he planned to jilt the unlucky lady?

Adults, Tabitha decided, had an enormous capacity for cruelty. But then again, so did children. Cruelty, she supposed, was one of those skills that ripened with age, but could be learned and executed quite well during any of life's stages.

As soon as the man was gone and his business firmly decided, Tabitha wondered whether working for a newspaper might be a satisfying, mystery-solving type of profession. It hadn't nearly the prestige of being an Inspector, but perhaps females (even one who happened to be an orphanage washer girl) might have a better chance of securing such a position.

Several hours later Mr. and Mrs. Crum primped and prepped each other in the art of fine conversation, with the order that Tabitha remain quiet. Mr. Crum wore a high, wing-collared shirt, waistcoat, frock coat, and top hat, and had also purchased an elegant black cane. Mrs. Crum wore an ankle-length skirt and long, tunic-like jacket that required a straight-line corset she forced Tabitha to squeeze her into. "It's the latest style," she kept grunting. She fidgeted with her new broad-brimmed evening hat, which featured an entire stuffed hummingbird in addition to several large feathers.

"We're wanted in the foyer. Come along," said Mr. Crum, tapping his feet.

Tabitha straightened her clothing. Mrs. Crum had bought her a black, knee-length dress in a shop for servants' clothes, saying it was cheaper than mud, due to an odd stain on the front. "Don't complain. They gave me this apron to cover it.

Put it on. And you can wear your school sweater on top."

With her shabby shoes, the too-big dress, too-tight sweater, and the odd gray apron hanging down, she looked more like a scullery maid than a guest. But the apron's pocket was handy for holding her mouse, and a small sweater hole would give Pemberley sufficient air, so she didn't say a word. She'd managed to pin her hair back on both sides, which helped a bit.

I still look ridiculous, Tabitha thought.

"You look ridiculous," observed Mr. Crum. "We want her to look poor enough to be humble, but not *that* humble."

Mrs. Crum sighed, as though having to purchase an excess of poverty for Tabitha had been a terrible burden. "You'll get the sympathy vote, that's for certain."

"Let's go, then." Mr. Crum picked up the trunk he and Mrs. Crum were sharing.

Tabitha lifted her carpetbag and followed her parents down the hallway precisely at a quarter to three. At the last moment, she'd fastened the tiny bittern pin to the edge of her dress collar to look a bit festive. Tabitha fancied the pin was good luck. Good luck needed for what, she hadn't the slightest idea.

The newspaperman in the telephone booth had been curious about the children, which was reason enough to believe that something very interesting could occur during the weekend ahead. Six children chosen to visit Hollingsworth Hall, seemingly at random, was apparently a story worthy of poking about for details. And from reading Inspector Pensive novels, Tabitha knew that small details often came full circle.

She took a very deep breath and watched her mum and dad descend the staircase to the hotel lobby. *Pay attention. Anything can be a clue,* she reminded herself. But a clue to what? The mysteriousness of this particular mystery was frustrating beyond pleasure until she realized what was missing—what was part of every Inspector Pensive mystery novel she'd read over and over again.

A crime.

4

Pay attention, Tibbs, to what is precious to people. Do they cling to paintings or pastimes or money? Do they shun the gifted items of others by shoving them into drawers instead of putting them on display? Remember that when a person leaves their home quickly, what they leave behind might be as important as what appears to be missing.

—Inspector Percival Pensive,
The Case of the Disappearing Dachshund

The Hotel McAvoy's lobby rustled and murmured as women in full skirts and feathers mingled with men in their dress coats and homburg hats. The doorman and desk attendant busied themselves with afternoon arrivals, and there was a decided feeling of anticipation to the place, marked by a corner of bunched luggage and flocked parents awaiting transport to Hollingsworth Hall. Even hotel guests who were not bound for Hollingsworth paid tribute to the milling group with silent stares and appraising glances.

Tabitha journeyed the steps slowly, observing the four children seated beside the reception desk, lined up along a bench like expectant soldiers. Clearly they were her fellow invitees.

Nearest the window sat a pleasant-looking tall boy with dark hair and a half grin directed at a flash of silver in his hands. The seat next to him was taken by a cherub-faced blonde with a cheery glow, and next to her, a yellow-haired boy slouched. He wore delicate spectacles and rested a book on his belly, his mouth moving silently along with the words. The seat beside the marble length of desk was taken by an elegantly postured but sour-faced child with lovely auburn curls who kept eyeing the front desk attendant as though she wished he would disappear.

All four children were immaculate, with the tall boy and sour girl wearing the finest clothes. *Oliver Appleby and Frances Wellington, based on Daddy's notes,* Tabitha guessed, *leaving the others to be Viola and Edward. Though it's best never to determine a person's identity solely by their exterior, Pemberley. Goodness knows what they make of me.* Tabitha took a very deep breath, determined not to show embarrassment over her own appearance.

"Frances, *do* put a pleasant look on your face, like the delightful child you are," a stylish woman called from across the room.

"Yes, Mother." A charming smile appeared immediately on the sour girl as she stood and curtsied to her mother, though her eyes remained annoyed.

The tall boy put away the pocket tool he'd been fiddling with and caught sight of Tabitha lingering on the fringes, but still standing solidly within the bubble of the Hall-bound gathering. He beckoned her to join the rest of the children. With no small amount of surprise, she hesitated, looked behind her, and finally nodded.

Don't bob your head like an idiot, she heard her mother's voice say. *A woman should nod demurely.* But Tabitha wasn't sure how to nod demurely, so she simply blushed at her own awkwardness and walked toward the bench. *None of them want to be friends, so that takes the pressure off,* she told herself. *And I've got my best friend with me already,* she added, giving Pemberley a quick pat.

The beckoner grinned and held out a hand to Tabitha. "I'm Oliver. Look a bit stiff, don't we all?"

Pleased to have been right about names, Tabitha sat. "Yes, you do all look a bit stiff," she whispered back to Oliver. "That is, I didn't mean to insult you, I'm sure you're all harmless, I just meant . . ." *Oh, bother! Why can't you behave normally?* "I just meant that I'm Tabitha."

Oliver's gaze shifted across the room as Barnaby Trundle's family made a noisy appearance. "I wouldn't be too certain about all of us being harmless. Some seem fit to win a game that hasn't even been announced yet. I say," he said, taking a fleeting but not unnoticed glance at Tabitha's apron, "you look quick-witted enough to know what the sport is. You're not some sort of spy, meant to throw us all for a loop, are you? If a sinister event occurs over the weekend, I shall blame you immediately," he promised, eyes twinkling.

Tabitha blinked. "Sorry?"

He smiled at her kindly. "Joking."

"Oh. Right. It's just that I'm very used to getting blamed for things, you see." She gave herself a mental slap for saying another idiotic thing. Oliver was joking, so she should joke as well. "Er, um, do I look the guilty type, then?" she asked.

Oliver narrowed his eyes. "Hard to say, hard to say." He cocked an eyebrow. "Perhaps we're all guilty of something."

Tabitha let out a fumbled laugh and felt herself longing for the simple glares and whispers of the school yard. At least those were straightforward. Why, oh why, was it so much easier to interact with Pemberley than with people? It was desperately confusing to both yearn for others to include you and half wish that they wouldn't.

As observation was familiar enough, Tabitha settled into Inspector mode. *Character study, Tibbs, is an integral and constant part of an investigator's modus operandi.* She watched the auburn-haired girl curiously from the corner of her eye. Ignoring the chitchat around her, Frances Wellington had lifted her hand casually to the marble desk. Her finely manicured fingers crept toward a small pile of short pens, which were next to an ink pot, which was next to the large leather guest book. She snatched a pen and stashed it in her elaborately beaded reticule before a full second had passed.

What would a rich girl want with a silly hotel pen?

Barnaby Trundle continued to stand next to his parents. His father, who wore a larger, bolder version of his son's signature sneer, was gripping Barnaby's arm. Quite tightly, it would seem from the pained expression on the boy's face. Raising a finger and jabbing it repeatedly into Barnaby's chest, Mr. Trundle gave some sort of instruction and then shoved his son toward the other children.

Barnaby bumbled over in a just-been-smacked-for-piddling-on-the-floor puppy manner that Tabitha had never seen from him. The sailor suit his mother had chosen for him was unfortunate. He aimed a hesitant smile toward Frances, nodding at the small open space between her and the front desk.

Lips pinched together as though appearing pleasant was becoming an intolerable and loathsome task, Frances scooted over so that all six were seated on the bench.

"Might as well introduce ourselves," said Oliver. "The name's Oliver Appleby and I'm eleven, near twelve. From London, attend Abbott Academy. My father is the head of Appleby Jewelry, so if you ladies are in need of a nice necklace or bracelet, he's your man." He winked and rolled his eyes.

Nobody laughed.

Oliver gave an embarrassed grin. "He likes to have me say that. I'm lined up to take over the business, though I'd rather be an engineer. I want to work with motorcars." He pulled the silver tool from his pocket and held it up for general view. "I nearly fixed a faulty engine just last week using the knife and metal toothpick from this." His lips twisted to one side. "Didn't work out too well, actually. Anyway, I'm pleased to meet you all."

"I'm Viola Dale," said the sweet-faced blond. Her voice was

light and breathy, but confident. She had a lovely green velvet bow in her hair and a smile that seemed eager to please. Her dress was a generous cut of matching green velvet, complete with buttons and lace from her neck to her knees, where the whitest of wool stockings were worn with a darling pair of black dress shoes. On any other girl, all those buttons might look excessive, but Viola wore the dress with such a casual manner that Tabitha liked her immediately.

"I'm eleven too," Viola said. "I go to St. Stephen's with Edward. We live in London, next door to each other, actually. Our mums and dads know each other quite well. And, let's see, what else? I love to research social services, and I'm learning French."

Frances tossed her hair, snorting like an amused piglet. "You're 'learning French.' How *new* money of you. My mother would love to take your parents on. She runs a finishing business for young ladies. Not that class or grace can be taught."

Nor can humility, Pemberley.

"Frances Hortensia Rathbourne Wellington, also age eleven, near twelve. I already speak French. I have a private tutor and live in London as well. The second we got the invitation, my mother used her connections to hire a former servant of Hollingsworth Hall. For a price, the woman blabbed everything." She frowned. "Which wasn't much."

"Out with it then," Edward said.

The others nodded.

Frances's mouth tightened. "Fine. She locks herself into her bedroom some nights, and she supports the women's movement, though not openly. Oh, and she talks to her staff like they're actually people—how ridiculous is that?"

Tabitha covered her laugh with a cough. *Scandalous,* she tapped onto Pemberley's back.

Next in the introduction line was Barnaby Trundle, who did not mention attending school with Tabitha or say a word about his tendency to be awful in general. Tabitha was tempted to add a bit to his introduction, but made do with realizing his sailor outfit was perhaps more of an embarrassment than her own clothing.

"Hullo," Edward said next, straightening in his seat. "Edward Herringbone. My parents work with the Dales. Like Viola said, they've all been the best of friends for years. We've spent enough Christmases and holidays together to be one big family. I like animals and poking bugs and reading thick books on history and medicine." He nodded at Oliver. "That little knife and toothpick of yours would have worked wonders on medieval battlefields. Instead people mostly had their wounds jabbed at with rusty nails or sizzled with hot irons or . . ." He trailed off, sensing a general lack of enthusiasm. "Anyway, not a clue what we're doing here." He rattled off a few sentences in French and awaited Frances's response.

Frances stared blankly.

"I asked if you knew why we're here," Edward told her. "You being a bit of a know-it-all."

"Perhaps Frances's old-money French is a little rusty," Oliver said, with a wink in Tabitha's direction.

"Shut up. I don't speak *peasant* French. Speaking of peasants,"

Frances added with a smirk, "who exactly are you?" She looked pointedly at Tabitha.

Simple is best. "I'm Tabitha Crum. I live in Wilting. My father works at a bank. I'm eleven as well."

"Tabitha keeps rats," Barnaby blurted. "I saw her playing with one at outdoor invigoration one day."

Tabitha glared at Barnaby and placed her hand over her pocket. "It wasn't a rat."

"It *was* a rat," Barnaby insisted. "You were feeding it something, like it was a proper pet."

"A filthy rat?" Frances said, recoiling to Barnaby's side of the bench. "Are you perfectly serious? You can't be, of course, but I can certainly imagine it. My God, Tabitha Crum, you are officially the most disgusting member of this party. You've edged Edward out of the spot completely."

"Edged me whatsies?" Edward asked, popping a pocket chocolate into his mouth.

"It was a mouse," Tabitha said softly. Perhaps the admission would cause her to lose any chance of making a close acquaintance among the group, but loyalty was owed to Pemberley. Tabitha had forgotten many of the rules of friendship, but that was one she felt certain of. "And he wasn't filthy at all." *And he's listening to us at this very moment.*

"I'm *sure.* Lovely brooch, Tabitha," Frances said, clearly not meaning it at all. "What is it? Some kind of insect?"

"I like animals too," said Viola, patting Tabitha's knee.

Tabitha's hand went automatically to the pin. "It's a bittern," she said, hating herself for the blush she couldn't stop. After all, there were *far worse things* than being insulted.

- having her hair pulled out, clump by clump
- sifting through a rubbish bin for rotten food to eat
- witnessing a carriage running over a kitten

"Oh, a bittern!" Viola exclaimed. "We just learned about those in our nature course. Our teacher said that they used to be found in the wet areas of England, but they've nearly all died out. It was so very sad to hear that I told her perhaps some have hidden themselves away. Perhaps they'll come back one day." She leaned over Oliver and looked at the pin more closely. "It *is* lovely. Do you know that the Countess has given away nearly eight thousand pounds to avian causes?"

"Birds are very big in jewelry design now. My mother has a piece almost exactly like that pin," Oliver said, glaring at Frances. "In fact, that design would fit in nicely at any of my father's stores. Where did you get it? I'll recommend the jeweler to my father."

Tabitha reddened once more. Oliver was just being kind, lying and trying to knock Frances down a bit. "My mother gave it to me."

"How nice. I'm sure it was her best piece, too," Frances said, keeping her eyes wide and innocent.

Tabitha gripped Pemberley lightly, willing his influence to keep her silent.

"The Countess is sure to like your pin," Edward said, having finished his treat. "There were swans on her seal."

"Oh! And we learned of something of swans in class as well. Boy and girl swans mate for life," Viola said with a soft smile. "You know, the Countess never remarried after her husband died. I think it's terribly sweet and romantic."

Edward pulled a worn envelope from his back pocket. He peered at the broken seal, trying to press it together. "Huh. Doesn't look romantic to me. They're the same size on this seal, aren't they? Boy swans are bigger than girl swans in real life, so I'd say these two are brothers or sisters, or maybe best mates, but not the best of *mates*." He chortled at himself, then scratched his nose. "If I recall, the Countess's husband was rumored to have been *murdered*. And I've heard the place is haunted with all manner of ghosts." He winked at Frances. "You're not the only one with access to rumors, are you, tea cake?"

Frances sniffed. "Good God, do you never stop thinking of food? And I suppose anyone with access to the daily tabloids knows of the ghosts. Former employees, bitter from being let go and looking to make money with their lies, Mother says."

Viola looked around the foyer before raising her eyebrows and lowering her voice to a whisper. "I don't have any information about the ghosts, but I heard something about her husband's death. It was probably in a grisly manner."

Oh my. Tabitha's curiosity bullied away her silence, and she found herself unable to remain quiet. "Um, sorry, but why do you say that?" she asked, wishing very much that she had either a writing tablet or Pensive's enormous memory to store the information in.

Viola cleared her throat. "Since moving to Hollingsworth Hall, the Countess has given five thousand pounds a year toward hospital care for injured constabulary workers across England, from city police to small village watchmen and parish constables. And the funds were marked only to care for the fiercest of injuries—manglings, blunt force wounds, slashed appendages, things like that. I don't know how much money she gave before she came to the Hall, because mother could only find donation records for the DeMoss name starting when the Countess moved there. But research shows that a consistent hospital donation of that size probably indicates some sort of traumatic injuries to an individual close to her."

"And why the police, do you think?" Tabitha felt a flush come over her. *Stop asking questions! This isn't the time to play Inspector. Take Mum and Daddy's advice and just stop talking altogether.*

But Viola didn't seem bothered in the slightest. Her lips twisted in thought. "Perhaps because they made proper inquiries. I overheard bits of conversation at a fund-raiser," she added. "Two ladies were discussing how best to appeal to the Countess's sensitivities, and one mentioned her moving to Hollingsworth Hall with only her son and sister. And apparently early staff members overheard the Countess speaking with her sister about their husbands' deaths. *A double murder.*"

Tabitha patted Pemberley gently, but he didn't appear to be trembling. Tabitha had read enough Pensive novels aloud, she supposed, that the word *murder* didn't carry too much of a shock with it. And the *Times* article she'd read had hinted at the possibility.

Oliver clucked his tongue, opening and closing items on his pocket tool. "That's awful."

"Yes," Viola said. "No wonder she wasn't ready for another marriage after that."

Edward shrugged. "Though I suppose none of the gossip ruled out the Countess and her sister doing the husbands in themselves. Seemed they came into enough money to buy themselves a Hall. Ha! Not too shabby, I say."

Viola gave a good-natured harrumph, followed by an affectionate smile. "Oh, Edward, you'll never be a romantic."

Edward popped another chocolate into his mouth and grinned. "Never planned on it."

Vaguely, Tabitha wondered what it would be like to have a close friend to trade barbs with, rather than a mouse. Not that there was anything inferior about a mouse.

A man in formal driver dress stepped into the lobby, straightened his coattails, and cleared his throat. "Transportation to Hollingsworth Hall, ladies and gentlemen. Children in the first carriage, adults in the second and third, please."

Lined up were three splendid black carriages, each with a driver and a footman. The dark veneer contrasted dramatically with the white horses set to pull them along. Even the horses seemed formal, stamping their feet with strength and dignity, trying to keep warm in the early afternoon air, which was growing colder by the hour.

They shuffled outside, the parents scrutinizing the children as they exited one by one. Mrs. Dale kissed Viola's forehead, and

Mr. Appleby shook Oliver's hand in a mock-serious way. Frances Wellington had brought a trunk and two cases and made herself busy by ordering an attendant to be careful.

"Doesn't even feel like there's anything in this one," said the man, lifting one of her cases. "A nice surprise and change from the heavier loads," he added, reddening under the influence of Frances's cool stare.

"Do hurry, please, children," said another attendant.

"Why don't *you* hurry," Frances told him, stomping up the short steps and into the double-benched space.

"Settle in, everyone," the lead driver called over the activity. "It may be a bit of a bumpy ride." He turned his face to the darkening sky, where white and gray clouds billowed and grumbled overhead. "We've got a few hours to drive, and the world looks fit to send something unsightly our way at any moment."

5

The very rich and those who long to be so,
Tibbs, are often odd birds, who only dirty their
cages when others aren't looking. Astonishingly
foul, the habits some people keep secret.
—Inspector Percival Pensive,
The Case of the Interrupted Ingenue

The Countess's property was thirty minutes at a fast clip from the last home they'd spotted, its isolation adding to the splendor of Hollingsworth Hall. Indeed, Tabitha's mouth hung agape as the carriages drove between two low stone walls, crossed a bridged stream, and finally came into view of the group's destination. It was a confident structure that had no tilting or looming about it, unlike Tabitha's future residence, Augustus Home. And it most certainly was not full of orphans.

No less than ten chimneys dotted the estate like top lookouts, and three small diamond-shaped windows perched closely together near the very top of the Hall. *I would deduce, Pemberley,*

Tabitha said silently, *that even the attic space in Hollingsworth Hall is certain to be true cozy quarters.*

"Ho! It's a country palace," said Edward.

It wasn't quite a palace, Tabitha decided, but it was still the most impressive home she had ever seen. She let her eyes follow the gables and sloping roofs downward, her gaze slipping and sweeping around the different angles of the manor. Lit by tall, glass-sheltered gas lamps, the lower half of Hollingsworth Hall was a somewhat unsettling study of shadows, with manicured trees and bushes queued up as though standing guard.

The horses came to an abrupt halt, jolting the children so that they were torn from their seats and flung together like trapped trout. It was a lumbering process, waiting for the adults to arrive behind them and then waiting while the children's bags and trunks were unloaded in the harsh weather. Though the rain that had pitter-pattered, then pelted the carriages during the drive had stopped, the ground was wet and boggy, sucking at feet as though hoping to keep anyone from ever leaving the estate. When nobody opened the large set of front doors, the group huddled together in a heap, not quite sure what to do next.

"What do you think we're doing here?" Mr. Dale asked Tabitha's father.

"Standing in the cold, aren't we," Mr. Crum replied. He sniffed. "If you're talking about why we were all invited, Dale, I don't know, and if I did, I don't believe I'd tell you."

Mr. Dale looked baffled. "Oh."

"We haven't a clue either," Mr. Appleby said, stomping his feet and stepping around his wife to block the wind from her. "Does anyone else?"

Murmurs of "no" and various speculations whirled into the wind and disappeared as they waited. The temperature had dropped several degrees since leaving the hotel and a cold, foreboding scent like frost and frigid things filled the outdoors, as though winter was arriving early and had chosen to make its first appearance at the Countess's home. Tabitha watched her father. Mr. Crum had a short fuse when it came to patience and shallow reserves when it came to politeness, so it seemed fitting that he was the one to finally shove the group apart.

"I suppose I'll see to the door," he said, "if there aren't any servants about." He grumbled about someone not knowing standards of decency if they were slapped in the face with them, but as he approached the wide set of carved wooden doors, he shied a bit at placing his hand on the knocker held within a brass gargoyle's jaws. Quickly, as though he might be bitten for impudence, Mr. Crum banged on the entrance.

Four solid raps echoed somewhere deep within the manor. Mr. Crum stepped back as the thick wood eased inward in slow motion. The door opened, revealing a statuesque butler standing at the fore of a marble-floored foyer. Tabitha noticed that his sideburns were meticulously trimmed and his eyes were brown and steady. A deeply clefted chin and a slight, involuntary lip twitch saved his face from being ordinary. He wore a black uniform with dark brown dress shoes.

"Good evening. Do come in." He bowed, showing a bald spot

on top of an otherwise-thick head of black hair streaked with a few bits of silver.

Mr. Crum straightened his jacket and peered around the man. "Yes, well. Who the devil are you? Where's the Countess?"

"*I* am Phillips. The butler. The Countess of Windermere does not answer her own doors, sir. Welcome to Hollingsworth Hall."

A rush of icy air blasted the crowd, which scurried in without further hesitation. A hush fell over the guests as they soaked in their first view of Hollingsworth Hall's interior.

On the foyer walls hung two portraits, one on each side, both of older gentlemen. Each oil painting was displayed under black curtains, pulled back with gilded ropes, and each portrayed a man sitting in an armchair, holding a large pocket watch. The men's faces were such that the eyes seemed to follow Tabitha across the open room. She watched them watching her, wondering if the paintings had been silent witnesses to any wandering spirits.

Dim lighting came from a massive, low-hanging chandelier. Most likely it was secure, but Tabitha stepped out of its path nonetheless. Not one, but three suits of armor stood guard, looking out of place but ensuring the utmost sense of occasion. There seemed to be only one significant thing missing from the scene, Tabitha thought. One significant *person* missing, rather, she corrected herself.

"Where is she?" Barnaby asked. "Where's the Countess? *Ow*, Mother, you don't have to—*ow!*" Barnaby rubbed his ear and glared at Tabitha as though she'd done the tugging.

Clearing his throat, Phillips took in the group with a single gaze and double lip twitch. "Her Ladyship is delayed in her rooms and will join us for dinner. I'm to take you to the parlor for light refreshments. Parents, you may settle yourselves from the journey while the children are shown to their rooms. Once they return, I'm to give you a brief tour of the property." He bowed again. "Agnes will take your coats and see that the children's things are deposited in the correct rooms." He clapped twice, like you might do when summoning a dog. "Ag*nes*!"

A cowering maid appeared, quickly disappearing under the load of thick dress jackets and coats piled upon her. Mrs. Wellington had worn a mink, which looked to weigh more than two stone.

"I say, Phibbits," Mr. Trundle said, "before we refresh ourselves with anything, what are we all doing here? We demand to know." He dug in his pocket and produced a shilling, holding it out to the butler. "Out with it, now, like a good chap."

Phillips studied the coin as though it were a piece of tummy lint. "Oh my, that is *most* unnecessary. Put it away, please, sir. And it's not my place to say why you've been summoned."

"So you know, then?" Frances asked.

"We demand to know as well," Mrs. Crum said. She slapped a hallway table for emphasis, rattling a Grecian mask. "First the hostess doesn't show up to greet us, and now the butler is flaunting knowledge that we don't have. I've never been so insulted in my life."

Mrs. Trundle clucked her tongue. "Perhaps not to your face, dear."

Frances whined like a squeaky vault door. "Give him twenty pounds, Daddy. I want to know *now*."

"Quiet, Frances, I've told you not to speak to me when I'm assessing the art." Mr. Wellington stroked his chin, gazing at the portraits. "Shades of Thomas Gainsborough's work, I believe."

"Follow me." Phillips began walking down a wide hallway, his shoes alternating between efficient clicks and a barely audible squelch. All of their soaked shoes were squelching a bit, Tabitha noticed, from the delicate heels on Frances to her own shabby pair.

With a dramatic roll of his arm, Phillips ushered them through a set of open double doors. Tabitha gazed at the finery in awe. Every surface burst with money, from elegant ivory effigies on side tables to the two large paintings hanging on either side of the fireplace mantel. Each showcased a single swan, swimming gracefully along a scenic lake.

"This is the high parlor. *Don't* touch that, sir," Phillips said sharply, swiping a silver apple from the hands of Mr. Crum and placing it back on an end table. "A ladies' powder room and a gentlemen's room are just down the hall. Children, you will be escorted to your rooms shortly. Parents, please feel free to seat yourselves." He pointed to a bound album resting on the lower shelf of a table near the fireplace. "There are more than three hundred thank-you notes cataloged in that album, if you would like to peruse them while you wait for the children. The Countess has been quite the benefactor."

"If she's so rich, why hasn't she got a fleet of motorcars?

Would've shortened the journey here," snorted Mr. Crum.

Phillips raised one eyebrow. "The Countess keeps five of the finest new motorcars with custom-added luggage racks in converted stables on the property. I can only assume she sent her finest horses and carriages to convey an older sense of class and elegance, perhaps a difficult concept for some to grasp. I'll be back shortly." He gestured to a stone-faced servant. "This is Jane. She's here to pour if you care for tea. There are assorted food items as well, though I should warn you that the Countess has quite a meal planned for supper, so do save room. She has"—he coughed into his hand, and a wrinkle appeared between his eyes—"spared no expense." He bowed and closed the double doors behind him.

Jane stood beside silver platters of cucumber sandwiches and smoked salmon sandwiches and savory-sweet ham sandwiches and open-faced sandwiches with thickly spread butter and fresh mint.

"Hello, *hello*, Jane!" Edward said, rubbing his hands together. "And *hello*, refreshments." But just as he reached for a butter-and-mint, two nervous-looking female servants appeared and approached the children.

One was no more than fifteen years of age, with tired eyes and blond hair tucked under a cap. "Tabitha Crum?" she asked, fingers twisting together as though knitting an invisible scarf.

Tabitha raised a hand. "Yes, that's me."

"Thank you, miss. Follow me to your room, please." She turned and began walking quickly down the hall.

Tabitha pushed gently past Oliver and Edward, hurrying to catch up. Stepping alongside the young maid in the hallway, she had the sudden idea of practicing the art of conversation. Surely it would benefit her throughout the weekend ahead if she could become comfortable speaking with others. And, though clearly tired, the maid seemed kind enough to be a suitable trial friend. "So, have you worked here long?"

"No, miss. I arrived just two days ago."

"And have you run into any ghosts?" Tabitha was joking, but the servant stopped at the base of the staircase.

Without looking at Tabitha, the girl spoke softly. "It's . . . not for me to say, miss."

Hmm. *A hesitant answer is one that always begs another question,* Pensive would say. How to encourage the girl? Tabitha smiled. "I'm not frightened of them, you know. I just like mysteries, and ghosts are quite an exciting mystery, aren't they?"

The servant looked at Tabitha as though she had grown a second head. She began climbing the staircase at a fast clip. *Oh dear, Pemberley,* Tabitha said silently, *I'm afraid I can't talk to people the way I talk to you.*

The servant was glancing down the long left hallway when Tabitha reached the top. "The rest will be in the west wing, that way," she said. "There were only five guest rooms on that side." Twisting her fingers, she turned right, hurried past a shut door, then turned down a short hallway that dead-ended with a single room. "Here we are. I'm so sorry you'll be separated. It's not my fault." She bit her lip.

"No, of course not. It's perfectly fine. And I'm sorry to have brought up ghosts. Perhaps you can't talk about things like that."

The servant gave her a long stare, deciding something. "Well, since I'll be leaving shortly and because you're staying in this room . . . it's probably best that one of you know that Hollingsworth Hall isn't all baubles and ten-course meals."

Pemberley shuffled, and Tabitha gave him a light squeeze. She was certain that he gave her a nudge back. *Yes, I know, sir! It's exactly like something a maid would say in a Pensive novel before revealing terribly important information. You pay attention too!* "Yes," she said, fixing her face with an open and encouraging expression. "Please go on."

"I've heard something the past two nights. I stepped out of my room to see what was what, and it was almost as though something was walking the hallways, making the air currents shift. I swear I felt a presence. Something's not right with this house.

"I heard rumors before I took the job," she continued. "Spirits calling for people in the halls. One poor girl even came back to the agency just to warn us not to work here. The voices, she said. The voices were moaning for an Anne and a George and a Victoria. Can you imagine?"

"No," Tabitha said, though she could. She had a very healthy imagination. She also knew that sometimes people liked to play tricks on those they thought naive. It was likely that somebody had been having a bit of fun with this servant, but it would be rude to suggest that. No, it was best to play along. "Who are Anne and George and such?"

The servant shook her head. "Don't know. Now," she said, opening the door, "it's not as large as the west wing rooms. I hope it will be acceptable, miss."

Tabitha thought of her attic dungeon. "I'm sure it's wonderful, thank you."

But the servant had already left, keeping her head low and muttering to herself. Tabitha reached into her pocket and let Pemberley scurry up her arm. "Fresh air, my little Inspector." She stepped into the room and froze. All thoughts of ghostliness vanished at the sight of her quarters, and then young Tabitha Crum felt a surprising wetness at the corner of her eyes and realized that she had been placed into a story after all, just as she'd wished for only one day earlier. "I have entered a fairy tale," she whispered.

And it was. There were luxuriant fabrics, elegantly carved wood, and a thick, rich rug with colors that beckoned her inside and wrapped around her lonely heart like a magically woven blanket and cup of never-ending tea. A canopy bed dominated one wall. It was hung with green gossamer curtains, covered in a gorgeous pale yellow comforter, and piled with embroidered pillows. It was a bed fit for a princess.

There was an armoire and a separate closet as well, with a simple chair resting between them. Tabitha opened the doors of the standing wardrobe, almost expecting to see a row of fine dresses made just for her. Instead there were neat rows of clothing—four plain dresses that looked like something a maid would wear (or, Tabitha thought, what someone like herself would wear to a special occasion at a manor house), four trousers suitable for a groomsman or lower houseman, four aprons, six blouses, six shirts, what looked to be a driver's uniform, and a variety of shoes and hats. All very organized.

"This must be where the Countess keeps extra servant uniforms," Tabitha told Pemberley.

A large dressing table, a mirror, and an elegant seat were next to the wardrobe. She touched the items on the mahogany dressing table, first letting Pemberley down to explore a carefully arranged plate of chocolate digestive biscuits. There was a silver brush set, a powder puff, and a small jewelry case holding several rings and tasteful pins. Among them was a simple silver finger band with a large, clear gem astride it. Tabitha picked it up as Pemberley scuffled onto the dressing table.

"This could make you a lovely collar, Pemberley." She slipped it over his head and placed him in front of the looking glass. If mice were inclined to primp and preen, then Pemberley was doing just that. Paws on the glass, he sniffed his reflection, then sat back for a better angle.

"Oh my, aren't we fancy, sir," Tabitha said. "Come, you can't wear it to dinner." She pulled him away, though an indignant squeak told her that Pemberley would certainly be back to examine his diamond collar later. While he scurried beneath the bed to investigate, Tabitha lifted a small frame from the dressing table and sat on the mattress. "Who's in this photograph, do you think?"

The picture featured a tall man, a plumpish woman, and a half-covered bassinet that revealed the lower half of a baby, whose two legs poked out of a blanket, feet spread far apart as though he or she had kicked off the confines of a too-tight wrapping. The image sent an attention-demanding prickle to her mind, as though it was hiding something of importance.

I wonder if I was bundled lovingly. Tabitha placed the frame on the bedside table and closed her eyes for a moment, trying to remember back to her days of being an infant. Did she kick off her blankets until her mother stopped wanting to bundle her at all? Had she been a poor fit, both in swaddling clothes and in her parents' lives, from the very start?

Pemberley dashed up the bedclothes and settled on her lap.

"What's that, Sir Pemby? I'm being tiresome? You're right. This, sir, is likely to be the most magnificent place we ever take lodging, so let's soak it in." She stretched herself onto the bed, folding both arms behind her head, studying the swirling design on the canopy and sniffing the air. "Though it smells like old lady in here, Pemberley."

Squeak. Squeakity-squeak.

"Yes, I meant musty, not like an actual elderly person. Really, it's a bit like Mr. Tickles's favorite chair." She sniffed again. "And pipe tobacco." Tabitha studied the one painting adorning the room's walls. It was a child sitting on a rocking horse, longish blond-red hair sweeping over his forehead and dangling into his eyes. He looked mischievous and happy. There was only one boy who had lived in the house with the Countess. Was this her son, or had the paintings already been there when the Countess purchased the estate?

A knock sounded on the door. "Time to meet for the tour, miss."

"Yes, all right, thank you." As Tabitha walked down the hallway to wait for the others at the staircase, she wondered at the chance of her being given the only isolated room. It was almost as though the Countess knew that she wouldn't fit in, while the others would be great friends.

Squeak!

"I know, I'm being ridiculous."

Still, as the others exited their rooms in the west wing, Tabitha couldn't help but notice how confident Frances was, how she casually whispered something in Oliver's ear, and how comfortable Edward and Viola were together.

"Tabitha, come with us." Viola held out a hand. "I simply can't wait to find out why we're all here! Isn't it exciting? I haven't a clue what's going to happen, but it's bound to be spectacular. It's like Bonfire Night, just before the fireworks light up the sky."

"Yes," said Edward, "except now we have to tour the house before we even find out what this business is about. Parlor this, drawing room that, here's money, there's money. It's like being invited to Buckingham Palace and then first having to tour the extra-special toilet facilities with perfumed—"

"Edward, stop." Viola's hand wiggled a little, her fingers brushing Tabitha's dangling ones. "Are you all right?"

"Oh, well, um, yes." *Stupid Tabitha, just take her hand!* Though her inner voice had been rather rude, Tabitha took its advice and lay her palm in Viola's.

Viola squeezed and leaned in to whisper, her breath a warm wisp of air against Tabitha's cheek. "Boring tour or not, I'm dying to meet the Countess, aren't you?"

"Dying," Tabitha repeated, thinking about Edward's words and an Inspector Pensive novel where a body was found in a water closet during a manor tour.

Pemberley rumbled about in her pocket, and she used her empty hand to free a piece of chocolate biscuit she'd hidden under her collar. She was just poking the morsel into her apron when she bumped into a very solid wall.

6

The number and quality of rooms touted in mansion tours is rarely as impressive and extensive as the wealth of secrets nestled within its walls.

—Inspector Percival Pensive,
The Case of the Enigmatic Encumbrancer

The wall Tabitha had just run into, as it turned out, was the butler. Black uniform fabric pressed against Tabitha's face, and she noticed that Phillips's clothes felt strangely cold in a manor that was such a furnace of wealth. He stood at the base of the grand staircase, staging himself three steps up so that he looked down on the parents, who were leaning collectively forward.

"Pardon *me*," Phillips said, gently pushing her into the parent clump with a slight bow of apology.

Tabitha let herself be squeezed into the cluster and was gradually pushed out of its backside. Viola had been right. There was an electricity to the air—a sense of anticipation and building pressure that had followed them from the hotel lobby and escalated. Even Pemberley was restless, scratching at Tabitha's sweater until his nose found the small hole.

They're all desperate to know why we're here, Sir Pemby. And I can hardly blame them. This whole manor feels like a powder keg, just waiting for a flame.

Inclining his head a very butlerish fifteen degrees to one side, Phillips inhaled and exhaled deeply, then nodded at the gathering. "Hollingsworth Hall was built in the fifteenth century. Many a wealthy man has owned the estate, but never has such a *charitable* woman come into its possession until Camilla Lenore DeMoss's purchase of the property in 1880."

"Are those two gentlemen the previous owners?" asked Mrs. Crum. She pointed to the portraits in the foyer.

Phillips sighed and wove his hands behind his back. "I really couldn't say, madam. The portraits were here when I arrived two years ago. Now follow me to the library." He strode directly down the middle of the group, parting them and turning to walk gracefully backward as he spoke. "In addition to private rooms, the Hall contains—"

Barnaby's mother nudged herself to the front of the group. "A library, study, drawing room, double parlors, a dining hall, a vault, and guest and servants' quarters," she recited. She eyed the two nearest rooms with a hungry expression.

Streaks of red crept up Barnaby's neck as he stared at his mother, but he remained silent.

At Mrs. Trundle's summation, Phillips merely lifted the non-twitchy side of his mouth and gave a stiff nod. "And a gallery that includes England's largest private collection of historical crime paintings, from the assassination of Julius Caesar to the Whitechapel murders of Jack the Ripper."

Oh my, thought Tabitha, her hand drifting down to cover Pemberley's ears so he wouldn't hear more if Phillips went into further detail. *What an unusual choice for a collection.*

"How *horrid*," Barnaby's mother said.

"Odd," said Mr. Wellington, the art collector. "Though if they're of significant quality, they might bring a very large sum at market."

"Is that right, sir?" asked Phillips, looking at Mr. Wellington with curiosity.

"Certainly," Mrs. Wellington replied. "There are all kinds of collectors looking to own unique pieces. There's absolutely nothing a person can cherish more than the right piece of art. Art is the most precious, important thing that a person could ever give birth to or nurture. Isn't that right, Frances?"

Frances stiffened and pursed her lips. "Yes, Mother."

"Edward," Viola whispered, gripping her friend's shoulder. "The Countess gives nearly three thousand pounds a year to art-based organizations, and I daresay I should be interested, but *do* say we won't go see those paintings."

Edward shrugged her off. "Not in charge, am I? I'd like to have a look at the Caesar one, myself. According to a riveting read on Roman medicine, the first recorded autopsy was done on him. Something like twenty-three dagger wounds. Physician named Antistius got to do it, lucky chap."

They passed through another door and into a wide room with three windows along one wall and scores of bookshelves along the rest. A neatly laid blaze crackled and popped in an enormous fireplace, lending extra warmth to what Tabitha had already decided was the best room in the manor. The fireplace's mantel was made of dark wood, finely carved and extended to the ceiling, glittering here and there with golden leaf adornments. To one side of it hung a small painting of a boy seated beneath a tree.

Viola's nose wiggled, and she sneezed three times. "Oh dear, I do hope I'm not getting sick."

"Allergic to the rug fibers, maybe?" Edward guessed.

Shaking her head, Viola sneezed once more. "No, it's probably a dreadful cold. Some of the people at the poorhouse we visited were ill, and I must have picked something up."

"Or perhaps you're allergic to anything with a smattering of class," Frances suggested.

Phillips cleared his throat until he had everyone's attention once again. "As you can see, the library contains the most ornate of the manor's seven working fireplaces. And the Countess owns more than two thousand volumes covering a variety of subjects."

Only seven fireplaces, Tabitha thought. But there were ten chimneys total. She'd counted.

"Nobody gives a fig about fireplaces or books," Mr. Crum murmured.

"I'm so sorry to be boring your unrivaled intellect, sir,"

Phillips said with an attentive lip twitch. "Is there anything at all related to the manor that you *would* give a fig about?"

"What about the ghosts?" Viola asked. "Will we be needing to say prayers against seeing ghosts this weekend?" She tugged on her mother's sleeve.

"Shh," said Mrs. Dale, smoothing Viola's hair and placing a kiss on her velvet bow. "Don't be silly, sweetheart. Please continue, Mr. Phillips."

While Tabitha tucked away the fantasy of having her own hair smoothed in a similar manner, she remembered to watch Phillips for his reaction to the word *ghost.*

To her surprise, the butler did not smile. Not a whit. Instead his lips turned inward and pressed together in what was either a grimace in regard to the question or a grimace in regard to the ghosts themselves. "I regret to inform you that rumors of ghostly occurrences in the Hall are not an approved tour subject. Nor is the reason that you've been invited. *That* you'll have to wait for."

While Phillips summarized the library's contents and the parents listened with thinly disguised impatience, Tabitha's eyes drifted to the view outside, which had taken a turn toward the ominous. An outdoor gas lamp must have been secured close to the windows, because Tabitha could see sleet pouring down. Bare, twisted branches of wisteria whipped back and forth in the wind, tapping against the glass with insistence. The center window was marked by three panes of diamond-shaped colored glass, reminding Tabitha of the three small windows she'd seen at the manor's highest point. That gable also had a chimney atop it.

Never hold back when the opportunity arises to address an oddity, Tibbs, Pensive had said in the very book Tabitha had brought in her carpetbag. *Unless it's concerning a woman's choice of hat, of course. By God, never address that sort of oddity.*

"What about the other chimneys?" she heard herself blurt out. "You said there were seven fireplaces, but there are ten chimney stacks."

Phillips stood on his tiptoes to locate the speaker. "Observant, aren't you?" he said, not phrasing it as a compliment. "Three of the fireplaces are in the locked rooms."

"*Locked* rooms," Edward said, elbowing Viola.

"Locked rooms!" Frances repeated, stepping closer to Oliver.

"*Locked rooms,*" Tabitha murmured, nudging Pemberley to make sure he had heard.

"Locked rooms," Phillips affirmed.

"What locked rooms?" Barnaby asked.

"The ones that have just been mentioned," Phillips said. "There are several rooms in the manor that the Countess keeps locked. They are not needed and are no longer in use and are not meant to be disturbed."

Mrs. Crum licked her lips and tapped Phillips. "And what exactly is in these locked rooms?"

Phillips wrinkled his nose at the touch and straightened his posture once again. "I wouldn't know, madam. They're *locked*, you see, which indicates that one cannot get inside. Her Ladyship has mentioned that one of the doors leads to the third floor, which is her son's former nursery, but that's the extent of my knowledge, I assure you."

Tabitha raised her hand, only to have it yanked down again by her father.

"Stop speaking, you twit," Mr. Crum quietly ordered.

But Tabitha couldn't halt questions from forming in her mind. *Were the rooms all of sentimental value? Did servants enter them to clean off the dust now and then?*

"And now for the gallery . . ."

Phillips's voice faded with the group while Tabitha dawdled in the library, her eyes petting the beautifully stained shelves. "See, Pemberley," she whispered, tucking a finger into her pocket. "That's two solid mysteries. What is in the locked rooms and what is the truth behind the ghost rumors mentioned by a maid and *not* refuted by Phillips. Oh, and why have we been invited, bringing us to a trio of mysteries."

Squeak!

"Yes, quite right, duly noted: And we still need a crime."

Squeakity-squeak.

Tabitha smiled. "Yes, *other* than Frances Wellington swiping hotel pens."

Footsteps clipped across the marble floor. Agnes, the maid who'd taken their coats, bowed her head and curtsied. "The Countess wishes you to sit for dinner. Oh! Where is everyone, miss?"

"The gallery. I was just heading there. Sorry. I was mesmerized by the books, you see." Tabitha gestured around the room. "I love to read, mysteries mostly, but I could spend hours exploring in here."

"Yes, well, you needn't look in the library to find mysteries at

Hollingsworth Hall," Agnes said, her shoulders shuddering with some invisible chill. "Let's find the others, miss. The tour will have to be cut short. The Countess is still in her room, but she requested that you be seated for dinner."

The dining room was dominated by a long, dark table with an autumn centerpiece of silken leaves and golden acorns, nineteen places set with gold-and-maroon settings, and more cutlery than Tabitha had ever seen. Dainty place cards marked the seating, with parents placed next to their child. Everything would have been quite lovely if it weren't for the rather shell-shocked elderly woman slumped in an armchair that was scooted up to the far end of the table.

Tabitha's end of the table.

"Is *that* the Countess? The maid said she was still in her room. What's the *matter* with her?" Barnaby said to his mother. It was a rude set of questions sandwiching an obvious statement, but everyone seemed to be wondering the same thing.

"Quite the sloucher," Mr. Crum murmured, nonetheless smoothing his toupee and plastering on a smile.

Phillips's head didn't turn to acknowledge the woman, but Tabitha noticed his nostrils flaring with some emotion. Disgust, perhaps. "Please do sit down," he said. "The Countess will join you shortly."

"This one must be nobody of consequence, then," Mrs. Crum said, sitting next to Tabitha, who was seated next to the sloucher.

The woman appeared to be drooling a bit, and one side of her

face was wilted into a frown. Her long-sleeved gray dress was simple and slightly wrinkled. Other than a marvelous head of snow-white hair, her only adornment was a thick, almost tube-like wooden bracelet, coarsely carved with some sort of inter-twined fantasy creature, serpents or some such thing. It was the sort of unique, inexpensive item that you might find in a crafts-man's market stall.

Everyone took their seats and began sipping from crystal water glasses and quietly gossiping. Nobody acknowledged the old woman, who did not have a place card to identify her. She sat limply, one arm tucked into her body at an odd angle and her head tilted to one side. Her blue eyes, however, seemed firmly locked on Tabitha's face.

"Hello," Tabitha whispered in a friendly voice while her parents argued over the cost of the table setting. "Can I get you anything?" She saw that the woman had only one earring, a tiny jeweled bluebird. It was a silver bird in profile, with three blue stones dotting the wing and a single jewel for the eye. The detail was impeccable. Tabitha wondered if the woman had had an accident while putting in the second one or was simply elderly and forgetful.

The woman's eyes lowered to her lap, where her hands were piled on top of each other. A grunt of effort escaped her as she turned one palm over. The other remained quite still. Her eyes swiveled back up, and they became the loneliest things Tabitha had ever seen, like baby swallows whose mother had flown away, never to return.

"There now," Tabitha said softly, patting the woman's hand. It was a soft hand. Soft and smooth, with long fingers and short, clean nails. Tabitha patted again and watched as a tear came dangerously close to spilling from one of the woman's eyes.

Tabitha unfolded her napkin to dab at the soon-to-be-shed tear, sensing that the woman couldn't do it for herself. "There now. I don't know your name, but we're at a lovely dinner party, and I . . . I feel lucky to be beside you."

Tabitha noticed Oliver looking her way and nodded at him. He was far down the table, in between parents who were chatting away with the Herringbones. Oliver shifted his eyes toward the woman beside Tabitha and raised his eyebrows in question. *What's her story?* he seemed to be asking.

Tabitha slowly shrugged her shoulders in response. *Haven't a clue.*

Oliver raised his glass and tipped it her way. *Cheers,* he mouthed.

Tabitha lifted her own water, letting the glass linger in the air for an extra moment while she committed Oliver's grin and raised glass to memory. She wondered very briefly what it might be like to be a girl who did not have a list of *far worse things* in respect to not having friends.

"Ehhllz," the old woman whispered. The dry rasp of a sound coming from her throat was what Tabitha imagined a mummy at the British Museum might sound like, if mummies were prone to speaking.

"What's that?" Tabitha asked. "What did you say, madam?"

As the woman's chest rose and sank with effort, a soft wind blew from one side of her lips. "El . . . behh."

Nodding encouragingly, Tabitha took her elbow off the dining table. "Oh, thank you for the reminder. I'm Tabitha Crum."

Two tears sank freely then, dripping down her seatmate's left cheek. Confusion clouded the blue irises, a trace of fear overlaying the sadness.

"I wish I could hel—" Tabitha began, but stopped at a peculiar whining sound. At first she thought it was coming from her tablemate. From the curious set of heads turning toward the mystery woman's part of the table, so did everyone else.

There it was again. A low moan.

Barnaby's chair scraped against the floor as he stood, peering from the other end of the room. "Is she trying to say something?"

Another sound. This time it was a muffled struggling noise, almost like someone being strangled.

"What the bloody hell is that?" Mr. Crum asked, moving his head back and forth as though someone were hiding in the air.

By the second mysterious uttering, Tabitha had confirmed that the sound was coming distinctly from the space *behind* the elderly woman. A static silence filled the room, each guest straining to hear something while also hoping very much not to.

"What is she saying?" asked Barnaby. He turned to his mother. "Why can't she speak properly?"

"It's not her," Tabitha told him.

"Ghost," Mrs. Herringbone whimpered.

"Shh, dear," Mr. Herringbone said. "Surely not. Noises from the kitchen, perhaps."

"Yes," Edward agreed, looking eagerly toward the serving

entrance. "Maybe they're doing lobster and we heard the death scream." He smiled at Frances, who looked ill. "Read about that in one of Mum's cooking books. It's actually the air coming out of its stomach through its mouth parts. Sounds quite exciting to witness."

Before anyone could comment further, Phillips entered with an echoing click that startled everyone's attention to the opposite end of the room.

"Eh-hem," he said, gesturing to the grand doors. "May I present a patroness of England and your hostess, Camilla Lenore DeMoss, Countess of Windermere."

7

"With the known tension among those present tonight, this dinner party will be absolutely bursting with information, Tibbs," noted Pensive, arranging his ascot in the mirror. "Aside from the food, I'd say there's a decent chance that the conversation will be poisoned as well. So in addition to your very capable mouth, please keep your eyes and ears open during the meal."

—Inspector Percival Pensive,
The Case of the Salmon Surprise

Perfume wafted into the room, filling the dining area with a swirling mélange of lavender, rose, and Devon violet. The Countess appeared soon after her scent, and everyone in the room stood and quieted to a respectful silence.

Her blue dinner gown was complemented by matching gloves and a fashionable webbed evening hat, and around her neck hung an enormous sapphire, cut in such a way that it glimmered beneath the chandelier's glow like lake water touched by sunlight. The Countess inclined her head with a graceful nod and stared appraisingly around the room until she had taken in every guest. And then, quite suddenly, her face broke into a delighted smile.

"Welcome, everyone!" she cried, clapping and laughing in cascading tones of delight. "Welcome to my home! I, of course, am Camilla DeMoss, and I simply couldn't be happier to see you all here."

The Countess's hair was a gray-brown that was elegantly fading in color, and she wore it swept up in a delicate knot. Her face was flawlessly powdered, eyes lined in a light charcoal, and her lips were glazed with color that brought to mind the most brilliant russet leaves of autumn.

"My goodness," said Edward, elbowing his father and nodding appreciatively at his hostess. "You're beautiful for an oldish person," he told her.

"And *you're* very kind, young sir." The Countess beamed benevolently at the group and moved toward the head of the table, carrying an oversize handbag. A large brass ring hung from her silk belt, strung with a variety of keys that numbered into the twenties.

"Younger than I would've thought," Mr. Crum said loud enough for the entire table to hear, clearly liking what he saw. He straightened his posture and smoothed his shirt.

The Countess's makeup was rather thick and heavy, Tabitha thought, as she got a closer look. The effect was a bit unnatural, but perhaps it was standard fare for women of title. Goodness knows her mother had come home raving about how this and that wealthy woman had the latest in powders, rouges, or false eyelashes. Or perhaps there was another reason. Tabitha put on her invisible Inspector hat and resisted the urge to take a pensive chew on her invisible pocket watch chain. *A burn victim, perhaps, who is self-conscious of scars. Or she used to be a circus performer and holds nostalgia for strongly applied blusher and eye shading.*

"Introductions are in order, I suppose," said the Countess, her voice low and warm, "but we can all read the place cards, can't we?" She bent to set the handbag on the floor next to her chair and rose slowly, her arms coming to rest on the back of her chair. "I assume you're seated in your spots, and I know most of what I need to through your family's files. Now, sit, sit!"

Viola's eyes widened, and she mouthed the word *files* to her parents as they settled into their chairs. Everyone seemed equally taken aback by the word, but Tabitha was delighted at the mention of investigative work by the Countess. Her Ladyship hadn't randomly sampled the British population to come up with the six children at the table; it had been a deliberate choice. Tabitha tapped softly on Pemberley's head to make sure he was listening. What sort of file could anyone have possibly filled with information about the Crums?

"Have files on us, do you?" Edward asked. "Glad to be sitting next to you, by the way. Edward Herringbone's the name, and enjoying this meal's my game." He smiled widely.

The Countess patted him on the head. "Aren't you a charming little gentleman? I do admire frankness, young man. Such a loud voice, which is perfect, since I'm just the slightest bit hard of hearing and this table is rather long, so please speak up, everyone, or I won't hear a word. And I am *so* looking forward to this meal."

Between the heavenly odors wafting behind the service door, the lighting dimmed for evening, and the Countess's gracious manner of speech, it was as though a relaxing enchantment had been placed over the gathering. Expressions of irritable impatience had smoothed into content curiosity. Even Phillips, who had stiffly positioned himself next to the dining room doors, seemed captivated by Her Ladyship.

"I do love charity, but another great love of mine is fine food," the Countess said. "I hope you all will indulge me a little excess in the form of a ten-course meal. Do you approve of excess, dear?" she asked Viola.

Viola nodded quietly. "Yes, Lady DeMoss, thank you."

"And the rest of you children? Do you mind being spoiled a bit?"

They all responded with hesitant head shakes, and Tabitha noted that even Frances was subdued under the presence of Camilla Lenore DeMoss.

"Oh, good. And I'm so glad your parents are joining us.

Good children can't exist without good parenting, isn't that right . . ." She leaned forward and peered down the table at the place card next to Tabitha's. "Mrs. Crum."

Mrs. Crum gave a vigorous nod of affirmation. "Yes, Your Ladyship. That's what I always say."

"Is it? How wise of you. Let's get on with the meal, then, shall we? After all, explanations are best served along with a full stomach. Now, now, don't look so disappointed! I promise you, it's something worth waiting for." As though the words were a summoning charm, the cook appeared and directed two kitchen servants as they served a first course of oysters.

A sigh of lament came from beside Tabitha.

"Can I get you anything?" Tabitha whispered to her seatmate.

The elderly woman didn't respond, but her eyes watered again and her hand twitched as though it very much wanted to be held. It was such a real manifestation of Tabitha's own feelings from time to time that she reached over to twice squeeze the poor hand before addressing the food being served.

The meal was delectable, with courses of consommé and leeks, cold poached salmon with bergamot mousseline sauce and cucumbers, curried game meats, mutton joint with savory stuffing, roasted duckling and pheasant and squab with herbed root vegetables, and so on. Tabitha, whose finest meals had consisted largely of tinned meats and powdered custard, nearly wept at the smells and textures and tastes flooding her senses.

Bits and pieces of carefully rehearsed conversation were attempted by all the parents, but it was rather like watching a boatful of fishermen scattering lines into the water with confidence, then reeling them in again when nothing of substance cared to take the bait. Tabitha noticed that the few times her mother tried to field a question, her response was thrown back like an underweight smelt.

It wasn't until the second fish course was presented by the cook herself that the room expressed any sort of intense animation. Banging through the service door with her tall, sturdy frame, the cook heaved the dish onto the center of the table in front of the Countess. The fish lay on a bed of dressed spinach and onion shavings and was surrounded by small glass dishes of both a clear and a light-pink gelatinous substance. Its lidless eyeball was as large as a sovereign, death causing it to stare at nothing and everything at once. Its expired mouth was open, and a row of sharp teeth was clearly visible.

Wiping a sweaty arm across her brow, Cook gestured to the platter. "May I present," she said in a deep voice, "the broiled perch with choice of rose or champagne jelly, Countess."

Mrs. Crum gave an involuntary shudder. "The *head's* still on it," she murmured.

"Good Lord, the size of it," Viola whispered, then smiled across the table at Tabitha. "What has it been eating, do you think? Look at it, Edward."

"I am looking, and it's looking right back." Edward grinned hugely, clapping his hands together and rubbing them. "Well done, Cook!"

Cook blushed and gave a small curtsy. "Eighteen inches

long, head to tail, straight from Lake Windermere."

"I don't like my food staring at me," Barnaby said. "Ow! Sorry, Mother, but I don't."

"Nor do I," said Frances, whose timidity and manners seemed temporarily frozen by disgust.

Yes, it might catch you nicking the silverware, Tabitha thought, switching her gaze to the Countess, who was making a small, unsatisfied grumbling noise in the back of her throat.

Cook frowned. "Is it not to your liking?"

The Countess touched her forehead and sighed deeply. "You've done it whole, Cook. I specifically said the presentation was to exclude the head, which you were supposed to have used to enliven the flavor of the lead consommé." Her fingers tightened around her napkin.

"Apologies, Your Ladyship. I'll fix it right up." Grunting, Cook reached forward to grab the dish.

"Just go," the Countess ordered a bit coldly. She dropped the napkin beside her plate, and her lips did an odd dance that ended in a half smile. "That is, you've worked so very hard, Cook. And being worn out, you might slash the flesh to pieces, leaving it looking like a stabbing victim. That wouldn't do." She smiled at her guests and once again, her beauty and flashing jewels seemed to cast an assuaging spell. "After all," she added meekly, "I may be a countess, but I'm not too high and mighty to get my hands a bit dirty. I'll do it myself."

And while her party members exchanged puzzled glances, the Countess of Windermere reached into her oversize handbag, produced a rather large knife, stood up, took careful aim, and with a single flash of metal, beheaded the fish.

Sitting delicately, the Countess wiped the knife on her linen napkin and returned it to the handbag. She nodded toward the divided fish. "You may take the head back, Cook."

Cook stared at her employer, her mouth hanging open, not unlike the beheaded perch. "Yes, Your Ladyship." She eyed the handbag. "I was wondering where the ten-inch blade had gone."

"It's with me, along with the paring knife," the Countess answered, holding up a small blade. "I *always* have them on me." Seeing the baffled expressions of her guests, the Countess tilted her head and smiled softly. "Oh, I know it must seem odd, but a widow likes to feel protected at all times, you know. It's the same reason I always lock my study and have my staff sign confidentiality papers. I've been a bit jumpy since the deaths of my loved ones. Anyway, I'm awfully fond of my knives."

It was a reasonable, if disturbingly eccentric, admission. After all, one must get terribly paranoid after having a husband killed. *Though she seemed awfully comfortable with that knife. Not a moment of hesitation,* Tabitha noted.

"Makes perfect sense to me." Edward nodded. "That was a lovely beheading, by the way. Human ones can be messier, you know. Did you know that the Countess of Salisbury was whacked eleven times at the Tower of London in 1541? Inexperienced axman, they say. Gashed her shoulder first, then took ten more blows to finish her off. Sixty-seven years old at the time, poor girl. *Executions and Medical Mishaps.* Rather nasty book, that one."

Nobody responded. Viola was kind enough to steer the conversation toward the Countess's philanthropic gifts to Lake District interests, and as the perch was rather delicious, the knife incident was slowly forgotten. But gradually, an uncomfortable silence settled around the table.

"Does anyone have any general questions about Hollingsworth Hall while Phillips fetches a little surprise?" the Countess asked. She gave a curt nod to the butler, who bowed and exited the room.

Barnaby Trundle, who had been sneaking glances at Tabitha's end of the table throughout the meal, was eager to oblige by blurting out, "Who *is* that?" while pointing to the elderly woman. He winced, no doubt suffering from a thick pinch given by his mother.

The Countess appeared pleased by the question. "Oh, I'm so glad someone's finally asked about *dear* Mary Pettigrew," she said. She rose and stepped the length of the table. She had a wonderfully determined, if slightly jerking, walk, Tabitha decided. Short, clipped steps.

Moving directly behind Mary, the Countess placed her hands on the woman's shoulders. "Perhaps you've heard of my tendency to switch out all my help every six months."

"But Phillips doesn't leave," Edward said. "He said in the tour that he's been here two years."

The Countess cocked her head. "Did he now? What else

did he share with you? I wonder. Anyway, I was in between staff on this past Monday evening when Phillips found my *dear, dear* maid Mary slumped over my desk. She'd had a stroke, poor thing, that much was obvious."

Tabitha couldn't keep her hand from rising. "Pardon me, but what was she doing at your desk? I thought you said you always locked your study."

"Precisely what I was thinking"—the Countess squinted to read the place card—"Tabitha Crum. Rooms that are locked are clearly meant to remain private."

Private for what purpose? Tabitha supposed that a study might hold the Countess's paperwork, something adults seemed to place a great deal of importance on. Pensive detested the idea of keeping private rooms and vaults. *What better way to announce the location of your valuables and secrets than to gather them up behind a locked door, Tibbs?* he'd said in multiple novels.

"But Mary wasn't in a state to be questioned," the Countess continued, "so I had Phillips take her to the servants' quarters for rest. I feel sorry for her, really I do."

"Let me see if I understand this, Your Ladyship. Your *maid* is joining us for dinner?" Mrs. Trundle asked with a frown. "Isn't that . . . kind." Her lips moved up and down, forcing themselves to end in an upright position. "You're so very kind. A maid . . . at dinner."

"She's not really eating," Tabitha quietly noted. The maid hadn't been served a single course. Pemberley shifted in

Tabitha's pocket, poking her tummy repeatedly with his snout. *Yes, Inspector Pemby,* she thought, *we need more information.* "I'm terribly sorry to bother Your Ladyship again, but do you know what sort of thing would cause a stroke?" Tabitha asked, enduring a harsh foot stomp from her mother.

The Countess lifted her hands from Mary and fixed Tabitha with an expression that adults often did when too many questions were asked. "I suspect it was the fault of too much sausage and bacon. Love the rich stuff, don't you, Mary?" She caught Mary's pale cheek with the palm of her hand in a delicate double pat. "She would try skipping the heavy items every other month or so, but in the end, I'm afraid too much pig is simply too much pig." Clucking her tongue, the Countess lifted her head to the group and smiled.

"Perhaps she saw a ghost," Viola suggested.

Edward wiped a lingering bit of champagne jelly from his chin and raised a hand.

A furrow formed between the Countess's thin eyebrows. "Yes"—she squinted once again to see the hand-raiser's name—"Edward Herringbone?"

Edward cleared his throat and gave a nod to the room in general. "It's true that strokes can be caused by clogged arteries due to an unbalanced diet consisting mainly of fats," he recited. "They often result in confusion and disorientation and one side of the body failing to react to basic muscle commands, from motor skills to speech. Read that in *Mason's Anatomy and*

Diseases. It's also true that stressful or frightening situations can increase the possibility of strokes, and um . . ." A slip of pink tongue brushed his lower lip, and his gaze rolled to the ceiling in thought. "That's all I remember."

"How awful," Tabitha murmured, briefly considering whether a stroke on the part of either of her parents might improve their personalities. *A stroke would explain what a strain it was for her to produce the word 'elbow,'* she noted, politely ignoring another series of grunts escaping from Mary.

Frances let out a single snort. "Fatty diets?" she said softly, so that the Countess couldn't hear. "Then you had better watch out, hadn't you, Edward? And your best friend Viola as well."

While all eyes turned to the Dales and Herringbones to see their response to such rudeness, Tabitha watched Frances's hand shoot forward to the centerpiece. A golden leaf disappeared, presumably into the beaded bag.

"We're just large-boned," Edward declared while his friend and mother and father blushed. "And we get plenty of vegetables, so a stroke's not likely for us." He pounded on his belly and grinned hugely at the room and then at his mother. "No worries, Mum."

"Shouldn't you fetch a doctor for your maid?" Mr. Appleby asked.

The Countess dabbed at Mary's mouth with the maid's untouched napkin. "I wouldn't really know about fetching someone. I've never been sick a day in my life."

Tabitha watched the Countess meet Mr. Appleby's

bewildered expression and shift her indifference to concern.

"I phoned a doctor, of course, and he said there's nothing to be done except rest. She's been with me for years, so of course I would never send her to the streets, begging for work. That"—she pinched Mary's cheek—"would have been very cruel indeed." The Countess's hand rose, smoothing her hair. "But enough about the maid. Is everyone having a lovely time?"

Hesitant nods went all around.

"Then I suppose I should tell you why your children were summoned. You must be curious."

Every parent and child shifted in their seat, their legs and eyes nervous with expectancy.

"Oh, good, you are! In that case . . ." The Countess paced slowly around the table, playfully raising and wagging a finger. She paused, mid-wag, and cracked the double doors a smidgen. "Phillips! Bring in the—"

Backing up, the Countess made way for the butler, who was carrying a very small trunk. "Well done, Phillips, quite prompt. On the table with it, then out with you."

After a long glance at the Countess, Phillips bobbed an obedient bow and made his exit. The black trunk sat, all eyes glued to it.

Countess DeMoss seated herself once more. "Children, I'm afraid I have some shocking news. Your parents have been naughty liars."

Any warmth in the room disappeared immediately, as

though an unexpected eclipse had blackened the sun. There was a slight flicker in the electric light.

Perhaps this was it, Tabitha thought. A thrilling crime was to be revealed. *Steady now,* she told herself. Recalling hours of training spent at the literary sides of Inspector Pensive and Timothy Tibbs, she took inventory of the adults who had just been accused of unspecified deceit:

A guilty start from her father
A choked cough from her mum
An impressively raised eyebrow from Mr. Wellington
A small, confident smile from Mrs. Wellington, who was checking her face in a pocket mirror
Polite but strained interest from both Herringbones
Puzzlement bordering on worry from the Dales
Panic from the Trundles
Confusion from the Applebys

Carefully sifting through the enormous brass ring, the Countess came upon a small silver key. With a dramatic flick of the wrist, she unlocked and popped open the trunk's lid, revealing a neatly organized series of folders.

Mrs. Trundle and Mrs. Crum lifted themselves up a bit, craning their necks to get a better look.

"As I said earlier, there's a file on each family present." The Countess took in a lengthy breath and let it out evenly. Then she chortled and raised a hand to cover her mouth, though her eyes remained sparkling. "Oh dear, that was unladylike, wasn't it, but this is going to be *such* good fun." With considerable effort, she adopted a more serious expression once more.

"Your parents, children," the Countess of Windermere informed them, "have been keeping secrets from you."

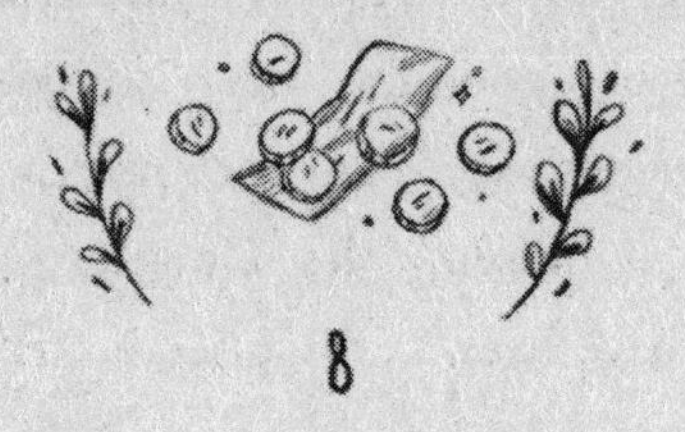

8

Money isn't everything, Tibbs, especially to those who already have it. That said, offering large sums to people can have a variety of effects: shock, suspicion, or pure joy, though the joyful ones ought to check their happiness, Tibbs. Nothing comes without attachments or a sacrifice of sorts, not even free money.

—Inspector Percival Pensive,
The Case of the Bilious Banker

Secrets, the Countess had said. The word echoed mutely around the table, overpowering the lingering smells of butter and roasted meats. Chandelier bulbs darkened, then fluttered back to life overhead, and the Countess eyed the flickering lights while sucking a small bit of lower lip into her mouth. "Storm," she murmured.

Lifting a piece of paper from a file, she paused, eyes reading over some sort of report. "But before we get into your family secrets and *such* a lovely piece of fun as well, you may wish to know a bit about my own sad history."

Edward lifted his spoon, swiping it across his neck and aiming a wink at Frances. "*Double murder*," he whispered loudly.

Frances shot her hand in the air. "Your Ladyship, with all due respect and humility, I'd prefer if you'd skip over any double murder."

The Countess stared blankly for a moment. "Are you talking about my husband and brother-in-law?" she said. "I've heard that rumor myself, though I'm not sure if I believe it. People slap the term 'murder' on everything these days, don't they?" She stared at the page. "Are you all ready to listen?"

The room's silence seemed an acquiescence.

"Twelve years ago my son Thomas ran off and eloped with a woman of no education or connections, embarrassing me to the point of estrangement. She, of course, was with child when they ran away. He fully embraced the estrangement, the fool, changing his name to God knows what. A little over a year later, they both died in a boating accident. Their six-month-old child was reportedly onshore with an attendant who clearly had no clue about my son's background. She sent the babe to an orphanage, a fact that took years to confirm."

Tabitha was reminded of Augustus Home. *That's where I'm headed. But there are far worse things than living in an orphanage, Pemberley.*

- living in a toilet
- living in Barnaby Trundle's room
- living in a haunted manor with vengeful ghosts

"You see, when Thomas and his wife died, I immediately put people on the hunt for my grandchild, but the attendant had disappeared, and I couldn't find anyone who knew where the child was taken. Only recently have I received solid evidence."

The Countess took a paper from the first file and read aloud. "The investigation has traced the point of abandonment to Basil House, London's Oldest Home for Orphaned Infants and Children." Dropping the paper, she pointed around the room at each of the children in turn. "You six children were the only ones dropped off at Basil House in May of 1895, at approximately six months of age. You were all adopted by your charitable and childless parents shortly thereafter." The Countess held both arms out and smiled hugely. "Tra-laa, children, surprise!"

An audible gasp, sounding very much like it came from Barnaby Trundle, echoed throughout the dining room.

Viola turned to Mr. and Mrs. Dale, dropping the spoon she'd been clutching with a harsh silver-on-china *clank*. "What was that? Mum? Dad?"

"I'm sorry, what?" Edward said pleasantly. His smile faded when the words sank in, and he turned to his mother and father. "What did she say? I'm . . . not your son, then? Well, whose son am I?"

Frances Wellington choked on her drink. Both hands flew to her neck, and her eyeballs became wide, white, straining things until she coughed up the water.

Oliver was silent, a slight grimace appearing on his face as though he'd had one too many dinner courses.

Tabitha did not gasp or ask questions or choke or grimace. Instead her hand drifted down to cup the lump in her apron, and she felt a slow compression occur within her. A sense of being squeezed and drained. Whether it was a healthy loss, like a snakebite being purged of poison (*I am not truly a Crum, Pemberley*), or a harsh loss, like feeling even smaller in the world (*I am not truly anyone at all, Pemberley*), she wasn't certain. Perhaps a bit of both.

"So you see, one of you is my heir." The Countess lowered the files. "Now, because I've been desperately looking for my relation all these years, I set up a substantial trust fund long ago on the off chance that I would one day find my beloved grandchild."

The room went abuzz with raised eyebrows and taken-aback facial expressions and the repeated words "trust fund," and the Countess clapped her hands rather gleefully. "Oh lovely! You're all surprised and thrilled to pieces, I can tell! You six are the only possibilities, and I absolutely can't wait to find out which one of you is my grandchild, so I can spoil the dickens out of you. You can stay the entire summer next year! I'm really quite sentimental, you see, and find myself in the sad situation of having every member of my family dead."

Pemberley scratched at Tabitha's tummy. *Yes, murdered, rather. At least some of them.*

The Countess smiled an awkwardly large smile, a bit of lipstick clinging to one of her front teeth. "So it's happy news. For one of you, at least. You'll come and have visits with me to make up for all the lost years, and you'll come into the lovely trust fund."

"And just how lovely is the trust fund?" asked Barnaby, wincing once again and glaring at his mother.

The Countess ignored him and dinged her glass repeatedly with a fork. "Cook! The champagne!"

Cook burst from the service entrance with a tray and gave every parent a flute of champagne and every child a tiny sherry glass full of bubbly drink.

"It's one hundred thousand pounds, loves." The Countess lifted her flute. "Cheers!"

"One hundred thou—" Mr. Trundle coughed and snorted, and Barnaby stared at the Countess with rapt attention. The Applebys and Dales and Herringbones exchanged impressed glances. Even Viola, Tabitha noticed, was transfixed by so large a sum of money, much larger than any donation she'd ticked off on her fingers thus far.

Frances raised a hand. "One hundred thousand pounds. Are you perfectly serious?" She looked between her mother and father, considering them. "And when will I be visiting next?" She pasted an angelic smile below her eager eyes. "Pardon, but it *is* me, isn't it?"

"I'm afraid I don't know, dear. Otherwise I wouldn't have invited all of you, would I?" The Countess looked among the adults. "Let's be quite open and honest, parents. You must have been given some sort of special knowledge about the origin of your son or daughter."

The parents exchanged puzzled glances, but no confession was made.

"No? Well, I'll give you some time to think about it, and then you can pass along any personal recollections to your children. Please do share everything with your child. For *their* sake. And for the sake of one hundred thousand pounds. I shall interview each child tomorrow, and we'll see what comes of it. For now, I'll just say once again how happy you've all made me by coming and being part of this blessed reunion!"

The Countess ordered another round of celebratory beverages to be poured. Everyone toasted and clinked and soon became rosy-cheeked with the wonder of the situation and the pondering of life possibilities that could be bought with an extra hundred thousand in one's pocketbook.

"One chance in six, then," Mr. Trundle quipped. "I like those odds. Barnaby would thrive here, and we could get by without him quite easily for the summer. Or longer if you'd like." Mr. Trundle either ignored or didn't see Barnaby's hurt expression. "But how will you know the right child for certain?" he asked the Countess, his expression more curious than concerned.

Yes, how will she know?

The Countess set her drink down carefully. "Obviously there will be some knowledge that the orphanage gave to the rightful heir's parents—a description of the mother and father that I might recognize, a story about their past that links the birth parents to Hollingsworth Hall, a token of some sort. And dear Mary will be assisting me to ensure that the correct heir is claimed."

Mr. Crum snorted. "I doubt that a strokey maid would be able to identify much at all."

Frances wrinkled her nose in Mary's direction. "And I doubt that she could judge which of us has countess blood." She straightened her posture and smiled. "Besides, I should think it rather obvious who your heir is, *Grandmother*." She glanced at Tabitha, Viola, Barnaby, and Edward. "Or at least to rule out who it *isn't*."

"Not really a matter of 'countess' blood, is it? She wasn't born with a title," Edward pointed out.

Yes, that's true. I do wonder at her history previous to her arrival at Hollingsworth Hall.

"Mary Pettigrew," the Countess stated firmly, "has seen the child as an infant and knew my Thomas well. And Mary was well acquainted with the woman my son ran away with, which I was not." She smiled at the maid. "Low class being acquainted with low class, and all that. I shall include her in the interview sessions to gauge her response to faces and such. Rest assured, by the end of the weekend, I will have a grandchild. Isn't it exciting?"

"To be perfectly clear, you've never seen this child?" Mr. Wellington asked. "And Basil House didn't keep records of who dropped off which baby?"

The Countess sifted through the first file and frowned at the paperwork. "Of course they kept records, but being an orphanage, there were times when children were simply left at the doorstep. That was the case for all the children here. So no, there are no formal records, other than drop-off dates."

"There's just one thing, Your Ladyship," Mrs. Appleby said

delicately. "I don't know that you can just claim one of our children as a grandchild and demand extended visits."

"You can claim Barnaby," Mr. Trundle said eagerly. "You'll get no resistance from us."

Lines of pressure formed around the Countess's mouth. She inhaled deeply, plucking her bag from the floor. "Everyone please calm down. I am a patroness of England, titled by my good friend, the *King*. Surely that's enough of a character reference."

Tabitha wondered how good of a friend King Edward could be to the Countess, and whether he knew that she kept knives on her person at all times.

"But why didn't anyone tell us we were adopted?" Viola asked.

Mrs. Dale squeezed Viola's hand and looked at the other mothers with empathy. "I'm sure that some of you know the pain of not being able to carry a child. There's no shame in not wanting the whole world to know your business."

Mrs. Appleby nodded and reached for her husband's hand. "We went to the Continent for a year," she said quietly. "Lawrence came back to get Oliver and then we stayed in Europe until our boy was one. Not a soul except the woman at Basil House knew he wasn't ours." She cleared her throat. "But he *is* ours now, and we'll need more time getting to know you before Oliver is left here for an entire summer."

Mrs. Herringbone raised a hand. "I'm sorry, Your Ladyship, but I agree with the Applebys." She turned to Edward and squeezed his hand. "Oh, my dear boy," she said, gesturing to the Dales. "Our best friends in the world adopted a child at Basil House and suggested we do the same. We wanted you and Viola to grow up together, so we picked children of similar age. And we didn't tell either of you about the adoption because there can be a silly stigma associated with that sort of thing and it really doesn't matter. You are *my* son, Edward."

The Countess fiddled with the stays on her handbag and gave an odd chirped laugh. "Oh, let's all just relax! Details can be worked out on Sunday. I'm a flexible woman, and I'm sure we'll all end up with exactly what we want. Cook! Dessert!" She smiled once more. "This is a celebration."

"She's right," Mr. Appleby said, patting his wife on the hand and nodding at Oliver. "We seem to have forgotten our manners, Your Ladyship." He stood and raised his champagne. "Glasses up once more, everyone." He waited for the room to follow suit. "To the Countess of Windermere!"

The room echoed him.

"To one hundred thousand pounds!" cried Mrs. Trundle.

Agnes walked in with a tray of gorgeous raspberry tortes, fruit sorbet, and pistachio ice. The Countess mingled among the parents and children, touching arms and patting heads, and once more the dining room became an enchanted place.

Tabitha looked at her parents, who were deep in discussion, with no indication that they needed her consultation. They, unlike the others, had not worn expressions of hesitant giddiness at any point during the trust fund announcement, which probably meant one thing: the Crums were absolutely certain that they wouldn't be coming into any money.

"I'll just visit the loo," she told them, leaving the room humming with excited, tense whispers behind her. She heard a small whisper of her own. It called to her faintly from somewhere between her heart and her mind.

There are far worse things than no longer having a family.

"Why, Pemberley," she whispered, drawing the mouse from her pocket, "wouldn't they ever have taken one from Basil House?"

Tabitha knew any thought of earning her parents' love was slim, but still she had tried. She had tried very hard. And buried far beneath her need to be part of a family, her desire to be loved, and her frustration at not being able to earn that love, was another feeling that she couldn't quite place. It sent hot bursts of blood from her heart to her toes and fingertips. The rogue feeling threatened to rush out and show itself in an uncontrolled manner, but Tabitha took a deep breath and made a logical and concerted effort to push all emotions aside.

A proper Inspector had no room for feelings. Tabitha had no inkling of being anything special and doubted she was related to the Countess, but if nothing else, she might use the time with her parents to discover why, exactly, she had been adopted by two people who seemed to shun the very idea of children. That was a mystery she'd like to solve.

9

If you want to know the true personality of a person, Tibbs, never go by how they treat you. Go by how they treat the butler and the maid. In every single case, whether the crime took place in a palace or a pauper's alley box, by God, find yourself a maid to speak with.

—Inspector Percival Pensive,
The Case of the Loitering Lord

Tabitha patted her hands dry on a lavender towel. "It's a lovely home," she told Pemberley, in what she hoped was a soothing sort of voice. She sensed that her mouse friend was feeling a bit apprehensive about the coming chat with the Crums and that he could use a burst of possibility. "And a grandmother *is* family. Perhaps I'm actually a lost DeMoss, and that's why my life has seemed like a dress that I simply can't fit into properly. Perhaps I'm to inherit a trust fund and I can buy you a cheese palace and—"

Squeakity-squeak.

"Yes, well, as I was saying to myself earlier, if that's the way of things, then perhaps I can clean floors here instead of at Augustus Home. Let's go."

The electric lighting in the hallway made Tabitha feel shadowed as they walked hesitantly down the carpet, passing more evidence of the wealth that would soon be shared by one of the children. Silver-framed paintings and gold-set mirrors crowded the walls, making it seem as though the manor was about to close tightly upon them, like a clever plant that had trapped a missing jewel in a Pensive novel Tabitha had read.

When she returned to the dining hall, it was empty, save for Mary Pettigrew and a server taking the uneaten desserts away. Mary did not look well. Slumping forward against the table, her eyes faced the painting on the opposite wall. Tabitha got the impression that Mary was far away, looking at a much different picture in her mind. The server looked up at Tabitha's footsteps.

"Is someone coming to get Mary?" Tabitha asked.

The server blushed. "I would think so, miss. The others have gone to the drawing room or the library or the foyer."

Sure enough, Tabitha found tight circles of parents and children scattered from the large entrance hall to the expansive library and the drawing room. The Trundles were grouped near a suit of armor, Mr. Trundle's hand gripping Barnaby's shoulder as he whispered with intensity. Mr. Wellington was just visible near the doorway of the drawing room, puffing at a thick, deep-brown cigar.

Tabitha wandered until she saw Mr. and Mrs. Crum at the

base of the main staircase. They were quite huddled together, and there was a decided look about them as she approached.

"Mum. Daddy."

They turned and glared at her in unison. When it was clear that neither of her parents would be starting a conversation, Tabitha took a deep breath. According to Inspector Pensive, it was common sense that whenever you were in a fix or at a crossroads in an investigation, there were always two choices: to do nothing and worry, or to take some sort of action and deal with its associated risks.

"I don't know if you've anything to tell me," she began softly. She paused, wondering whether to clarify her meaning by adding *other than why you decided to abandon me and poor, sensitive Pemberley to an orphanage. Or why you adopted me in the first place if you were just going to throw me away.* "But I am to be called into the Countess's study tomorrow. Is there anything you remember about the day you got me from Basil House? Anything at all?"

"What's to remember?" Mrs. Crum said. "The only thing that chafes my memory is that you had a frightful shriek and I couldn't get you to shut up and you gave your father an insufferable headache."

Mr. Crum nodded. "An ingrate from the start."

As a small child, Tabitha had thought ingrate was a pet name. A loving term. She'd known better since checking at the library several years ago. *Ingrate* meant that she was ungrateful. A self-seeker. Thankless. It was seeing those words in an official book that cemented Tabitha's belief that perhaps she was at fault somehow in the mysterious case of her parents not loving her.

Mr. Crum harrumphed loudly. "And it seems that you still can't keep your gob shut. Now you're badgering us with preposterous questions." He threw a piece of paper at her.

Tabitha picked it up. "A train ticket?"

"Yes, after this weekend you can find your own way back to the station and that will take you to a stop within a few miles of Augustus Home. You'll walk there." Mr. Crum shook a single finger at her, then ran his hand carefully through his toupee. He bent over, leaning close while his eyes looked somewhere beyond Tabitha. "I can't *believe* we delayed our trip for this rubbish. We've stuck our necks out for you on the chance that we'd get something out of this weekend. It was supposed to be *profitable*, and now it seems the payoff comes with a ridiculous condition."

Mrs. Crum snorted her agreement. "Ridiculous. Hopeless, even. Imagine *Tabitha* being related to a countess." She looked at Mr. Crum. "Teacher, wasn't it?"

Tabitha stiffened. "What?"

"A teacher," Mrs. Crum repeated. "The orphanage said the note left with you indicated that your mother was training to be a schoolteacher or some such rubbish. Not a maid. And there was no mention of a father, so *no*, you are not anybody's heir, nor have you ever been." She gritted her teeth. "You've been nothing but a waste of time."

Tabitha felt Pemberley shift inside her apron pocket. Inspector Pensive was always brave in front of Tibbs, even if he later confessed to not feeling quite as valiant as his actions had suggested at the time. "Perhaps you're wrong and the orphanage was mistaken," Tabitha said very quietly, issuing the challenge for her mouse's sake. "Perhaps she *is* my grandmother."

"You? Come from gentility and money?" Mr. Crum's outstretched index finger returned, this time to poke her in the chest. He leaned forward until Tabitha smelled a combination of onion, fish, and raspberry torte. "The only thing that came with you was the blanket you were wrapped in and the promise that you had a beautiful mother. We thought we'd get into some money by marrying you off for your looks to some fool of a rich boy."

Mrs. Crum nodded. "Men are idiots and will fall in love with anything pretty. My own mother rose from a poverty too heinous to tell us much about, and how? By marrying up. And if I hadn't fallen in love with you, Mortimer, I could have married a prince before the strains of motherhood aged me prematurely."

"Too right, darling," Mr. Crum lovingly agreed, "you deserve the world." He sniffed as though he smelled something foul and grunted at his daughter. "That's the only reason we picked you, Tabitha. We had a solid plan based on you being a beauty. But what a joke that turned out to be. The orphanage woman probably said that about all the wretched babies."

Tabitha stumbled back as though she'd been slapped. "Well," she replied, cheeks aflame, "the haircut certainly hasn't done me any favors."

Mrs. Crum shook her head miserably. "I was going to let it grow out when you came of age. I didn't want you catching any boy's eye too early. And now . . ." She blew her nose, unable to continue. "Oh, Mortimer, now I'll never be an upper-class member of London society!"

Mr. Crum gently stroked his wife's arm. "There, there." He finger-brushed his mustache and breathed in, then let out a pained sigh. "We don't need London, dearest. On with the plan, I say."

Tabitha looked between them, the two people who had plucked her from a life without parents. At least Mrs. Crum had the decency to look disturbed, but that turned out to be because Tabitha was standing on a bit of her foot. "Do get off, Tabitha."

"I'm sorry," Tabitha whispered. The apology sounded very far away even to herself, like the voice of a very small person stuck at the top of a very large mountain. Like a person who wasn't sure how she'd gotten stuck in the first place and whether Fate was to blame for the unfortunate situation, or if being cold and alone was somehow secretly her own fault. She peered at each of her parents' shoes in turn. "I'm very sorry I'm not what you intended."

Mrs. Crum dabbed at her eye makeup. "Stop being difficult."

Slowly, fingers trembling, Tabitha unpinned the bittern her mother had given her the day before. She carefully stroked the pin's brass feathers in farewell and handed her mother the brooch, realizing it would be the final time they touched. Her parents would not be coming back after one year or two years or three. They were leaving forever. "I don't know how things will work out on Sunday, but you can have the bittern back. It's a symbol of leaving. I don't believe I want it anymore."

"How *bizarre*," Mr. Crum muttered. "Get rid of that ugly thing." He snatched it away from Tabitha and pitched it aside. The brooch went skittering across the foyer floor, passing through shadows and settling in some dark place.

Tabitha refused to let her gaze follow its path.

Her mother stepped forward, tilting Tabitha's chin until their eyes met. "I want you to know, Tabitha . . ."

"Yes, Mother?" Tabitha leaned forward, surprised and nearly hopeful. *Here it is. A piece of advice to guide me in my years ahead, wherever they might be spent.*

Indeed, Mrs. Crum's eyes softened, and she brought a hand up to cover her mouth for a moment before speaking. "Tabitha," her mother said, "I want you to know what a disappointment you turned out to be. Now go, Tabitha. Disappear."

The Crums avoided her beseeching stare and strode in a confident manner through the foyer. Tabitha could see snow falling on the other side of the large front windows. Soft flakes flurried down like pieces of frozen beauty. The unlucky ones touched the glass and turned instantly to water. Tabitha was struck utterly numb as she watched them fall, as though she'd been tossed into winter itself. As though she, too, were a solitary snowflake surrounded by glass, paralyzed as she floated down, knowing that she had no power to stop herself from melting.

From disappearing forever.

Think of far worse things than being told to disappear, she urged herself in between aching, raw breaths. *After all, you never actually believed they would come to love you.* Her chest seemed to be collapsing upon her heart and the pressure, oh, the truth's pressure was overwhelming.

Oh dear, I suppose there was a piece of you that did think that very thing. Even after they told you about Augustus Home. Stupid, stupid Tabitha. Her parents only wanted her as something they could one day use to raise their social status. And that was all they'd ever wanted from her. She herself, as a daughter and a person, as a gangly and poorly shorn child named Tabitha Crum, was worth nothing.

Finding a small corner between a set of armor and a foyer table, Tabitha let herself sink to the floor, tucking her knees in tightly and wrapping both arms around. *There are far worse things than this, far worse things, far, far worse things.* Pemberley fussed and squeezed out of his pocket. Up Tabitha's apron he scuttled, stopping at her shoulder, where he uttered the tiniest of squeaks.

"They're wrong? My existence isn't pointless, you say?" Tabitha whispered. "Oh, Pemberley, I'm not sure I believe you this time."

The large entrance doors opened and Phillips stepped in, his hair covered in white powder. "The motorcars are here. You're to take three of them, so there's plenty of room, no need to crowd in. Parents, please get your things."

Still feeling lost, Tabitha couldn't even summon a particle of panic as she felt Pemberley run down her leg and scurry toward Mortimer Crum.

"It's bloody *snowing*," observed Barnaby's father with a haughty look. "It shouldn't be snowing." It was difficult to know who he blamed: the weather, the Countess, or the butler.

"A little early for snow," Phillips agreed. "But not entirely unusual. The cars will get you back safely and far more quickly than the horses." He bowed to Mr. Crum. "So you see, you'll get to ride in one of the Countess's fine motorcars after all, sir. Perhaps they'll let you press the horn or steer the wheel for a moment or two."

Mr. Crum narrowed his eyes. "Are you being serious or cheeky?"

"I don't think a butler is allowed to be cheeky, dear," Mrs. Crum answered.

"We had a cheeky butler once," Frances said. "Father fired him immediately."

"I assure you, sir, madam, and miss," Phillips said, "a quality butler's cheek is never noticed."

"So were you being cheeky or weren't you?" Mr. Crum demanded.

The Countess appeared in the foyer, smiling and looking like her captivating self. "Everyone ready for a cozy night?" She patted the stuffed hummingbird on Mrs. Crum's hat. "This fellow's already cozy as the grave, isn't he?"

"Ow!" Mr. Crum bellowed, shaking his leg and knocking down one of the knights, sending metal clattering, scattering, and echoing throughout the front hall. "What in God's name just *bit* me?" He jerked up his pant leg, and a small trickle of blood streamed down. "I've been *bitten*!"

Tabitha lowered her chin and watched her father clutch at the tiny wound, as though it could possibly hurt more than the loneliness she'd felt the majority of her life.

"My guess is that the Countess's knight 'bit you,' sir," Phillips said, raising one hand to his mouth in what was certainly mock concern. "The Countess's sincere apologies, I'm sure."

Pemberley made it safely back into his pocket space, his little mouse heart beating against Tabitha's stomach.

"Well done, friend," Tabitha said, her voice cracking. "They really never loved me at all, so well done." She spoke under her breath so that nobody would hear, and though her words held strength, Tabitha's lips still quivered at the same pace as Pemberley's heartbeat. There was no sense of triumph or closure in having fixed her parents' dismissal as fact, or in solving the mystery of why they didn't love her. Instead her heart felt more permanently off-kilter than ever, unable to claim a suitable beat.

A whole child's beat.

Phillips made shooing motions at the parents, driving them toward the exit like a herd of unruly sheep. He pressed the back of Mrs. Trundle's mink, scooting her into the developing blizzard, where two bundled footmen were waiting to open the doors to the motorcars. The parents piled in, flakes of white whirling in headlights as the cars drove away. And when the door closed on the swirling, freezing, snow-filled air, every single electric light in the manor went out.

"Candles," the Countess's panicked voice barked. "Get the candles!"

Footfalls scattered across the entrance hall, and someone bumped Tabitha on the shin. Jostling and murmured words of dismay filled the air.

"Quiet! Everyone just be quiet and stay where you are until we get some light in here!"

In the silence that followed, there was a sound of low creaking. Tabitha got her bearings and decided that the noise was coming from her front left. No, wait.

It was moving.

The creaking stopped near one of the portraits, where it turned into a soft moan. Tabitha had the distinct feeling that something in the dark was watching her. Perhaps, she thought, remembering the servant girl's words, the portrait was of a man named George. Perhaps his ghost was haunting the—

The lights flickered on again, and every child's eye was drawn to their hostess, who was standing in the middle of the room, ten-inch knife blade poised high in the air.

10

Horrible things happen every day, Tibbs. Every single day. For instance, I was having a perfectly lovely day off when I noticed a rather large beetle in my meat pie. Disgusting. But a rather poorer day for the beetle, I suppose.

—Inspector Percival Pensive,
The Case of the Slippery Salesman

The Countess blinked hard and breathed heavily, her bosom practically bursting from the decorative lace on her dress. Turning a slow circle, she raised her eyes to the foyer chandelier and finally halted her movement facing Barnaby Trundle.

"Oh God, don't murder me," he begged in a hollow whisper.

The knife lowered and disappeared back into the Countess's handbag. "My apologies, young Bartleby," the Countess said, patting the frightened boy on the shoulder, ignoring his flinch.

"Barnaby," he whimpered. "My name is Barnaby."

She gave a hesitant laugh and licked her lips. "I was a bit

startled, children. The boy bumped me and I . . . was startled. That's all."

"Perfectly understandable, Grandmother," Frances said, her voice shaking ever-so-slightly as she assessed the Countess's oversize reticule. "You've lived alone too long."

"It's just the storm, messing about with the electric light," Edward said. "Do you know that a single jolt of electricity could fry a man from toes to eyebrows? In fact—"

"No frying, Edward," Viola quietly ordered.

His cheeks rose with a nervous grin. "Fair enough."

The Countess nodded slowly. "That's right, Frances. I've lived alone too long. Just the snowstorm, nothing more. Phillips, see the children to the second parlor. Agnes, see that the imbecile cook I've hired brings in some hot cocoa, tea, and sweets. Those are things made with sugar, not salt, in case she needs clarification. The children and I will get to know one another a bit more, I think."

"I'm the only one worth knowing," Frances muttered.

Oliver reached over to give Tabitha's hand a single squeeze. "That went a bit beyond eccentric, wouldn't you say?" he whispered.

Tabitha stared between Oliver's hand and face, feeling a pleasant glow in her chest and a rush of . . . she wasn't sure what, but it was a very nice, warm feeling in the midst of a very cold, uncertain situation.

"We'd better do as she says," he said, dropping her hand and offering a formal arm and clearing his throat. "'Into the fray, together we go, out of the warmth and into the snow.'" He blushed. "Or parlor, rather. That was from a poem we read in class. Some sort of soldier bit."

She nodded her appreciation. "Into the fray," she repeated.

Though not quite as grand as the one they'd seen during the tour, the second parlor held an impressive array of furniture and features. Paintings hung on the walls, most of them parlor scenes with people mingling, playing cards, and the like. By the time the children had settled themselves near the central table, a tea service and a delightful stack of goodies were displayed for the taking. A jittery-handed Agnes took the liberty of serving each child an individual assortment, while the Countess sampled tiny bites of each type of dessert and Phillips stood by the door, waiting to be needed.

"Oh, lovely. Sweets, Viola!" Edward took a bite of a dark dessert bar ribboned with chocolate. "Ah, excess," he said happily.

The little room became cozy and warm with dancing light and heat from the hearth. At least it *would* have been cozy, were an uncertain tension not sandwiched within the atmosphere like a thick layer of slightly-off buttercream. And if Tabitha herself had not felt so very unanchored. She roiled with mixed feelings from the conversation with her parents and felt as though she were trying to keep steady upon an empty ship that was to be her new home.

Had yesterday's fog been a warning of her becoming quite lost in the world, just as the bittern had been a sign of her parents leaving? *Oh, pish-posh, you really must stop dwelling. It's not as though you were that poor fellow in the Pensive book, tied to the sea piling with high tide coming in.*

That's right, Pemberley scratched. *There are ghosts and oddities and lost heirs to be investigated. Chin up, you adore a good mystery!*

Touché, dear partner, she scratched back. *Onward with the evening.*

As though agreeing with Tabitha, Pemberley wiggled his way out of her pocket to nibble on dropped sweet crumbs. He scurried beneath a claw-footed table and disappeared.

Frances stood and glared at the children until all side conversations halted. Only then did she turn to the Countess with a humbled expression. "Hollingsworth Hall is so very lovely, *Grandmother*, and I don't believe I've properly thanked you for the invitation," she said loudly, offering an exaggerated curtsy. "My sincere gratitude is yours. I absolutely cannot wait to visit whenever you'd like. I'm sure we'll have a wonderful time once all of these . . . imposters are out of the manor." She sat down, primly folding her hands in her lap.

Pemberley soon appeared, scooting along the edge of the cushion behind Frances with a rather guilty twitch about his whiskers. *Oh my,* Tabitha thought. *I've seen that look before.*

Frances picked at her cookie. "Chocolate sprinkles," she murmured.

"Where?" asked Edward, his eyes darting to everyone's plates. "I didn't get one with sprinkles."

Tabitha felt the pressure of tiny claws as the mouse made his way up her leg and into the safety of her apron pocket. Horrified, she noticed Pemberley had left sprinkles on the side of Frances's plate in addition to the cookie itself.

"I suppose that's because you're not special like me, Edward."

Frances swept a finger along Pemberley's leavings, licked her fingers, then popped the cookie into her mouth. "Delicious. Now, let's talk about something else that's special. Hmm . . . I suggest ridiculous haircuts." She smiled at Tabitha. "Yours looks like a lake bird attacked a woman while she chopped your hair with a kitchen knife," she said, nodding to herself. "Anyone else agree?"

"We've all got our faults, Frances," Edward said good-naturedly, reaching for another non-sprinkled cookie. "As I'm sure Granny"—he winked at the Countess—"will find out by tomorrow if she hasn't already. Tabitha's poorly dressed, I'm too fat, Viola's too concerned with charitable nonsense, Oliver here has little in the way of personality—just so far, old chap, I'm sure there's more to you in there somewhere—and as for you, Frances . . . well, I didn't want to say anything, but I believe your eyes are a good half-inch too close together. Poor breeding, I'd say, if there wasn't the chance that you were related to Her Ladyship."

The Countess watched the exchange, chewing with a thoughtful expression before spitting a bite of walnut fancy into a napkin. "Too much flour. Phillips, I do believe Mary's been left in the dining hall, poor thing. Bring her in here, will you?"

The butler wrinkled his nose. "Yes, Your Ladyship."

Her gaze sank to his feet, and the Countess inhaled sharply. "Phillips, why are you wearing *brown* shoes with your uniform?" Her lips fell into a slight pout. "I went to a considerable amount of trouble asking one of the servants to shine up your black ones."

Phillips cleared his throat and shuffled a bit. "That's a lovely thing to do, Your Ladyship, but the servant seems to have kept them. I haven't a clue where they are."

Looking extremely put out, the Countess touched her sapphire and straightened her posture. "Well, do find them or I'll have no choice but to think you don't really care. And if that's the case, Phillips," she said, her voice breaking slightly, "maybe I'll . . ." She noticed the children watching her. Barnaby Trundle's eyes were glued to her handbag. "Well, as it is, you look improper, like a man from the vortex of filth from which you came. Sprang out of there like a diseased cat, didn't you? It all turned out, though. We've both done well for ourselves, I daresay. I'm all for rising above one's station." She walked forward and patted him on the cheek.

Phillips stumbled back a step, his lip twitching incessantly as he left the room. Tabitha wondered exactly which "vortex of filth" he had come from.

"Now," the Countess said, turning to the children with open arms. "Which one of you is the key to keeping my fortune, I wonder?"

"Pardon, but don't you mean *passing down* your fortune?" Tabitha asked.

The Countess took two steps toward Tabitha and crossed her arms. "You ask a lot of questions. If it turns out to be you, I'd like you to stop. Especially as the chosen child will be living with me after the weekend."

"What?" Oliver coughed and pulled at his collar with a finger. "I'm sorry, Your Ladyship, but did you say that your grandchild will be *living* with you?"

The Countess peered across the room to a window, which was being pelted by heavy snowfall. "If this horrid storm wasn't about, I'd have the signing papers here already."

"Um, papers?" Viola asked politely, her shaky teacup returning to its saucer with a rattle.

"Yes, papers to make me the child's legal guardian. Permanently."

There was a moment of shocked silence at the remark. Tabitha, having been told of her definite non-heir status, was able to take in a more clear, Pensive-like view of the room. Oliver and Viola both looked as though they'd eaten a bad piece of fish, Edward was openmouthed, and Barnaby appeared to have lost several shades of pigment.

The Countess frowned and rubbed her necklace jewel. "Well, really just until he or she comes of age, of course, and then the child can do as they please. Barring a nasty case of accidental death, of course."

"Accidental death?" A piece of chocolate wedge fell from Edward's hand. "What's that now?"

"I'm *joking!*" The Countess smiled and laughed, until Frances and Barnaby weakly joined in. "Nobody will be dying accidentally. I was just trying to provide a little levity for you young ones, but I can see that none of you have a sense of humor." She whirled at the sound of a high-pitched squeak, relaxing when she saw it was only one of the children. "What?" she asked. "What is it, Viola?"

Viola squirmed in her seat. "Well, it's just . . . I suppose I'm not certain that I would want to leave my parents."

"And I won't leave my parents," Edward said firmly. "Though," he belched quietly, "I'd be happy to stay with you on the odd weekend if you are, in fact, my granny. Grand food and setup you've got here, despite the noises in the walls and rumors of ghosts and ominous locked rooms and collection of horrific murder paintings." He uttered an uneasy laugh. "Anyway, you can't legally force our parents to sign us over."

"Oh, but I *can*." A slightly manic grin wobbled on the Countess's lips. "And I *will*. Connections with the king allow you to get away with all manner of things, don't they? Yes, I believe they do." She stared at each of them as though daring anyone to disagree.

No one did, and Tabitha suspected that each child was attempting to process the change that had come over England's finest philanthropist. Even Frances, stiffly maintaining her elegant posture, wore a disquieted expression. All sense of hospitality had disappeared from the Countess's face. It was as though the celebration had ended for the evening and someone had turned off the festive twinkle lights, replacing them with uncertain shadows.

Viola raised a shaky hand. "I feel as though . . ." But at the sight of her hostess offering a skeptical smirk, Viola did not finish her sentence.

The Countess smiled her approval. "Ah, *quiet*," she said. "That's much better. I don't really care how any of you *feel*. Do you think a chance like this comes along every day?"

"No?" Oliver guessed.

"That's right, Mr. Appleby. I fully intend to reclaim one of you as my own. And one hundred thousand pounds is a great deal of money. I need to be certain the money goes where it's supposed to and not into any of your parents' pocketbooks just because it was released to their child's name. If I'm the child's legal guardian, I can be certain where the inheritance goes." She paused, closing her eyes while taking a deep breath. When she looked upon the room once again, her features had morphed into a kinder expression.

Tabitha squeezed Pemberley to ensure he was paying attention to the personality shift. *She's back to the kind Countess. She's either unusually moody, social awkward, or . . . something else.*

Frances raised a delicate hand for attention. Her chin was held at a high, determined angle, as though she were still resolved to "win" despite the unexpected and rather dubious development. "Your Ladyship, I'm certain that my parents wouldn't mind who I belong to on paper. They often say that their focus is on artistic vision, and that legal business is beyond their concern."

"Do they? I do believe we'd get along grandly. Here's hoping it's you, dear. I've *so* missed out on being a grandmother. The arrangement is to the advantage of everyone, so if you'd cooperate, that would be lovely. Now *do* eat your sweets, children. Sweets for the sweet, that's what I say." She raised a cookie as though it were champagne and started chatting at a terrified-looking Barnaby.

The rest of the children were equally unsettled, exchanging apprehensive glances. Viola's fingers worried themselves around a bit of her velvet skirt as she turned to Tabitha. "I suppose she's just . . . very floundering with people," she whispered. "And she's used to directing her money, that's all." Nibbling a corner of hardened pink frosting, she managed a smile and nod. "Yes, that's all."

Tabitha nodded back. "I'm sure you're right. And the Countess can't *really* keep a child whose parents want him or her." She didn't mention that in her own case, it was a moot point, as her parents clearly didn't fit that mold. "That can't be possible."

"No, I can't believe King Edward would sanction that sort of thing," Edward said. "Viola's right, the Countess has just gotten herself worked up about the money."

And perhaps she's right to keep control of the money. Goodness knows my parents would have taken it with them on holiday. And speaking of control, isn't it odd how the Countess seems to be losing a bit of hers?

The Countess clapped her hands as Phillips and Mary appeared. "Ah, here she is! Sit her right next to me, Phillips, and then you may leave. I'm not afraid of mingling with filthy commoners like Mary, am I? Only kidding, pet." She pinched the nearly catatonic woman's cheeks. "You can look at the pretty vase if you're not up for talking."

Mary looked helpless as ever, slumped to one side, leaning on the arm of the sofa with her head tilted until it was nearly touching a large violet vase. She was clearly unable to speak, but her eyes . . . her eyes were slowly rolling around the room. Lingering on Oliver as he politely smiled back. Focusing for a moment on Tabitha. Studying Edward, who had momentarily stifled his face stuffing. Staring at Viola. Examining Frances and Barnaby, whose matching freckles made them look like nasty siblings.

A few heavy breaths sent a thin spray of Mary's spittle onto the vase.

"Poor thing," the Countess said, gritting her teeth. "I'm afraid she's not going to make it too many more days."

"She's right there," Tabitha said softly. "You needn't say such things."

The Countess smiled. "We're going to play a little game. It can be called either 'You needn't say such things' or 'Tell me all the nasty things you know about each other.' Speculation or truth, I don't care."

"Funniest grandmother I've ever met," Edward muttered, picking up a mechanical dragonfly on a side table. He wound it and set it on the floor, where it buzzed in circles until Frances stood up and crushed it beneath her foot.

Frances's hand flew to her mouth. "So sorry, Countess," she said. "I was startled into thinking it was a rat," she said. "Tabitha Crum keeps rats, you know." She curtsied and sat down.

"Rats?" The Countess stood, looking almost murderous. "I despise rats even more than I despise cats and smoking."

Viola's mouth fell open. She sneezed twice, then raised a hand. "But you gave three thousand pounds just last year to Feral Feline Fancies Street Cat Rehabilitation, didn't you? Or was that a misprint in the donation records?"

The Countess rolled her eyes. "A mistake, clearly. I get so many requests that sometimes funding for idiotic causes slip through."

It's also funny for someone to have cigars available when they can't stand smoke, Tabitha thought. *Perhaps they're only for guests who indulge.* Pemberley squirmed and squeaked softly. *Or for would-be victims of the Countess's kitchen knives?* Tabitha gave him a gentle squeeze. *Pemberley, I don't know where you get these awful ideas. I shall have to stop reading you mystery novels.*

"Rats are spreaders of disease," said the Countess. "Phillips hates rats as well. He jumps like a schoolgirl just at the sight of mice. Plague-ridden terrors. I would like nothing better than to gather all the rats and mice of the world and make a large stew of them, and then feed it to anyone who thinks well of a rodent."

She's getting raw now that the parents are gone, Tabitha noted. Pemberley shuffled upward, and she poked him back down. *No, I'm not sure I'd want her to be my relation either, Pemberley.*

Mary lurched a little. Her eyes rolled around, locking onto the children in turn. She was pleading for something, Tabitha was sure. The elderly woman looked desperate.

The Countess moved back to the sofa and patted her maid on the head. "No opinion yet on who's to be my future companion? Well, perhaps a night's rest will bring some clarity." The Countess tapped Mary's knee and turned to the parlor door. "Agnes! Get in here."

Agnes scurried into the room and Phillips followed close behind, uncertainly holding a short chain attached to an enormous boarhound. His eyes drifted to the Countess's handbag. "There's another telephone call for you, Your Ladyship," he said, slightly out of breath. His lip fluttered several times before he managed to calm it down with his free hand.

The Countess shook her head. "Probably a reporter. Tell whoever it is that I'm entertaining for the weekend. We agreed that I wouldn't be taking phone calls."

"I've already done so, Countess," Phillips said. "But this gentleman is rather *insistent* that he speak with you. It's not a reporter, it's a Mr. Simmons, Your Ladyship. The second time he's called. He wishes to speak with you 'immediately, if not sooner.' Seems rather concerned and claims to know you personally."

A small crease appeared between the Countess's eyebrows. "Tell him I'm indisposed. Terribly rude, these random callers, lying about knowing me and whatnot. Probably trying to guilt me into handing over money for some ridiculous cause."

Repeated telephone calls from someone named Simmons, creaking in the front hall. If she could only be allowed into a room, Tabitha would spend any time alone jotting down the oddities of the evening, excluding any interaction with her parents. Yes, all she needed was a piece of paper and a pen and that business about being forever abandoned could be properly forgotten. Tabitha swallowed hard. For once, she would have something more interesting to list than *far worse things*. Instead she would list *noises heard at the manor*:

- Phillips's squelchy shoes during the tour
- Muffled strangling sounds from somewhere in the dining room or kitchen
- Creaking and soft moaning in the foyer

- Ghostly voices heard by a servant calling for Anne, Victoria, and George

Cook entered the room, her apron and hands floury, her expression harried. She carried two candlesticks and placed them on the center table along with several long matches. "Electricity has gone out in the kitchen, Your Ladyship. I thought you might need these if the same happens in here."

"And what did you need me for, Your Ladyship?" Agnes asked.

"I want you to—"

But Camilla DeMoss didn't finish saying what she wanted, because once again, the entire manor was plunged into darkness.

It took three long seconds before the screaming began, and then the room turned into a wild place full of grunting, shuffling, bumping, sneezing, fluttering, banging, crashing, gasping, and shrieking.

"Don't bloody push me!" yelled a boy.

"Aaaaeeee!" shrieked a girl. "Get off me! Get off!"

"No!"

"Come on, then!"

"Ghost! It's a ghost!"

"My hand!"

"It's got me! Who's got me? Dear God!"

"It's not God, it's me Edward! Who is—aaaaaaaaah!"

Attempting to avoid the banging and slamming and whacking, Tabitha knelt on the floor, where she'd heard one of the candlesticks roll. Trying not to absorb a rather colorful string of street swear words that she wouldn't have guessed Cook capable of, she reached around and felt for it. *There, got it.* Perhaps she could find the matches on the table. A dry hand tore the candlestick from her grasp, and a foot (belonging to the same body or not, Tabitha wasn't sure) kicked her to the side. A raucous crash sounded close by, its sheer volume momentarily halting all human noises.

When the lights flickered back on several moments later, a motionless body lay draped across the center table.

11

People's reactions to the unexpected or the upsetting say so much about their character and their role in a mystery. A burst of anger, a bark of nervous laughter . . . study these things well, Tibbs, but also keep in mind that a reaction may be as rehearsed as the dastardly deed itself.

—Inspector Percival Pensive,
The Case of the Mistaken Martyr

Mary was splayed chest down on the table, a thin line of drool glistening along the cheek that wasn't pressed firmly against the polished wood. A stain marred the back of her dress, like someone had pressed it with a wet cloth. One of her hands barely covered something beneath her. *A hint of brass . . . her bracelet? No, that was wooden.* The visible portion of her neck appeared to be reddened in places.

Tabitha's mind took a quick inventory of the scene as though she'd been preparing for such a thing since birth.

Indeed, months of reading Inspector Pensive novels had her memorizing each individual's stance and manner.

Phillips, breathing hard, rubbing his head, and looking furiously around the room; a large, angry scratch on one of his cheeks

Agnes, openly weeping and holding the tea tray, stepping on pieces of the broken violet vase

Cook, breathing heavily and looking at Agnes with concern

Viola, cradling her right fist in her left hand

Edward, looking rather fascinated by the body, a pastry smashed over his face

Barnaby, frightened and wild-haired

Frances, fiddling with her purse and looking as though she might vomit

Oliver, looking at the Countess's hand

The Countess, pale but calm, her right hand fidgeting slightly as it gripped and regripped a brass candlestick

And myself, Tabitha added, *with my left hand shoved protectively inside my apron pocket. Holding a mouse.*

Edward walked slowly toward Mary Pettigrew's body. He picked up her wrist, and not a soul objected when he placed two fingers over her skin to take a pulse. Concentrating, he held very still for a full minute before shaking his head.

Mary's hand hit the table with a sickening thud.

A second thud sounded as the Countess, having fainted, sank to the floor.

"My God, that old woman's dead!" croaked Cook, ignoring the Countess.

"What do you know? You're just the maid," snapped Frances.

"Cook," Tabitha corrected.

"Fine, she's just the cook!"

Viola clasped her hands together, then grimaced at her right fist, which appeared to be dripping. "And I'm *bleeding*." She gasped. "Oh! Oh dear, I've gotten some blood on poor Mary's dress!"

"Barnaby's hair grease is on the back of the dress as well," Tabitha said quietly.

"That it is," Oliver said, bending down for a sniff. "Smells like it, anyway."

"He did it," Frances announced firmly. "Barnaby Trundle killed the maid."

Barnaby, appearing panicked, tried to edge his body behind Edward. "I couldn't see where I was going. I didn't mean to knock into her! I didn't—"

Oliver frowned. "Don't be ridiculous, Frances, she's died of natural causes. None of us had a reason to kill Mary Pettigrew."

Tabitha cleared her throat, ignoring Pemberley, who was frantically scratching at her to keep quiet. "That's probably the case, Oliver, but actually, we all have a very good reason. Mary Pettigrew may have had the ability to identify the true grandchild.

With her dead, any of us might convince the Countess, thereby coming into one hundred thousand pounds."

"That money should go to charity!" Viola shouted. "And I don't even *want* to live here."

"Neither do I," Oliver seconded. "But—"

"Quiet!" Everyone turned to Phillips. "Just wait a bloody minute while I have a think. Her high and mightiness, the Countess here, thought this might happen."

They all looked around, aghast.

"She . . ." Agnes tried to control the tremor in her voice. "She thought Miss Pettigrew might be murdered?"

Phillips eyed Mary and shook his head twice. "No, no. She was very sick, after the stroke. The Countess was certain Mary could die at any moment, having never said another word in her life. She had a cousin with a stroke, you see, who never regained any sort of understandable speech, so we thought—"

"Are you familiar with the Countess's history then?" Tabitha asked curiously. "Where she came from before buying Hollingsworth Hall?"

Phillips reddened. "I believe the Countess said for you to restrict the number of questions you ask. And I'm not sure you'd like the answer to that one, anyway."

"The smallest shock can cause a second stroke," Edward stated. "Even a physician telling you that you've just had a stroke could cause another stroke." He shook his head sadly. "How's that for a misguided treatment?"

"Then perhaps *you* decided to give her a shock," Frances said.

"It could have been the small matter of the electricity going out twice, Miss Wellington." Phillips surveyed the room. "Although there *may* have been foul play."

He bent over Mary Pettigrew and lifted her head. "I assume this lump at the front of her head was from the fall, but perhaps it was something more sinister." He peered at her back. "In addition to this rather pungent cream on her back, there seems to be a bit of frosting."

Edward swallowed hard. "It was dark. There was pushing all over the place. I would *never* push an old lady, especially not a strokey one."

Viola nodded. "He wouldn't, I'm sure of it. He's only ever pushed me in jest."

Phillips pulled aside the back of Mary's collar. "There's some redness on her neck and a large mark on the side of her shoulder here, almost as though someone struck her with a fist. Is your hand quite all right, Viola?"

Viola squeaked. "It was dark," she whimpered. "And I thought there were ghosts. I must have hit the corner of an end table. I wasn't anywhere near Mary Pettigrew, I swear!" Doubt crept around her mouth and downturned eyes. "At least I don't think I was."

"And traces of powder here and there." Phillip kneeled to the floor eyes drifted down. "It's on the rug as well."

"Flour," Tabitha guessed.

Cook put both hands on her hips. "I was pushed and shoved as much as anyone, but I had *no* part in a murder. And a maid's not the one I'd be after to get rid of, anyway," she mumbled. "There's others that's making their way up my list, if you get my meaning."

"Fine, Cook. That's enough." Phillips gently moved Mary's hair aside. "Let's see, there's more redness around her neck, and—"

"It was her!" Frances bellowed, pointing a long fingernail toward Viola. "You all heard that lump at dinner. She's obsessed with learning about the Countess's charitable nonsense! She launched herself at the maid so that she could claim to be the grandchild and give away all the money. She caused the shock!"

Viola's lip and chin trembled. "I didn't! I wouldn't! And I'm not a lump. Mother says I've got a statuesque bone structure."

"That's right." Edward squeezed his friend's shoulder. "Large-boned and healthy as oxen, we both are."

Viola removed his hand. "I am *not* an oxen."

"Ox, then."

"Don't call me that, Edward!"

"No, I just meant that one of us would be an ox. Together we're oxen, but just you alone would be a—"

"It's the butler!" cried Barnaby, backing away from Phillips. "It's always the butler in these types of situations!" All traces of bully were gone from his persona, whisked away by circumstance. What was left, Tabitha noted, was nothing but a frightened and whiny little boy. She could hardly believe that she'd ever let him bother her before this weekend.

"Settle down." Phillips's face had nearly reached the shade of a cherry. "We shall have a doctor in to determine the cause of death as soon as the weather allows. There's nothing to be done."

"Not nothing," Edward said. "You might take those knives out of the Countess's purse before the lights go out again and she accidentally chops off someone's—"

A hush fell over the room as the Countess woke. She rubbed her head and sat up. Her eyes jerked to the body of Mary, still slumped on the table.

"She's dead, then?" the Countess asked, her face a mixture of panic and fascination. Scanning the floor, she located and clutched her handbag, her eyes settling on Phillips. "Is she gone?"

Phillips stared straight into his employer's eyes, and Tabitha thought she noticed his jaw tighten. "She is, Your Ladyship."

Fingers playing with her necklace, the Countess eyed the tray in Agnes's hands. "Was it you, dearest? Did you whack poor Mary?"

Agnes inhaled sharply. "I didn't—" The tray fell from her hands. "I thought the ghost was attacking us all." Her eyes fell to the candlestick that was still in the Countess's hand. "B-begging your pardon, but you were trying to defend yourself as well."

The Countess sent a searing glare in Agnes's direction "The only thing I attacked was the vase, while you've killed a *living* thing. You were probably hoping to give me a thump. You and my terrible excuse for a cook have probably been plotting against me since your arrival, planning a mutiny with the stable boys."

"The stable boys are *gone*," the Cook said, "and all the house and kitchen workers have fled with them. That's the other thing I was coming to tell you. Everyone's gone, due to your hideous behavior and your horrible haunted house. If you're not more careful, Countess, I do fear for your reputation." She gave a conspiratorial nod to Agnes. "People hear things, you know. Rumors get picked up easily enough. Besides, how can I be expected to produce fine cuisine when the walls are rattling and I'm kept awake half the night by mysterious moaning?"

Agnes's eyes widened, and she buried her head in Cook's shoulder.

"The moaning is nothing. It's the wind, nothing more. And what do you mean, 'everyone's gone'?" The Countess's head snapped over to Phillips. "What does she mean?"

Phillips barely corrected a glower before answering. "She means that the rest of your staff seem to have taken the last working motorcar. The only one left won't start properly."

"Ridiculous," the Countess spat. "We would have noticed a motorcar leaving the property."

Despite her derisive tone, Tabitha had been paying close attention to the Countess and noticed the slightest tremble. *Of fear, perhaps?*

"It's snowing quite a bit, and we've all been rather preoccupied." Phillips cleared his throat. "Ridiculous or not, Your Ladyship, there remains the small matter of having no staff left at the manor house."

"Well," said the Countess, "we have Cook, however shoddy she is, and Agnes will be head of household. That will be sufficient. And you, of course, Phillips. You three may need to take on additional duties over the weekend until this blasted storm gets under control."

Cook huffed. "And what if we choose not to work? You've made it quite clear my cooking isn't up to your standards."

"If you choose not to work, Phillips will throw you outside and lock all the doors so you can't find shelter."

Cook narrowed her eyes, but Agnes whimpered at the threat.

"Phillips," the Countess said, "see to the body."

"Yes, Your Ladyship. I'll just . . . go check for a proper place to put her."

"'See to the body'?" Agnes asked as the butler left the room. Her cheeks turned ashen, then green. Tabitha sensed she was nearing a breakdown. "And what do you propose he do with her, Countess? Stick her in cold storage? Pack her in ice with Cook's steaks?"

The Countess walked calmly over to Agnes and stood inches away.

"Sit her in the back garden and turn her into a snow statue?" Agnes continued. "There's an entrance to the garden straight off the kitchen, so why not have him fix you an evening plate of something on his way back in?" She was babbling now, verging on hysteria. "Wait until she freezes solid and use her as a door guard to deter newspapermen?" Agnes blubbered herself to tears, only halting when the Countess's slap silenced her into shocked, heaving breaths.

"You're tense," the Countess said. "I can see that, but there's no need to be stupid. There's no room in the cold storage. The back garden will do nicely for now. We can't leave her in here or she'll start to stink. She's nothing but a shell, so don't be squeamish."

"Her spirit's gone to join the other ghosts,"Viola suggested.

Agnes nodded miserably. "That's probably true. The ghosts have banded together and now we're all in for it."

Tabitha put her hand up. "Do you think we should have a moment of silence, perhaps?"

The Countess stared blankly.

Clearing her throat, Tabitha tried again. "Don't you . . . don't you care at all that your beloved maid is dead?"

With a lengthy sigh, the Countess smoothed the top of her coiffed hair, tucking a loose strand back into the disheveled bun. "Of course I care," said Camilla Lenore DeMoss, greatest philanthropist in the whole of England. "I care a great deal. Not that I killed her personally, but I've been waiting years for the old biddy to die. It's dreadfully difficult being charitable to those you don't like."

For a moment, nobody moved. They waited, not daring to speak after such a statement.

The Countess stared back at them for a silent moment, a line forming between her eyebrows. "What? Do none of you value honesty? I'm not saying I *wished* her dead, I'm just saying it's not the most appalling thing I've been a part of."

"Right you are," Edward agreed. "Just buying that one Jack the Ripper painting had to be more disturbing than having an already-sick maid die in your parlor. Quite disturbing the way he was creeping along that alley. Can't say I was too upset when that part of the tour was cut short for dinner."

Viola elbowed him. "Of course you aren't required to like

everyone, Your Ladyship. It must be very hard being kind to all types of people, but your generosity is *so* very appreciated. Perhaps you might donate toward a house workers' union in Mary's memory?"

"At the very least you needed her to help recognize your true grandchild, didn't you?" Tabitha asked.

The Countess shifted her steely gaze back to Tabitha. "We'll make do. I'll use my own instincts in determining who's best suited to the role."

Role. Another odd word choice, Tabitha thought.

And that was when they all heard it. A low shuffling, like someone brushing leaves in the ceiling, and then in the wall along the mantel by a long, painted parlor scene.

A soft wailing accompanied the noise, almost as though someone was crying. Faintly, as though coming from even farther away than death itself, the sound was joined by smaller cries. High-pitched ones, like the sounds a pained child might make.

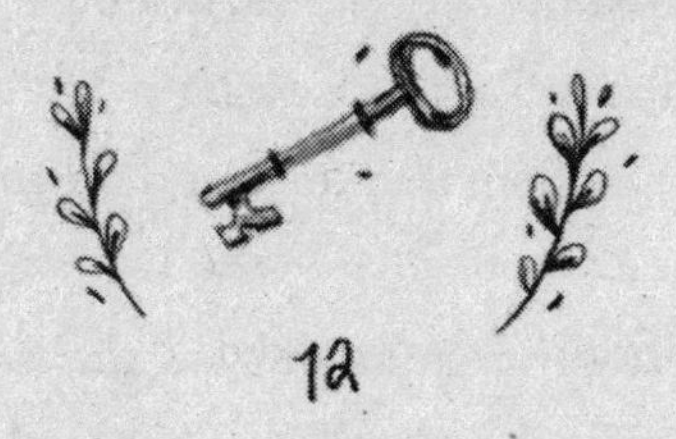

12

The trouble with motives, Tibbs, is that they are quite slippery, not unlike this plate of escargots. They have layers, you see, and you often have to look beyond the obvious hard shell and seek the heart of the perpetrator. The impetus of a crime often lies far deeper than expected.

—Inspector Percival Pensive,
The Case of the Cyanide-Crusted Crab

The cries subsided, leaving the room in terrible silence. Oliver caught Tabitha's eye with a grim expression, Frances stroked a lock of hair with both hands, and Viola looked as though she were doing a mental inventory of the Countess's charitable donations to remain calm. Barnaby fussed softly as Edward ate what was left of his chocolate wedges.

"The ghost!" Agnes cried. Her head jerked around, settling on the still body of Mary Pettigrew. "It's Mary's ghost, no doubt, joining the other spirits!"

"There are no such things as spirits," said the Countess,

walking to the fireplace. She drummed shaky fingers along the mantel, peering at the hearth. "No such things."

Phillips entered once again, looking a bit gray in the face. "The telephone is out from the storm and the upstairs electricity is faulty."

"Fine, it's time to retire anyway," said the Countess. "To the west wing with everyone. Candles only for the children. Cut them down to nubs for the bedside holders and make sure they have no oil lamps. Breakfast is at nine o'clock." She leaned toward Cook, managing to work up a sneer despite the ghostly turn of events. "Will I need to come show you how to poach an egg or do you think you can manage?"

"I can manage," Cook answered. "And I'll try my very best not to let any stones get into your food. Wouldn't want you choking."

"Stop that," Agnes hissed, and stepped forward. "I'm so sorry, Your Ladyship, but it seems Jane had to prepare a room in the east wing as well."

The Countess jerked her head around. "Which room? Those aren't proper bedrooms."

Agnes looked at the Countess as though Her Ladyship had lost her memory. "One of them is. The only door in that short hallway. It's a bedroom, Your Ladyship. Thought maybe it was storage, but it looks to be a suitable bedroom for a less important guest, as I'm sure you know. I noticed it wasn't being used and had Jane prepare it. I believe Tabitha Crum has that room."

The Countess's eyes flared with anger and confusion. "The

door was unlocked? You were told not to enter that hallway, if I recall. That door is *always* locked. How did you open it? Have you opened the others? And where did you find the key? Give it to me immediately!"

One of the locked rooms. Oh dear, Pemberley. We're to stay in one of the locked rooms.

Agnes blinked hard, as though stung. "But it wasn't locked, Countess. Must've been loose all along. I just had to jiggle it. I was just trying to be thorough," she managed to say through quivering lips. "Otherwise, there's the servants' quarters. With everyone gone, there's plenty of beds to be had, though I can't say much for the state of cleanliness."

"I should think not, given the state of you and the rest of the worthless staff." The Countess looked through the parlor doors and placed a gloved finger to her mouth. "The east wing room will have to do. I'll check to make sure it's suitable in appearance."

Agnes balked. "Oh, no, Your Ladyship! It's my job to see to the rooms, and I would never—"

"Silence. It is my house. I shall see to it, along with the girl." The Countess raised an eyebrow at Tabitha, as though challenging her to refuse the company of a titled hostess. "But first I have something to attend to, so wait here. Phillips, come with me. Leave the body here for now. Mary and Tabitha can watch over things," she said, smiling sickly. "You two." She pointed to Cook and Agnes. "Get moving with the other children. Do sleep well, dears," she said in a slightly sweeter tone. "I so look forward to our conferences tomorrow. Soon, for a lucky one of you, this will be your home. Your permanent home." She frowned. "You all look frightened." She turned to Phillips. "Am I frightening them, do you think?"

"Perhaps it's the matter of the dead body, Your Ladyship," Phillips answered.

"Oh," she said, as though the thought hadn't occurred to her. "Well, that's all over now. A shame, but one less person for Cook to poison." She laughed a high-pitched cacophony of notes that died out when nobody joined in. "It was a joke, children. Good night."

Tabitha waved good night to Oliver as he, Edward, Barnaby, Viola, and Frances were led out of the parlor. "Pemberley," she whispered, trying hard not to stare at the corpse, "in more ways than one, it's just you and me now."

And the dead body of Mary Pettigrew.

And the ghost or ghosts.

"We've got better ways to spend our time than blubbering and pouting."

Squeakity-squeak.

"Too right, Sir Pemby," Tabitha said. "I adore when you bring up a Pensive maxim: 'When hope has left your side, carry on with the assumption that it simply went to fetch a quick bite to eat and will return shortly.'" She nodded to her partner. "Quite appropriate, sir." She felt much resolved in spite of the facts that no parent would ever love her and poor Mary Pettigrew was still quite dead and quite close by.

With a very deep breath, her motivation was rekindled. "This is our first serious and real mystery. I may not be heir to a fortune, and I might be heading straight for Augustus Home after this weekend, but we must rally, sir." She stood. "In the words of my unloving nonfather, a game is afoot!"

Squeak! Pemberley scurried happily to Tabitha's shoulder.

"Perhaps we'll recount it to Scotland Yard at an interview one day if they ever decide to take women on. We must concentrate on scenes, clues, possibilities.

"So, Pemberley." In the absence of a pocket watch chain, she nibbled one of her knuckles as she paced. "The question isn't so much a matter of how Mary Pettigrew died. I'm guessing she was inadvertently startled into a second stroke. The question is *why*. *Why*, that is, did the Countess act as though Mary Pettigrew was a faithful servant, but seem indifferent, even glad, about her death? And what was Mary doing in her study when the first stroke occurred?"

Tabitha inventoried her knowledge of the Countess: a mysterious and death-ridden past, a philanthropic streak that began with her purchase of Hollingsworth Hall, an attraction to gruesome crime paintings, an affinity for knives . . .

Stepping over to the body, Tabitha once again noticed a glint of brass poking out near Mary's overturned hand. "*Why*," she asked, bravely leaning forward for a closer look, "did the Countess feel the need to keep such a close eye on this woman, even after she'd fallen ill?"

Cringing slightly and whispering apologies, she turned the woman's wrist and stared at her wooden bracelet. The entwined heads of the carved creatures had separated, revealing that the tubelike design concealed a secret space.

"Pemberley, what a very clever clasp. When Mary fell, her body's impact must have caused it to pop open. Exposing *this*." The metal item she'd seen was a small key, the majority of it still hidden inside the bracelet's hollow interior.

Quickly Tabitha slid the key from its hiding place and tucked it into her apron pocket. "Company for you, sir," she said to her mouse. She closed the bracelet's clasp around Mary's wrist and backed away from the body, scooting around the sofa to study the parlor paintings. Breathing in and out to calm herself, she meandered around the room, peering at the paintings from a distance.

She concentrated her gaze on a gentleman with a bird perched on his shoulder. He had startlingly realistic blue eyes. They were painted in such a lifelike manner that they seemed to follow her around the room, as the two portrait paintings in the foyer had done. She glanced at the gentleman from three different spots, and his eyes always seemed focused on her. Tabitha had just stepped closer to examine the technique when footsteps approached.

"Come!" the Countess barked. Holding a large unlit candelabrum, she led Tabitha up the main staircase and along the east side of the manor, turning down the short hallway. She stopped at the door just as the lights went out for good. Cursing, the Countess fumbled with a match and lit each candle, the four flames casting a menacing gleam on her cheeks.

With the other children an entire wing away, they were very much alone. The Countess placed a finger under Tabitha's chin and cocked it up. "My dear Tabitha Crum of the Wilting Crums. Are you the one, I wonder?" Her expression was not that of a rich, generous patroness or a warmhearted grandmother, but of someone who was after something.

When interviewing suspects, the most direct questions are best posed at unexpected times, Pensive would say. "You must miss them very much," Tabitha said.

"What?" The Countess frowned. "Who?"

"Your husband and your son and your sister."

"Yes, of course I do." The Countess bent to examine the lock, peering doubtfully between the keyhole and her ring of keys.

"And you want a piece of them back, is that it?"

"Unlocked all along, was it?" she murmured. "What are you mumbling about?"

"Why do you want your grandchild?" Tabitha asked in an authoritative tone, crossing her arms for emphasis. "And why are you seeking us all out now?"

The Countess hesitated, and it was the manner of the hesitation that told Tabitha that it was certainly not love. Her Ladyship reacted to the question with what was almost a guilty start. Between that, the small hints at anger and impatience, and her lack of compassion for Mary Pettigrew, Tabitha felt certain that something else had motivated the invitations to Hollingsworth Hall.

Perhaps a grandchild was not wanted, but *needed* for some

reason. But for what? A status symbol? Something to relaunch her reputation as a nurturing figure? Or for a darker purpose that she'd rather not think about, for dear Pemberley's sake?

"Cheeky," the Countess said. "That's none of your business. At least not until your worth is determined."

With a halting hand, the Countess reached toward the doorknob. Her shoulders tightened as the knob turned easily in her hand. She gave a dubious glance to the black room with a pinched expression, the candles' flames allowing only three or four feet of view. "I want you to think seriously about what you shall say to me tomorrow. Your future depends on it. Pleasant dreams, dearest."

Taking one candle from the stand, she handed it to Tabitha and walked back down the hall, her footsteps muffled by the roll of thick, exquisite carpet. Listening very hard, Tabitha thought she could hear the slightest metal-on-metal tinkling of the two knives scraping together in the Countess's handbag.

Loneliness can be quite the stimulant in terms of producing criminal theories. Some, of course, must be dismissed as paranoia, which is to be expected from those who spend time talking only to themselves, walls, photographs, and their supper.

—Inspector Percival Pensive, *The Case of the Harried Hermit*

The hallway was now pitch black, other than a lone glow. The Countess had forgotten to shorten Tabitha's candle, and it would last an hour, maybe more. And the oil lamp by her bedside was half-full. Careful not to lose her flame, Tabitha ventured into the room and tilted the candle until the lamp was lit.

"I am alone in one of the locked rooms," she said. A pocket shuffle argued otherwise. She pulled her furry friend out and held him to her cheek. "Of course I didn't mean that, Pemberley. I'm so glad you're here with me, and besides, we already established that the Countess keeps extra servant uniforms in the armoire, which is a perfectly valid reason to keep a door locked. I just meant that—"

A low creak sounded in the room or in the hall, Tabitha couldn't tell. She froze and waited. "The wind moving the house a bit, I think. It's turned into quite a violent blizzard, Pemberley. I do hope the motorcars made it to the cottage without incident. And I hope the other children aren't very frightened."

Squeak.

"Oh, all right, I suppose Frances could do with a bit of a shock. Perhaps there'll be a mirror in her room, and she'll insult the person she sees before realizing it's herself."

Squeakity?

"What? Oh! Yes, the key." Tabitha reached into the apron pocket and pulled out the small brass item. "Now, whatever might this open? Hmm. In Inspector Pensive novels, people hiding keys and such generally kept three things in mind:

1. Hide the item in an unlikely place.
2. Hide the item somewhere personal enough to remember.
3. Hide the item in a room where you'll go naturally and often, so as not to appear odd when retrieving it."

Squeak.

Tabitha sighed. "That's true. Mary's key was hidden in her bracelet, which means the keyhole it belongs to could be anywhere at all. Well, I think a thorough deducing session can be best done in the light of the morning." She brought the carpetbag to one side of the bed and fetched Pemberley's mustache tonic tin. Switching quickly into her one nightdress, Tabitha cleaned her face and hands in the small alcove containing a half-full water pitcher and washing basin.

"Here, Pemby. Wash up, as good dreams are seen more clearly when your dirt's been scrubbed away. Shame there's not a mouse-size basin. Perhaps when we set up our own Inspector agency, we shall get you your own alcove. Here," she said, pouring a bit of water into the soap dish, "use this." She watched, amused, as Pemberley scrubbed his muzzle and looked up expectantly. "Much better. Aren't you glad you have me to play mother?"

As she crawled under the heavy sheets and rich comforter, Tabitha again noticed the photograph on the bedside table. By all accounts, it appeared to be a quite normal and happy family of mother, father, and baby. What was odd about it? Once more, she had the distinct impression that *something* wasn't quite right. Was it something about the bassinet, or . . .

She looked at the painting of the boy on the wall, ignoring a gentle chill that seized the muscles in her neck and shoulders. "Hello, boy. You've probably been facing this photograph for years. Can you tell me what's odd about it?"

Squeak, shuffle, squeak.

"Yes, Pemberley, I know the boy is in a portrait and won't answer." With heavy eyelids (it had, after all, been an extraordinarily emotional and busy day), Tabitha looked more closely at the beautiful, long-haired, full-figured woman next to the bassinet. Her eyes held hope and love. A handsome man had his arm around her, and his smile was wide enough to stretch off his face.

"Pemberley, will we ever be this happy, do you think, now that we have no family?" Tabitha cupped her cheekbones.

Squeak.

"Yes, I'm being overly sentimental. Anybits, Mum and Daddy won't miss me at all." Tabitha bit her lip deeply and stared until the image became blurry. "But they aren't my parents anymore, and I mustn't care. I mustn't."

Squeak.

"Sir Pemberley," she said, cradling him. Bundling him. "Listen to me carefully." She kissed him softly, lifting the little mouse until they were nose to nose and she was quite certain he was paying close attention. "I found you on a Tuesday evening last November, after having been locked in my attic for burning supper. I was feeling cold and alone and frightened, and then I heard a rustling noise coming from one of the beams. When I found you nestled among your brothers and sisters, my heart filled up and my sadness was forgotten. Your existence brought me joy from the moment I met you. I shall never forget that day or think it ordinary. You made that day special."

Squeak?

"Yes, really. Pemberley, don't ever let anyone tell you that you're a dirty thing. Or an unwanted thing. Or a useless thing, do you hear me?"

Pemberley sniffed Tabitha's hand, looking for food.

"You are very much adored and very much needed. You are a gallant knight among mice, and my only friend to speak of, and I love you. Isn't that good to hear? I love you." She held up a crumb. "Will you twirl?" The mouse made himself go around in a circle one way, then the other, before standing on his hind legs to reach the nibble. "Bravo!"

Making a pile of her sweater on the bed beside her, she tucked Pemberley's tin far inside, where it wouldn't be immediately visible, in case anyone should come into the room before she could hide him the next morning.

"A story?" Tabitha yawned and placed the mouse into his bed. "Oh, fine. I'll read you a bit from *The Case of the Duplicitous Duke's Doorway*."

Squeakity.

"Oh, I'm so glad, it's one of my favorite Inspector Pensive novels too."

With three layers of blankets, it was a heavy lift to raise all the bedding at once in order to reach for the book in her carpetbag. She dug around for the familiar shape, but instead of grasping a book, her hands settled around the sheath of loosely rolled papers that her mum had stashed in the bag back in Wilting.

Smoothing the papers on her lap, Tabitha soon realized she was looking at several bank documents covered in numbers and figures. She didn't much understand the documents, other than to know they were probably not approved by Mr. Crum's employer. There was also a description of a villa on the coast of Spain and some accompanying financial gobbledygook.

"Travel papers," Tabitha told Pemberley. "They're leaving us for sunny Spain. Oh, Pemberley, why do you think—"

Squeakity-squeak!

"You're right, you're right. No point in dwelling. It's probably best to try for some sleep, anyway. You look awfully tired out from the day. Tomorrow we'll work on this key business." She clapped her hands together for a quick prayer. "Dear God, please bless poor Mary Pettigrew and everyone else who needs blessings, and thank you for Pemberley and Inspector Pensive, the end, good night."

Presently Tabitha's breath began to slow and soften. She was nearly asleep when an unmistakable cry of terror broke through the room's walls.

Bolting upright, Tabitha snatched Pemberley to her breast and ran to the door, where she listened intently. Hearing nothing, she opened the door a crack. A series of thuds and a scattering of objects tinkled faintly up the staircase. The noise was coming from far below. Somewhere else in the house entirely. She crept to the end of her short hallway. The west wing rooms appeared black and silent. No other child had awakened.

Silence.

Awful, deafening silence.

Tabitha tiptoed to the landing at the top of the staircase, searching the darkness below and waiting.

Not a single soul stirred.

"Did that just happen?" she asked Pemberley. "Did I imagine it?" She breathed in and out, calming her heart. "Was it all a nightmare? Am I sleeping?"

Pemberley remained silent, but Tabitha felt him shaking. Or perhaps that was her own body.

"I've heard of such things," Tabitha told herself. "Waking nightmares." Giving herself a quick pinch, she was disappointed to feel no different. "There are *far worse things* than having a waking nightmare, right? Shall we list a few?" But she could think of nothing worse at the moment than having an odd nightmare attached to a disturbingly realistic scream. "Logically, we should go back to bed, right, Pemberley? And it's best to be logical. Inspector Pensive values logic."

Part of Tabitha cursed her cowardice in not investigating matters further. It was very easy to be adventurous when reading books, but rather more difficult to address perilous situations off the written page.

"Don't be frightened," she said, returning to her room and setting a chair beneath the doorknob. Tibbs was prone to doing that in nearly every Pensive novel she'd read. *Ridiculous, Tibbs,* Pensive would say. *If a murderer is going to murder us, a silly chair won't stop him. Most likely we'll simply be poisoned in the morning.*

"I'm afraid that I'm unsure how to comfort you," Tabitha whispered to Pemberley as she tucked them both beneath the covers, feeling the mouse's trembling form. "I'm afraid that I'm feeling rather trembly myself. From the nightmare, you see." She nodded in the dark. "From that silly, silly nightmare. It's a shame neither of us have our parents' bed to run to." She frowned, sadness tugging on her fear. "I suppose I never did."

Soon after, stimulated to the point of exhaustion, Tabitha

Crum fell asleep with images of her fellow invitees, an imposing duke with secrets, cold carriage rides, calculating Countesses, East London accents, Hollingsworth Hall, orphanages, ghosts, and poor Mary Pettigrew all swirling about in the disappearing fog of Inspector Pensive's pipe smoke.

14

I'm not dismissing the possibility of spirits, Tibbs. What I'm *saying* is that the majority of spirit-related activities that I've encountered can be traced to those who are in possession of rather still-beating hearts and ill-smelling body odor.

—Inspector Percival Pensive,
The Case of the Grimauldian Ghost

Three firm knocks awakened Tabitha. She pushed the comforter to her waist, stretched up to the ceiling, then reached out to her still-covered toes. The knowledge that it was a new morning and the sight of elegant canopy curtains took away a bit of the previous night's eeriness. What a horrible and lifelike nightmare she'd had.

"Wake up, miss," Agnes called, cracking the door open. "I've come to bring you fresh water. Breakfast is nearly ready, and I daresay you could use something in your stomach. You didn't eat any of your parlor sweets last night, not that I blame you."

"Very observant of you. Thank you, Agnes," Tabitha said, rubbing her eyes.

The maid lingered in the doorway with a pitcher. "Miss Mary has been moved, so you won't be running into her. I was worried about that myself," she said. "The poor, poor woman. I hope she didn't die in much pain." The pitcher dipped a little, threatening to spill over.

Tabitha could see that reassurance was in order if she was to be given her washing-up water. There were ghosts and mysterious keys and unclear motives to be dealt with. "I'm nearly certain she died of a second stroke, Agnes. Natural causes. Any other disturbance was unfortunate, but not ultimately intentional."

Straightening with a pained smile, Agnes switched the room's pitchers. "Thank you for saying so, miss. Do you think you might be the Countess's grandchild?"

"Thank you, and no. I'm afraid that I came with no token or other information that might be of use. I'm not sure the Countess is the type of grandmother I'd like to claim, though. She seems to have . . . secrets. Do you know of any?"

Agnes startled, spilling some water and bending to mop it with a hand towel. "Clumsy, clumsy Agnes," she breathed. "No, miss, I don't know a thing." With a wavering smile, she curtsied and left the room without closing the door.

Tabitha watched the maid's shadow retreat before addressing Pemberley. "Time to get up, sir. Are you ready to face the day?"

Squeak.

Barnaby and Oliver were missing from the breakfast table, but the electricity was present and accounted for. The lights of the dining chandelier and the side table lamps seemed too bright, though. Falsely bright, as though they were posing as comforts and failing terribly.

"Good morning, Tabitha," Edward said. "Hope you're ready for another proper tuck-in. Cook tried to serve us in courses again, but I told her to just bring the lot."

"Oh," said Tabitha, approaching a chair slowly. She heard her father's words from just two days ago: *Don't say "oh" like an idiot.* But by the time she was finished remembering those words, the moment to say a few more of her own had passed.

The same elegant slab of wood where they'd had a pleasant dinner followed by celebratory conversation was once again piled with food. Still standing, she listened while Edward presented the trays of sliced melon and grapes, baskets of muffins, hard-boiled eggs, spiced mushrooms, poached eggs on toast, and porcelain bowls filled with sweet buttered peas. He took a breath and then pointed to boar sausages, beans, and hot cereal, which sat next to a platter of steaming beefsteak.

Edward made a grand gesture toward the final dish. "That one's deviled lobster. Told you that noise from the kitchen last night could have been a death scream. Poor bloke. Tasty, though."

Tabitha surveyed the feast before her but found that she had little appetite. Nor, it seemed, did Frances, who was sitting across from her, blank-faced. The foul little Wellington hadn't even the energy to sneer at anyone, not even an empty-plated Viola.

"Hello, Tabitha," Viola called. "Sit next to me?"

Tabitha was taken slightly aback. Why was Viola being so very nice to her? Did she consider Tabitha to be a charity case? It was only when Pemberley moved in her pocket that she remembered to answer. "Yes, thank you." She sat.

Viola smiled, then let out another series of sneezes.

"Oh . . . are you still feeling ill?"

"No, just itchy. I was doing better, though. Those sneezes came out of nowhere." She held up a hand to protest when Edward offered her a sausage. "I'm not terribly hungry."

"You can't let circumstances allow you to lose your health, Viola," Edward said, scooping a pile of beans onto his toast. "Got to keep your strength up."

"That's right," Oliver said, entering the room. His steps were slow. His hair had been combed, but one or two strands refused to stay down. He took a seat next to Tabitha, looking around the table warily. "Sorry I'm so late," he added, looking at the clock. "Agnes had to come twice to fetch me. Good morning. Or simply morning, I suppose."

"It's good so far." Edward nodded, reaching over to pour Oliver some juice. "No dead people and no accidental stabbings from paranoid women of title," he joked. "I say, have you all heard of Elizabeth Bathory, also known as the Blood Countess? Nasty woman. Liked to torture young girls in particular. Used blood to keep her skin young, which is a silly sort of thing. Soap would've been fine, don't you think?"

Nobody answered, but Viola looked distinctly ill.

"Do you know that one of her servants once stole a *pear*, and Elizabeth Bathory had her beaten so badly that the poor Countess had to change her shirt? Was standing too close and caught the blood spray. Around ten pints of blood in the human body, you know." Nobody responded, and Edward reached for another sausage.

Frances, who had managed a bite of toast, finally gained her strength and scowled. "Are you as stupid as your bum is big? You'd do well to show some respect to the Countess. Not that you could ever deserve one hundred thousand pounds."

Cook entered, snorting either at the comment or the lack of eating. "Something the matter with my food again? The boys are the only ones eating?" She snatched Tabitha's empty plate and began loading it. "All this other nonsense aside, you're lucky this food is even here. Drivers to the cottage seem to have raided my kitchen. Nearly half my eggs and tomatoes were gone this morning, and I'm only three days into my order week. We'll make do, I suppose, for as long as we need to. Here you go, miss."

Tabitha managed a smile. "Thank you. We've all been rather rattled by poor Mary's death, I suppose."

"Agnes and I have been rattled as well," Cook said. "There was a loud scuffling and shouting in the kitchen last night."

So it wasn't a dream.

"Stop talking," Frances ordered. "Do your business and be gone."

Cook whirled on Frances with a full fork. "I've had quite enough out of you, miss. In case your pretty ears and pretty eyes were removed from your pretty head last night, there was a death that took place." She flung four fat sausages onto Frances's plate.

"Oh, no, thank you," said Viola, placing both hands over her plate before Cook could drop eggs onto it.

Cook frowned and put the eggs back on the table, grabbing a tray of melon instead. "Maybe the awful noise last night was Phillips's beastly dog," she said, slipping fruit slices on Viola's plate. "Or else it was just a nightmare. I suppose none of you heard anything." She halted, eyeing them each in turn.

Edward and Frances shook their heads.

"I heard it," said Tabitha.

"I may have heard something," said Viola. "A yell and a crash of some sort. But I'd been dreaming of terrible riots in a poorhouse, so I just assumed it was part of the dream."

Oliver looked around. "Um . . . has Barnaby been down yet? Please say yes. Please say he's in the loo."

The Countess glided into the room before anyone could reply to Oliver, locking eyes briefly with Cook, who was suddenly in a hurry to return to the kitchen. She looked remarkably rosy-cheeked and well rested and was wearing a black gown with matching gloves. "Greetings, children. The interviews shall begin shortly. Where is Barnaby Trundle?"

"Not here yet, *Grandmother*," Frances said, her gaze glued to the Countess's multiple bracelets. "If you ask me, he's rather lazy and not at all suited to being in a household of such quality. No sense of class structure whatsoever."

"Well, I shall certainly take that into consideration when conducting his interview."

The door flew open and Agnes rushed in, her maid's hat slightly askew and her apron crooked. She slid into the table and collided with a bunch of grapes, barely missing the Countess.

"Careful, idiot girl!"

The poor maid could barely open her mouth, let alone speak, and Tabitha felt immensely sorry for her. She knew from experience that it's exceedingly difficult to communicate when you're busy processing a verbal attack.

"Well?" the Countess demanded. "Out with it!"

Still unable to speak, Agnes flapped her jaw uselessly, her eyes watering with panic.

Tabitha touched her hand, thinking it might calm the young lady into words. "Thank you again for the water this morning," she said. "It was very kind."

"B-B-Barnaby," Agnes whispered.

"Yes, where *is* Barnaby Trundle?" the Countess repeated.

Agnes jerked her hand back wildly. She fell to her knees, staring Tabitha directly in the chest. "He's missing! He's been taken! The manor's spirits have claimed him for their own and there'll be no getting him out ever and he's been turned to a ghost himself and I swear I heard the poor child moaning away when it happened but I thought it was a horrid dream so I did nothing!" It all came out in one large burst that left her chest heaving considerably.

"He's *missing*?" asked the Countess.

Phillips arrived, out of breath. He held a short leash on the large, mean-looking hound from the previous night. "I've just finished looking, madam. There's not a trace of him anywhere. Burgess here couldn't find the boy, and that was after sniffing his bedsheets. He was in the kitchen for certain. Burgess seemed frustrated to no end and kept going in circles as though Barnaby had disappeared."

"What do you mean, disappeared? Why is no one making sense? What was he doing in the kitchen?" The Countess marched to the serving door and pushed it open. "*Cook! Cook!* Stop burning things and get in here this instant!"

"The boy is gone," Phillips said, still breathing hard. "Burgess is completely reliable. He could track a thick wallet in a crowded square. . . ." He stopped talking, turning red.

Tabitha eyed him with curiosity. He looked flustered from the search, uniform slightly askew and properly matching black shoes shifting up and back along the floor with anxiety or nerves.

Cook entered the dining room, glaring at the Countess while her mouth curved up in a frozen smile. "And what can I do for you now, Your Ladyship? Make you a special dish?"

"Ghosts!" Agnes clutched at Cook's apron. "The spirits have taken Barnaby!"

"Have they, do you think?" Viola said, likewise clutching at Tabitha's sweater and nearly squeezing Pemberley's head off in the process. "Have they taken him?"

"I couldn't say," Tabitha replied.

"I could," said Oliver, distinctly whiter than he'd been minutes before.

All eyes turned to him.

Oliver focused on the table as he spoke. "He came into my room last night, to see if I fancied a late snack. Said he couldn't sleep. I let him go downstairs alone."

There was a brief silence, followed by soft, breathy whimpers from Agnes. Unease filled the room like an invisible fog, wrapping around each child in a stealthy manner until they were all paralyzed.

"Interviews begin shortly and will each last 30 minutes to an hour," the Countess said, her voice weak and cheeks paled. "Barnaby, it seems, will be forfeiting his chance to be my heir due to his pointless decision to hide himself. The boy is frightened of me for some ridiculous reason and is clearly trying to remain out of sight until his mummy and daddy arrive. Nobody's been snatched. Burgess will sniff Barnaby out eventually." She cupped one hand around the absurdly large diamond, emerald, and sapphire peacock brooch on her chest. "There's no one here, other than us." She turned to leave, but paused at the door. "No one at all."

Another beat of quiet pulsed through the room.

"Edward Herringbone," the Countess said, "come to my

study in ten minutes. The rest of you, find a way to amuse yourselves. Keep to the lower rooms and Phillips will find you when it's your turn. The order will be Edward, Frances, Viola, Oliver, then Tabitha."

While the others wandered the manor's parlors, drawing room, and gallery, Tabitha waited her turn in the library, gently petting Pemberley in her skirt pocket, occasionally knitting a bit of scarf, and attempting to whistle. The sight of the books helped her to relax, and she let her eyes drift over the shelves until her heartbeat became slow and steady once again.

She was used to cruelty, so the Countess's rather callous behavior didn't put her off nearly as much as it did the others. And she was shaken and saddened by Mary's death and Barnaby's disappearance, that was true, but there was a nagging feeling that all could be explained if she could just put the pieces together. She tapped her finger to her temple. That sort of thing appeared in Pensive novels and always seemed to help the tapper, though Tabitha was uncertain why. Perhaps it jarred the area of the brain assigned to clue retention.

Having had a few hours of what Inspector Pensive would call *observance of character*, Tabitha found the Countess's indifference to her maid's demise most curious, and it led her to wonder at the history between the two. *It's dreadfully difficult being charitable to those you don't like,* the Countess had said. But why would she need to be charitable at all in those cases?

Perhaps Mary Pettigrew had been a family maid, passed down from a previous generation, and therefore deserved a hint of special consideration.

Oliver walked into the library with his hands shoved deep in both pockets. He glanced around the room. "No rogue kidnappers here," he joked weakly. His face was paler and more drawn than it'd been the night before. "Hullo."

Tabitha stopped pacing and pulled her hand away from Pemberley. "Oh, um. Yes, same to you." *Stop being awkward.*

"Know what you'll be saying to the Countess?"

"No," Tabitha said, smoothing her skirt and taking a seat.

Oliver sat beside her. "You don't talk very much, do you? You're rather quiet and shy."

Tabitha couldn't help but smile and think of her conversations with Pemberley. "Not really."

Standing in a fidgety manner, Oliver plucked a book from a shelf and flipped through it without glancing at the pages. "I once got mad at my parents and threatened not to speak to them ever again." His eyes crinkled. "How long do you think I lasted?"

Tabitha shook her head.

"Three hours. My father says that if you stay quiet too long, you'll lose your voice. Funny sort of thing to say, isn't it?"

She shook her head again. "I think I know what he means." *Keep talking. That's what people do, so say something else.* "I don't think it matters much what I say to the Countess."

Oliver stepped toward her. "What do you mean by that?"

Don't say the wrong thing, and for God's sake, don't say a word about Augustus Home! Tabitha let her shoulders lift and drop. "Just that I'm not the heir. If I was, my parents would have flung themselves on the opportunity to take advantage of it, I'm certain. They were fixed to leave the country before the invitation arrived, and I daresay their plans haven't changed. And what will you say to the Countess?"

Oliver shrugged and studied the shelves. "Do you think she's read all these books? Maybe I'll ask her about them. Or about those gallery paintings." He frowned. "Do you think she's a bit . . . mad? And is that sort of thing inherited, do you think?"

"I couldn't say. Edward might know." And if madness could be inherited, Tabitha thought, perhaps it could be acquired by life experience as well. What sort of life would drive a woman to lunacy?

Shuffle.

Yes, agreed, Pemberley. It certainly wouldn't be a pleasant one, but we don't know anything about the Countess's past, and would you mind very much not pestering me with thoughts right now, please, as I'm attempting to interact with another human?

Carefully avoiding the topic of Barnaby Trundle's disappearance, they spoke of other things, namely what sort of cake they would have for their birthdays the following month when they turned twelve. Tabitha hesitantly played along, enjoying herself and placing orange slices and candy flowers on her imaginary treat. She knew very well there would be no birthday celebration for her. Oliver stayed for a half hour or so, then decided to explore the manor.

"Sure you won't come?" he asked. "Perhaps none of us should be alone after . . . you-know-what."

He's just being kind. He'd probably rather be by himself. "No, thanks. There's plenty for me to explore in here." She waved him away, secretly wishing that no one else would come in. A whole library all to herself, and with no tour to catch up with this time.

But without another presence in the room, thoughts of Barnaby's disappearance kept her company. The Countess's increasingly odd behavior idled around her mind as well. And the feeling that there was something not quite right about Hollingsworth Hall.

"Secrets, Pemberley," she said. "This house is full of secrets."

The mouse nuzzled her thumb. *Squeakity.*

"Yes, let's do explore anyway. Perhaps we'll discover something about our illustrious hostess." Nervously glancing about every time the wisteria branches brushed the library's windows, Tabitha gave herself a tour of the room. The lovely furniture, exotic rugs, paintings, and sculptures took fifteen minutes. An enormous standing globe took ten minutes more to spin and admire. And then, of course, there were the books, which overpowered her unease by sheer number and scope.

The Countess's books were all wonderfully organized, accessible from floor to ceiling by marvelous rolling ladders attached to the shelves. Taking care to peek once into the hallway, Tabitha made a running start toward a ladder and leaped onto the second rung from the bottom, sending herself flying across the back shelf. She ignored Pemberley's squeaks.

There were historical tomes on the Romans and Greeks and British. Thick volumes on philosophy and science. Architecture and useful crafts like woodworking and knitting. A section on scientific methods and forensics. Almanacs of weather patterns, atlases of the Far East and the Near East and Europe and America. Psychology and human behavior. Plays and art and poetry. Epic poems of Homer. A thin copy of short verses and Shakespearean sonnets. An even thinner book of parlor limericks and humor.

One shelf near the floor held a number of children's picture books. *How very odd for someone who doesn't seem to like children at all.* Perhaps they had belonged to her son long ago. That must be it. Perhaps the Countess had not always been so cold. Could life change you and turn you cold without your permission? Or was it a matter of whether you let it?

"I say, sir, now that's a curious book." Tabitha tilted her head to study a chest-high shelf. The rest of the books were strictly in place, but there, buried in the middle of a set of Inspector Pensive novels (how wonderful!) was a book that clearly didn't belong. It was faded, for one thing, and slightly more worn than the others. And the title was in a dull silver color. She peered closer—no, it actually *was* silver. Unshined, but still some sort of metal. Turning her head, she read, "*The Case of the Dowager's Descendant.* Never heard of that one."

With a glimmer of excitement over the discovery of a new

Pensive novel, she started to pull the book out and gasped. It wasn't a book at all, but a solid piece of wood. Pulling harder, Tabitha watched in amazement as the entire shelf came forward. There was a slight popping noise.

The shelf released from the wall.

15

Often overlooked is the fact that secret passages are not necessarily meant to hold secrets themselves, but to permit a person to hear and see the hidden agenda of others.

—Inspector Percival Pensive,
The Case of the Speckled Spyhole

Just inside the wall, there was a low bench and a shelf with several lamps, candle stands, and matches. Hidden passages were something that every great lover of mystery novels longed to encounter, and Tabitha's reaction was no exception.

"Magnificent," she said softly, struck by the unexpected gift and grateful to be alone with it. Before she could peek her head in even farther, footsteps echoed in the front hall. The sound stopped abruptly, and Tabitha thought she heard the armor being adjusted.

In or out? Bold or timid?

Feeling rather like Tibbs after listening to one too many

brilliant deductions about the necessity of good timing, Tabitha eyed the clock. Assuming each meeting would take at least half an hour, there would be nearly two hours until her turn arrived.

"Being badgered into submission by my sensible voice has not brought much excitement over the years, Pemberley," she whispered, slipping behind the open shelf and shoving it back into position until she heard a satisfying click. Sitting on the bench in total darkness, she felt her way to the matchbox, grateful for all the hearth fires she'd been told to start in the complete darkness of early winter mornings. With a scrape and a sizzle, the flame burst to life, settling into a yellow-orange glow that Tabitha quickly transferred to a lamp.

"I do hope we don't get smoke sickness, Pemberley. Now," she said, lifting him to her shoulder, "whose passage do you suppose this is?"

Approximately six feet high and three feet wide, the passage was quite passable indeed. Tabitha supposed that manor houses, even renovated ones, might have passages that went unnoticed and unused for years. Did the Countess even know about it? Making a note to address that question during her interview time, she reached a hand to one of the spare lamps and gave it a hesitant finger swipe. No thick layer of dust.

"Well, *somebody's* been here relatively recently. Thank goodness ghosts and those up to no good prefer the night hours, Pemberley," Tabitha murmured. "Otherwise we might be frightened. No reason now, though. No reason at all, right? Right."

"Oliver? Viola?" The voice rang into the passage clear as a bell. "Is anyone in here?"

Frances.

"Good," Frances said to herself, her shoes clicking into the library. "Now where shall I put it?"

Tabitha saw small points of light shining at intervals from the shelf she'd closed behind her. Peepholes.

"Shh, Pemberley," Tabitha whispered. "No squeaking." Sticking an eye against a hole, Tabitha made out the back of Frances Wellington as she sauntered along the bookshelves.

She moved to a corner, and Tabitha saw her profile, grimacing. "Where to put it?" she muttered again. "Poetry. No one reads this rubbish." She pulled a book aside. "William Wordsworth. Never heard of him."

Frances took a very thick envelope that had been tucked into her skirt. She shoved it quickly behind the book, just as Viola walked in.

"Hello. What are you doing?"

"Well, Viola," Frances said, spinning casually and walking deliberately to the opposite shelf. "This is what they call a library. I was contemplating reading a book. I don't suppose they teach you about reading in the charity circles your people belong to."

Viola kneaded her hands as though she'd very much like to offer Frances an uncharitable greeting with her fist. "If nobody gave money to charity, hope would be gone for a large number of people. Not that you'd care, Frances. But now that you know we were both orphans once, we have that in common, at least. I would think you would have some sympathy for those who are without."

Frances let out an unladylike cackle. "Don't flatter yourself, dear. I'll never be grouped with you for any reason, parents or no parents. And don't fool yourself either. Just because you're not poor doesn't mean your parents are actually accepted by the rich people they invite to their gatherings. Asking people for money is terribly low class, no matter who you're asking for."

"I beg your pardon?"

"See, there you go begging again. What are you doing, anyway? If you're here for that tray of cookies Agnes left, then you might as well say so." Frances clomped out of the room.

Viola sat on the sofa and grabbed a cookie.

Cringing, Tabitha realized that she wouldn't be able to pop back out without creating a bit of a scene. There was no choice except to explore further and hope a different exit presented itself. After a few paces down the passage, a spiral staircase curled up beyond view. "That goes to the second floor, Pemberley."

Shuffle-shuffle.

"Yes, and perhaps the third floor that Phillips said was a nursery. I think we'll stay away from there, as we've spent quite enough time exploring our own attic." There were two routes on the main floor, each one branching off within yards.

Following the second passage in a cautious manner, Tabitha found that it matched the walls perfectly, curving around the library shelves. Remembering her yarn, she trotted lightly back to where she'd started. Bending down, she placed an empty lamp on the ground and tied one end of the skein around it. In Inspector Pensive novels, there were always twists and turns to hidden passages.

"We don't want to get lost in the walls," she reminded Pemberley.

The two investigators moved forward cautiously. Every now and then, a tiny hole allowed Tabitha to see smidgens of a room or hallway.

"Stinky in here," she whispered to Pemberley. "It's almost a familiar smell, like . . . oh, I don't know. Let's go."

She took a right, then a left, and down a few steps (underneath that high library window, she deduced), then up, across, and down a staircase that seemed to mimic the room divisions. The path branched off, and the left side went on fifteen feet before leading to a dead end. The candlelight flickered as Tabitha searched the wall, finding a small square of wood. She touched it, and the wood rotated to reveal a single diamond shape. *Another peephole.*

Peering through it, Tabitha saw a large desk, messy with piled papers and teacups. Its bottom right drawer was badly battered and scratched, as though it had been attacked with a fire poker. Backing away, she raised the candle and saw the outline of a door in the passage. She pushed against it to no avail, then squatted, looking for a keyhole and finding only a latch that was turned to a locked position. Whatever room she'd looked into held another entrance into the secret passage, perhaps with a keyhole on the other side.

Squeak.

"My thought exactly," she said, patting the key in her apron pocket. "But I don't know what room it is, Pemberley. Best to leave it alone for now. Let's try the other way."

Tabitha backtracked to the main path and periodically checked the walls for more signs of a door, but found nothing. As she turned left, passing by what she guessed was the second parlor, another small block of wood caught her eye along the otherwise smooth passage walls.

It twisted easily, revealing two small holes, and Tabitha found herself staring at Frances and Oliver. They were seated in the armchairs in the second parlor room, avoiding the sofa where Mary had been the night before.

A sudden chill of realization crept up her neck, then sank down to her toes, numbing her into a frozen stance. *Dear Lord,* she thought. *I'm looking out of a painting.*

"Now, Pemberley, just because this is here doesn't mean that those *were* someone's eyes I saw last evening. It doesn't mean that only hours ago, someone was standing in this very spot. Painters can do amazing things with artwork now. Incredibly lifelike things." Saying the words out loud, Tabitha felt her toes tingle back to life. After all, she had years of experience pretending things were quite normal when they clearly were not. Even so, Tabitha was very glad that she didn't have access to dusting powder for fingerprinting that Tibbs had introduced in one of the later Pensive novels.

"I'm hungry," Oliver was saying.

Frances sighed, as though bored with the conversation. "Why didn't you eat more breakfast?"

His heel tapped on the floor, and he shook his head. "Too nervous. And I'm a bit worried, I suppose."

Frances laughed. "Don't be. I've already won the whole thing." She frowned and picked up a crystal bowl. "My parents always say that nothing in life is more valuable and precious than a work of art. Nothing at all." Her jaw tightened. "And now I'm worth one hundred thousand pounds, aren't I? Serves them right. The Countess will be taking me on in no time with the load that I told her. She probably won't even call you in."

"I'm not talking about that. A woman died last night, and it's possible that she was accidentally killed by one of us. And the Countess seems to have lost any sense of true kindness. It's not normal to demand that one of us leave our parents to live with her. It's as though she's got some sort of plan to . . . I don't know what, but it's eerie. And now Barnaby is missing." He stared at Frances. "That doesn't frighten you?" He shook his head and sighed. "I should have gone to the kitchen with him." He stopped heel tapping and stood. "And besides all that, there may be spirits about."

"Nonsense. Just because you're afraid to live with a woman of title doesn't mean that I'm not up to the prize." Frances twisted a finger through her curls. "Believing in ghosts is idiotic, and Barnaby is probably quivering in some corner, sucking his thumb. And if he's not, my money's on Cook. It was her kitchen and she's positively foul."

"Perhaps it was the Countess," Oliver guessed.

"Perhaps Phillips's dog ate him up," said Frances lightly. "Not likely, though. He would have been far too sour to stomach. Barnaby was terribly low class, pretending to be high class. That's the worst kind, I think, don't you? At least Tabitha Crum knows she's inferior."

"Tabitha is not inferior," Oliver said, his face turning red.

Thank you, Oliver.

Frances dug through a small decorative porcelain box. "Mini eggs." She wrinkled her nose. "How dull. And no, it doesn't make me nervous because I didn't do a murder and I didn't stick that smelly Barnaby anywhere."

"What was your hair doing on her, then? On Mary, I mean. I saw long pieces of reddish hair on her back. You can't pin that on anyone else."

Oh, well noted. Tabitha hadn't observed that particular bit of evidence. Perhaps Oliver had the makings of an Inspector about him.

Frances's hands crept to her purse, and she began playing with the clasp. "We were all being shoved about. And there are no such things as spirits."

Now, Tabitha knew it was quite possible that Frances might have deep reasons for her horrid behavior, but the girl was still a bit of a nasty-pants. Before she could stop herself, she let out a ghostly moan. Frances nearly fell from her armchair.

Tabitha's hand jumped to her mouth. "Did I just do that, Pemberley?" she whispered. "I probably frightened her terribly. And poor Oliver went all flinchy." She felt guilty for a long moment before a soft chortle slipped out. "Rather bold of me, wasn't it? If only I'd known the satisfaction of executing well-timed mischief earlier in life, I daresay I might have had loads of fun with my unloving nonfather's toupee."

But before Tabitha could fully enjoy her trick, the most delicate *swish* whispered behind her in the passage, and a light wisp of air moved past. She stiffened and listened, hearing nothing. Slowly, carefully, she turned her head both ways, seeing nothing in either direction by the low glow of lamplight. "Imagination," she murmured, forcing herself to return to the peephole. "Nerves." Nevertheless, she decided that perhaps it wasn't the time and place to be impersonating ghosts.

"It's Oliver's turn!" Edward called, stepping into the parlor with Viola. "I just ran into Phillips and he said to—oh! Wouldn't figure you for a clumsy one," he said to Frances, who had just bumped into the doorframe on her way out of the room. He bent to help gather the contents of her spilled purse.

"Stop! Stop that helping!" Frances said. "Don't touch my things with your filthy hands," she snapped.

Still visible on the floor were the hotel pen, one of Viola's velvet dress buttons, the piece of decoration from the dining table, a large green jewel, a cigar, an ivory-carved heart, and the miniature eggs she'd just sneered at.

Viola clapped. "You've found my missing button! I was wondering where it popped off to." Her face fell. "Oh *my*," she said, pointing at the rest of the items on the floor. "Some of those things belong to the house, don't they, Frances?" Viola shook a finger at the foul girl. "That's a bit cheeky, even for you."

"Seems spot-on to me," chirped Edward. "Right on target for her lovely character."

Frances gave a furious toss of her curls. "Shut up, you filthy *toad*."

"Frances." Oliver rose. "You must put everything back."

"Quiet," Frances hissed. "I borrowed the jewel from my parents and those other things were lying on the floor. I picked them up absentmindedly to return later, I tell you. All of it will be mine at the end of the weekend anyway." She straightened and walked a slow circle around the other three children. "This is all a misunderstanding, *understand*?" She pointed a finger in each of their faces. "If any of you say a word about this to the Countess, I will end you." She stalked out of the room, leaving the rest of them to gossip.

Though she desperately wanted to stay where she was, Tabitha thought it best to take advantage of the empty library to exit the passageway. She kept moving down the hidden path, thinking it might circle around.

A right, up narrow stairs, straight for a bit, then a left. Down the stairs, around a corner.

A dead end. And another door, complete with a locked latch, with an herbal, meaty smell wafting behind it. She'd found her way to the kitchen. She peered out of the keyhole, but could only see the far wall. A smidgen of storage cabinetry and a painting featuring a young boy leaning against a tree and staring at a lake.

"Drat. If only I had more time to explore. And what is that smell?"

Squeak!

"No, not the kitchen odors, something else. It's been all along the passage. Oh, never mind." Tabitha backtracked toward the library, pausing only to see that Viola and Edward were still in the parlor room. *Oliver must be with the Countess.*

She tripped right before reaching the library entrance, the oil lamp coming dangerously close to bursting into flames on the ground as her head banged and rubbed against the passage wall. Tabitha barely kept the lamp in her hand. Breathing heavily as she pushed herself up, she noticed a glint of metal on the passage floor. Bending, she picked up an earring.

A bluebird earring.

Hastily Tabitha found the inside latch, slipped back into the library, and shoved the bookshelf back where it belonged.

The next half hour was spent deducing and feeding bits of cookie to herself and Pemberley.

"So, Pemberley, Mary Pettigrew was in the secret passage earlier this week, shortly before her stroke. The Countess found her practically catatonic on Monday evening, so let's say she was last in here around Monday morning."

Squeak.

"Why? Because," she said, scooping him into both hands and bringing him to eye level, "a woman, especially a maid, does not lose a beautiful earring and not notice for more than a day." Tabitha stood and paced along the book-filled walls. "So she was in the passage on Monday and discovered in the Countess's study that evening.

"Sometime after that, the other staff arrived, but they've all left by now due to ghostly noises or because of the Countess's cruelty. And on Friday we all arrived and were told that one of us is her grandchild. The grandchild is to live with her permanently and will receive an enormous trust fund."

She stopped at the row of books concerning human behavior. "We know that the Countess keeps gruesome paintings, has a nasty (but explainable) habit of keeping knives around her person, and locks her extra servant clothes in an upstairs room. We know that there are ghostly noises in the halls, that a Mr. Simmons, possibly a reporter, has been calling repeatedly, and that a maid, who knew about this hidden passage, has died. What else?"

Squeak?

"Ah, yes. There is a family photograph in my bedroom with something odd about it that I can't pinpoint, and paintings of a boy in several places throughout the manor. And we mustn't forget the disappearance of Barnaby, whether by his own design or due to something more sinister."

She stopped pacing. "And the Countess wants her grandchild, but not simply for the sake of having a loved one returned. What can we make of all that?" she asked, plucking a reference book from the shelf.

It was no use. All the information was in a muddled pile. She couldn't stack it into a discernible story. Not three seconds after she'd plopped onto an armchair with *Psychology of Deviant Behavior, Volume 1*, a shadow appeared in the doorway, followed by its owner.

"Miss Crum," said Phillips. "Do come along."

She returned the book. "Coming." Tabitha followed him, realizing a moment before she stepped into the Countess's study what the particular smell had been throughout the hidden passage.

Burned toast and rotting cinnamon.

Barnaby Trundle's smell.

16

Defensive people use offensive maneuvers
to buy time. That's right, Tibbs, criminals often
reach a point in their plan when they are quite
out of control and are only stalling until their
next move becomes clear. It is our job
to catch them before it does.
—Inspector Percival Pensive,
The Case of the Swindling Sommelier

Camilla DeMoss offered the briefest of false smiles as Tabitha entered the study. "Sit down," she ordered, reaching for a glass dish of peppermints and popping one into her mouth. Between the deep furrow dividing the Countess's eyebrows and her vigorous candy sucking, Tabitha guessed that she either hadn't determined her heir yet or she was attempting to lose weight, and was becoming irritable with the effort, as Mrs. Crum did upon occasion. Perhaps both were the case.

"What's that?" the Countess asked, peering at Tabitha's head.

She reached forward and rustled a sprinkling of fine dust from her hair. "Dear God, I hope that's not lice."

"No," said Tabitha. *It's from your secret passage,* she added in her mind. *The one that you may not know exists. The one your maid, Mary Pettigrew, was bumping about in.*

"Well, what is it?" The Countess removed her gloves and reached for a silver container on the desk corner. Lifting the lid, she dipped her fingers into a thick lotion and began to rub it into her rough, dry-looking hands. "Go on."

"It's just, um . . . well, y-you s-see—" Tabitha rummaged through her brain for the right words. She had to find out if the Countess was aware of the passages, without drawing suspicion. What had Pensive said about reactions revealing knowledge?

The Countess squinted at her. "You're not here to show off a dreadful stammer." She sniffed. "Or your general lack of hygiene."

"Yes, Your Ladyship," Tabitha said. "It must be a bit of wheat germ that Cook gave us to sprinkle on our oats this morning. Edward was playing around a bit. Speaking of playing around, wasn't this a marvelous manor house for your son to grow up in? He must have loved exploring for hidden passages and such." Tabitha watched carefully for quickly smoothed-over eye widening, any movement around the mouth, and what the Countess did with her hands.

Had there been a total absence of reaction, that would have been an indication of deliberately masking a feeling as well, but instead the Countess looked distinctly bored. "That, my dear, is the most idiotic thing I've heard coming from your mouth thus far. Hidden passages," she scoffed. "Those don't exist outside of novels, and I don't care for reading."

"But you have an entire library full of books," Tabitha said, watching her hostess carefully. "I was so delighted to find that you had a shelf of mysteries."

The Countess waved a dismissive hand before putting both gloves back on. "I don't touch the things. They were here when I arrived. But really, do children always talk this much? With Frances it was 'How much is this worth?' and 'Can I get my money early?' and with Viola it was 'Oh, but you *must* feed the poor!' I've fed enough people to last a lifetime, I'll have you know, and none of them were sufficiently grateful, if you ask me."

So she doesn't know about the passages. So Mary Pettigrew must have discovered them and used them for . . . Tabitha was at a loss.

The Countess forced a pleasant expression to smooth its way up her cheeks. "Now, dear. Just tell me what you know. Might you be my heir?"

Tabitha forced a smile of her own. "I know nothing. My parents said there was no token given when I was handed over. I'm afraid I'm not your grandchild."

It was as the Countess turned to refill her tea that Tabitha noticed the desk. It was the same one she had been staring at just hours earlier. Quickly searching the walls for any interior sign of the peephole that she'd looked through, Tabitha saw nothing. And the wallpaper was patterned, making it difficult to locate a keyhole.

Hanging on a wall beside a rather large wardrobe (*odd thing to keep in a study, Pemberley*) was a framed oil painting of a small boy in a hand tub, being gently washed by a pair of arms that extended out of the picture. It was a profile image this time, and the child was much younger, but Tabitha was almost certain that the very same child had been in the painting in her bedroom. And the kitchen.

"No token?" The Countess flipped through papers in front of her. "I would think your parents might have thought up a lie, but no matter, dear. I'm afraid I'll just have to choose whoever I feel best fits my needs, other than Barnaby. I wonder where that dreaded boy escaped to. Not that you're high on my list, but I wouldn't try to run away like him. I don't have to remind you that Phillips stuck Mary Pettigrew in the garden because he was certain she would freeze there. In this weather, you wouldn't last one hundred yards beyond the manor. I do hope Barnaby's not gotten himself frozen solid down the road somewhere." She offered a strained grandmotherly smile. "Now run along and enjoy your day."

As Tabitha stood to leave, the painting caught her eye once more. It was at the right level to be covering the passage's keyhole. She had to find out if the key in her apron belonged to the secret passage door. But how to knock the painting from the wall?

Shuffle, shuffle.

"Oh bother, my shoelace." Tabitha knelt and squeezed Pemberley four quick times (*Good thinking, sir*). She set him on the floor and nervously cleared her throat to utter their secret cue phrase for distraction. She and Pemberley had used it on occasion when they needed to sneak provisions due to Tabitha being forced to skip dinner for nonsensical reasons.

She prayed for the ability to speak quickly, as the Countess seemed more the type to advance in violence than recoil in fear.

"Inspector Pemby, on duty," Tabitha announced in a clear voice.

Immediately the clever mouse ran to a wall.

"Inspector Who?" The Countess turned.

Squeakity-squeak, squeak!

"What's this about an inspecto—mouse! Rat! Mouse!" Springing to her tiptoes, the rich philanthropist danced around the room yelling, "Kill it! Kill it!" while Pemberley dashed from the wall toward the desk.

"A rat!" Tabitha echoed the words, adding, "Oh my, don't touch it. It could have a horrible rat disease! Foaming pustule influenza or scabies!" She moved behind the desk, both to shield Pemberley a bit and to examine the painting. The woman's hand gently scrubbed with a yellow cloth while the child tilted his chin up, gazing back at his mother.

Who says it's a mother doing the washing? the inner Tabitha argued. *Has anyone ever lovingly bathed you like that?*

I've actually never had the occasion to ask Mother how she bathed me, and she's gone forever now, so close your tea lid.

Oh, stop with your ridiculous inner arguments! Does the painting cover the keyhole or not?

Flailing wildly, Tabitha gave a little shriek and spun, successfully hitting the edge of the gilt frame. The painting landed picture side down while she frantically searched the wallpaper. There it was! Nearly blending into the pattern was a small keyhole. Now, if she could quickly reach into her apron and—

"Move!" the Countess ordered. "I heard what Frances Wellington said about you. Use your disgusting affinity for filthy rats and lure it in so I can smash it. I'll kill it myself!"

A terrible thumping noise came from somewhere above them in the house.

The Countess let out a bark of annoyance. "Stop jumping on the beds, you awful, *awful* children!"

A crash followed.

"What's going on!" the Countess shrieked as Pemberley tickled the back of her ankle on the way to a better hiding spot. "Bwah! Beastly thing! I'll cook you for Cook's dinner once I catch you!" She reached for her handbag and pulled out the larger of the two knives, throwing it fiercely at the wall and narrowly missing Pemberley's tail. "Blast!" She threw the smaller knife, embedding the blade into the wall next to the first. "Double blast!" Bending at the waist, the Countess tried to pull her weapons from the wall, but blessedly, they were in too deep. She rummaged through her key ring impatiently. Her eyes were crazed and glazed with the prospect of mouse murder. With stunning efficiency, she tried several keys before shouting, "Aha!"

Twisting the key in the bottom left drawer and thrusting her hand inside, the Countess came out with a box. And reaching her hand into the box, she came out with a revolver.

The Countess turned to the door. "Phillips! Where are you? Get in here now and shoot this mouse!" She bellowed something incomprehensible, ran out the door, and slammed it shut behind her.

Jarred by the sight of a revolver, Tabitha was nonetheless clear-headed enough to know that

1. the Countess didn't seem to be as confident in its use as she was with knives, and
2. she was likely to be gone long enough for a brief investigation to take place.

Tabitha contemplated the wise words of Inspector Pensive: *Some people hoard secret documents in elaborate vaults, Tibbs, but you'd be surprised what you find simply lying around a common desk.* Before diving into a hurried investigation, she slid the key from her apron and placed it in the passage keyhole.

It was a perfect fit, which meant Mary Pettigrew had been regularly creeping along the houses passages for some reason. Had she stolen the key or had it been passed down by other family maids or—

Squeak!

Yes, time for that later. The desk. Check for clues.

There were two files. One held a short stack of information about the Crum family and the other was thicker. Scanning its contents, Tabitha saw that it was a formal investigation report about the missing grandchild. There were search documents, interviews, and a background statement signed by the Countess of Windermere. It was basically the same information the Countess had shared with them the evening before. Tabitha dismissed the file and inventoried the rest of the desk.

There was wax for melting and an ink pot for dipping and three identical seals for stamping and cream-colored envelopes for addressing. Two drawers were on the right side of the desk, the bottom one battered, just as she'd seen from the passage. Up close, Tabitha could see that a considerable amount of banging had marred and dented the wood, and that the small keyhole had been tampered with, scratches on the side indicating that someone had been attempting to pick the lock. "Who's been trying to get in here, and did they succeed?" Tabitha asked Pemberley. "Was it Mary Pettigrew, do you think?"

Squeak?

"Quite right: More importantly, what's inside? But there's no time to speculate now." Unable to open the bottom, she opened the top drawer and found herself staring at two pieces of paper.

The smaller piece was simply a list in beautiful scripted handwriting that Tabitha recognized from the invitation:

Appleby, Oliver
Crum, Tabitha
Dale, Viola
Herringbone, Edward
Trundle, Barnaby
Wellington, Frances

The other paper looked to be a hastily drafted letter, the handwriting badly shaky and the paper crumpled in one corner as though it had been clutched in a fist.

My dear Hattie,

I've found the attendant and traced the delivery to Basil House, London. The list of children is comprehensive and contains the only possibilities. It is time to bring our speculation to an end. I must tell you that I have already contacted the adults, telling them to bring the children to Hollingsworth Hall. I have no doubt the parents will be pleased to hear about the one-hundred-thousand-pound trust fund that will be released to the family on the twelfth birthday.

Sweet Hattie, I know that you must have mixed feelings. I know what guilt you've harbored, but do remember that children are typically the most forgiving of people.

Before you say that I've acted in haste, know that I have grounds to be hasty. The doctor has said I don't have much time left. I have grown weaker by the day (indeed, I feel weakness coming over me even now), and I don't wish to leave this world before bringing our most important endeavor to a close. Grandmother is as important a title as Countess. I sincerely believe that Thomas would want this.

Yours always,

In glorious crime and justice,

Countess Camilla Lenore DeMoss

Tabitha replaced the list and letter, set Pemberley on the Countess's chair, and began to pace around the desk.

Squeak.

Tabitha nodded at her partner and held out her palm for him to climb onto. "No, quite right, it doesn't add up. Let's review, sir.

"Firstly, Pemberley, why did she tell us that the money wouldn't be given to the family? She must have changed her mind. Is it a simple matter of lack of trust?" she asked the mouse. "And she's dying and wants guardianship to ensure that she'll get plenty of personal time with her heir?"

Squeakity.

"Yes, moving on to point two, the Countess doesn't appear weak at all. Crazy, but not weak. What was that she said at dinner—'I've never been sick a day in my life.'

"And third, what's that bit about justice? Crime and justice . . ."

She lifted Pemberley to her shoulder and bent to examine the beaten drawer.

"I wonder . . ." With a thrill of investigative adrenaline dousing any nerves, Tabitha slid Mary Pettigrew's key into the lock and held her breath. She turned it.

And heard a click.

Knowing her time was limited, Tabitha excitedly sifted through a series of carefully labeled files. Were these the family files? But no, they were larger and more formal-looking than the ones in the small black trunk had been. And there were more than thirty of them.

Each file was marked with the letters *MPS* followed by a single surname and date. Pulling out the first, she saw that it contained a short newspaper clipping and three sheets of paper. It was a typed report of some sort.

"Oh dear, Pemberley." A young boy had run away from his home and was found in a back alley of London, his skull fractured and several bones broken. It was unclear whether he had fallen from a great height or if something else had caused the damage. The article mentioned that speculation was leaning toward murder. "How very sad. That poor boy and his poor parents."

As she scanned the contents of the other files, a cold, cold feeling came over her.

Oh, how horrid . . .

Oh, my, but here's another, more terrible than the last. . . .

Oh God, Pemberley, no, no, you mustn't look. . . .

They were all murder files. Carefully documented, dutifully

detailed accounts of murders that had taken place over a number of years. Elderly, young, males, females. Chokings, back-alley bludgeonings, poisonings, drownings, shootings . . . stabbings. Her heart became nearly audible in its booming as she checked the year on each one. Not a single murder file was after the year 1880. The year the Countess came to Hollingsworth Hall.

Which was the year that her charitable records started, according to Viola.

"Pemberley, why would someone start to be such a generous woman after years of not giving any traceable donations? And why would that same woman keep a gallery full of gruesome murder paintings?"

Pemberley made no sound whatsoever, no doubt struck speechless by the twisted turn of events.

No, Tabitha thought. *It can't be true.* But it could, and she knew very well that the evidence was stacking up in support of the ugliest of conclusions.

Camilla Lenore DeMoss, Countess of Windermere, was a former murderess.

"Well," Tabitha said, hoping for an explanation to strike her. "Perhaps she's changed? Been rehabilitated?"

Squeakity. Squeak! Squeak!

"Oh dear, you're right," Tabitha said miserably. "Mary Pettigrew must have found the files and had a stroke. But maybe they aren't the Countess's files, Pemberley," she said, hand shaking as she locked the drawer and stood. "Perhaps it's a matter of interest. The crime paintings, the murder files . . . everyone needs a hobby, right? Something to pass the time?" She stared at the painting of the boy. Poor Thomas, who had grown up, who had run away, and who had died.

Oh God, who had died in a *drowning* accident. Had it really been an accident, or had the son been deliberately dispatched? Tabitha recalled the Countess's words from the night before: *Nobody will be dying accidentally.*

"Pemberley, I don't mean to frighten you, but this is very, very bad." Tabitha sank into the Countess's chair and let herself tremble. "We are trapped in a house with someone who has a penchant for murder. She could kill any of us at any moment. I mean, she hasn't yet, and there are parts of her that seemed fairly normal, but—"

Squeak!

"I don't know! I don't know what's going to happen! Just take a deep breath, Pemberley, and *don't panic*. Oh dear. I don't know what to do."

But Tabitha did know what to do. Or at least Inspector Tabitha knew. She would act normally—as normally as possible under the circumstances. Any odd behavior would mark her as trouble that would best be disposed of.

"Pemberley," she said, forcing three deep breaths into her lungs and pushing them out before continuing, "this is *it*. We are firmly entrenched in foul play of the most dangerous kind. This is Inspector Pensive territory if ever I've seen it, and while we are not actually in a mystery novel, we have seen this type of situation before. Our goal must be twofold: to provide occasion for an arrest and to do it without anyone in our party getting killed."

Before Tabitha could deduce the best way to do that, the door handle jiggled madly. She jumped as the door burst open, but it wasn't Phillips who swept inside. Instead the pallid face of Agnes appeared, lips pawing at the air as though trying to find words to grip. "Oh," she finally said, sucking down a fresh breath of air. "Where's the Countess? It's terrible!"

Tabitha stepped quickly toward Agnes, grateful that she seemed to be hunting around the room for the Countess rather than appraising Tabitha's previous position at the desk.

"What's terrible, Agnes?" Tabitha asked.

The Countess hurried through the open door, the revolver still in her hand. "Yes, what's terrible, Agnes, other than the state of you, and the fact that I can't find Phillips, and the other fact that you've probably let a diseased mouse go flitting around the manor?" The Countess strode over to Agnes, looking her up and down (allowing Tabitha to scoop Pemberley into a quick recovery).

"It's happened again, Your Ladyship. Another child is missing! I couldn't get in! It was locked!"

Cook came running, as did Phillips and Burgess.

"What?" The Countess stared at each of them, baffled. "Who's missing?"

"I was tidying your room, Countess, and went to the laundry for fresh sheets. When I came back, the door was locked. 'Who's in there?' I asked, but nobody answered. And then there was a yell and she cried for help!"

"Who?" Tabitha asked.

Agnes clutched the desk with one hand and her chest with the other. "She said she was being taken! And then she stopped. Phillips came and broke your door down, but she was already gone!"

"Who?" demanded the Countess, this time shaking the revolver.

"Oh!" Agnes finally noticed the weapon and backed into the study wall, knocking her head and sinking to the floor. "Oh!"

"Oh, for God's sake, don't be stupid, the revolver's for a mouse, not for you. Who's missing?"

"Frances Wellington," Agnes cried. And then, unable to take any more drama, she fainted onto the carpet in a rather crumpled pile of overworked maid.

Tabitha's mind whirled with the new information. She gave a silent pat to her mouse, who no doubt felt the meaning and urgency in her fingers. *The plot thickens, Pemberley.*

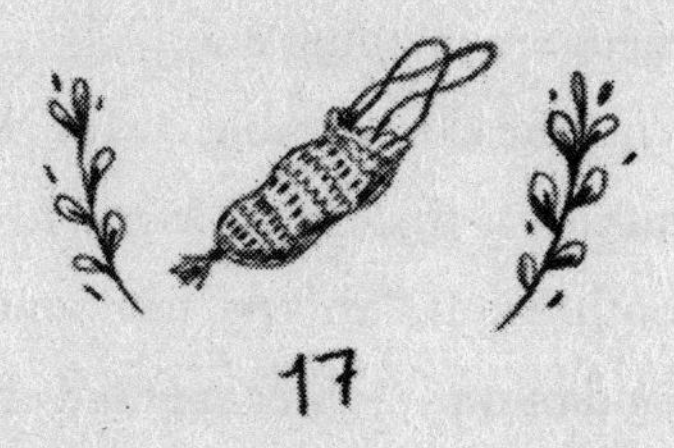

17

When a member of a party dies, there is sadness and sometimes speculation. When a member of the party disappears, the speculation is accompanied by fear. When the members of a party turn to fear, Tibbs, quite anything can happen.
—Inspector Percival Pensive,
The Case of the Beleaguered Boatman

Within moments of Agnes's recovery, the small party transferred themselves to the Countess's enormous quarters, where there was, indeed, a sign of struggle. Drawers of clothing were open and dresses were strewn about and the closet door was ajar, revealing a most un-countess-like row of sensible shoes and Teagan McTeagle's Best Foot-Soaking Salts. Every cream jar and makeup brush and perfume bottle appeared bothered, and three jewelry boxes on the dressing table were opened and in a state of disarray. The room was scattered nearly to bursting with an excess of personal items. But Frances Wellington was nowhere to be seen.

Cook patted a recovering Agnes on the hand. "There, there, dear. Do you remember anything else?"

Agnes shook her head miserably. "Miss Wellington seemed angry in her shouting at first. Then frightened." The maid buried her head in both hands. "So very frightened. And then more noises—thumps and bumps—and a muffled cry, and then silence. It all was over in a matter of seconds, really. It was ghosts." She nodded to herself. "They've spirited her away."

The Countess seemed more upset at the invasion of her privacy than at the disappearance of a child. "What was she doing in here in the first place?"

While Phillips looked under the bed, the Countess began ripping aside all four sets of heavy curtains, checking behind each one and muttering to herself. She marched across the room to slam the closet door shut. "All I want is a horrid little grandchild. Why is that so difficult? Stop staring at me, Cook, and get out of here! Get out and start preparing your unpalatable excuse for a luncheon."

Cook plastered an obedient smile on her face and curtsied in an exaggerated manner.

Tabitha felt ill, thinking of the horrid criminal acts she'd just read about. For the first time since she'd met him, she very much hoped that she would see Barnaby Trundle soon, and in one piece. Frances Wellington, too. She wouldn't even begrudge them an insult or two. *Stay calm,* she ordered herself. *Pay attention.*

The Countess seemed as perplexed as everyone about the children's whereabouts, but even if she was innocent of child snatching, Tabitha reasoned that anger and frustration and confusion and knives and murderous histories mixed up together in a manor house would not make for a pleasant outcome.

She felt Pemberley moving about and casually pinched at her sweater. *Yes, that's exactly what we need. A distraction.* Inspector Pensive had been very clear about that in the very first novel in the series: *Always give the suspects a decent length of rope with which to hang themselves, Tibbs, and shift your focus to someone else when possible. One who believes himself to be completely free of blame and attention will often relax to the point of idiocy, and thus prove himself guilty of all manner of things.*

Oliver, Viola, and Edward appeared in the doorway, hesitantly peeking into the room.

"Does anyone need assistance?" Oliver asked. "We thought we heard a scuffle."

"This room is absolutely huge!" Viola said, gazing around the Countess's quarters. She clapped a hand over her mouth, then relaxed. Then her eyes grew wide and she let out an enormous sneeze.

"Frances has vanished," Tabitha informed them gravely.

"Gone, is she?" Edward looked rather pleased. "That's the two bad apples out, then." He saw that nobody was smiling. "Well, wouldn't you say so, Oliver? I mean, no offense to them, but the rest of us are decently pleasant and Barnaby and Frances are rather—"

"Oh, stop!" said Viola, appearing guilt-stricken. She grabbed Edward's hand. "It's awful enough that I used her as an example of how bad things happen when children are spoiled with an excess of money, and how, how . . ." Viola's left eye twitched, and her mouth opened for a long second. "How . . . ahhhhhh-choo!!" She began an impressive series of seven full sneezes, before raising her head with watery eyes. "It's even worse in here than in the Countess's study! What on earth am I allergic to?"

"I suppose we can rule out Frances, her having been snatched by the ghosties," Edward quipped.

Viola shook her head miserably, then tightened her grip on Edward. "Don't you *dare* go anywhere without me from now on."

"Must go to the facilities eventually," Edward stated logically. "So, Phillips, what have we got here? What's the what?"

Phillips clipped over in his black work heels, examining the four remaining children. "Sometime in the last thirty minutes, Agnes began cleaning the Countess's room. After going to the laundry to fetch fresh sheets, she returned to find Frances locked in here. Do any of you know how that came to pass?"

"Maybe you should ask the Countess," Edward suggested. "It being her room and all."

The Countess came very close to slapping Edward, halting her hand inches from his face. "I didn't do anything with the child, is that understood? I'm not hiding anything."

Not hiding anything. That seems unlikely. The Countess's behavior had been increasingly erratic since they'd arrived, as though some sort of facade was gradually melting to reveal an unknown truth. If Her Ladyship *was* on the verge of becoming unhinged, it was best to put her attention elsewhere. Tabitha watched her search behind the final curtain. It waved back and forth, its edge brushing against a painting.

A painting of a child.

Tabitha felt an Inspectorish tingling sensation. A deduction fluttered on the edge of her consciousness. What was it about the paintings featuring that small boy? There was something about the paintings and the Countess saying that she wasn't hiding things. Hiding things . . . hidden things . . . *hidden things like passages.*

Tabitha scoured the walls for disturbances that might indicate a passage door. One wall, two walls, three walls . . . wait! The rug! A rich Oriental square near the dressing table was slightly off its mark, revealing a small dust corner. Tabitha followed the rug's length, keeping an eye on the wall, and there it was. The rich wood paneling was such that the dividing lines weren't noticeable unless one was looking hard for such a thing. And periodic bits of ornate carving let the keyhole blend seamlessly into the darkly stained images of wings and feathers.

But it was there.

At that moment, Tabitha was certain. She was certain the same way that Pensive was taken by sudden inspiration to make wild connections. There had been a painting of the boy in the library and the study and the kitchen. *Pemberley, don't you see? Each room with a child painting holds a door into the hidden passage.* The disappearances were no coincidence. The children were being taken by someone. Or, she thought, thinking of the ghosts, *something.* And if the passages could be used to make people disappear, perhaps they could aid the children's own escape.

"The Countess didn't snatch Frances," Tabitha agreed.

"Then who was it?" asked Viola.

"Don't tell me," Agnes whispered weakly. "I don't have the energy to faint again."

"She came up here on her own." Tabitha took a deep breath, mentally weighing the card she was about to play. "Frances was stealing. She has a bit of a problem."

"She's right," Oliver said, looking at Tabitha with wonder. "That must be why Frances came up here."

The Countess turned to Tabitha, who'd led the accusation. "Explain," she ordered.

Tabitha eyed her audience, silently summoning the wisdom and confidence of her literary mentor. "Well," she began, "Frances has a habit of thievery. She was found with certain household items in her reticule."

Agnes gasped. Oliver and Viola and Edward stared at her with puzzled curiosity, no doubt wondering how she knew about the stealing when she'd been absent from the parlor at the time Frances's purse had spilled.

All eyes were on Tabitha with marked attention for perhaps the first time in her life. "Phillips, did you actually hear Frances's voice?" she asked.

He frowned. "Well, no. But Agnes said—"

"I fear that Agnes," Tabitha said, feeling a bit bad about her next words, "may have misheard something. She's been under a good deal of strain. I believe that Frances is safe and sound, probably hiding with Barnaby Trundle along with a bundle of stolen items."

The Countess clenched her hands and jaw. She swallowed hard. "Go on."

"I believe, Your Ladyship," Tabitha continued, "that Frances responded to your invitation with the sole intent of grabbing every valuable you possess. She even brought a spare suitcase to smuggle things out," she added. "You'd best check her room thoroughly."

This was not altogether false. Frances *had* brought a rather light extra suitcase, according to one of the drivers. It was probably filled with harmless items by now—napkins and knickknacks and such, as well as the occasional item of small value. But checking Frances's room wouldn't distract the Countess for long. Tabitha would need more time with the others if they were to assemble a plan. "And you might check any areas of the manor her parents were in. I believe they became acquainted with the Hall's gallery during the excellent tour that Phillips gave."

The Countess pulled Oliver forward from the line of children. "Is this true? Oliver Appleby, you attest to this behavior on the part of Frances?"

"I know that she's swiped a few trinkets," Oliver said, glancing at Tabitha. "I couldn't say about the rest."

While Agnes, Phillips, and the Countess all faced Oliver, Tabitha took a step out of their lines of vision and innocently reached a hand out, tapping the clock on the Countess's dresser. *We need time*, she mouthed to the other children.

Viola took the hint. "I believe her parents spent a good deal of time in the library as well."

Tabitha shook her head furiously. *No!*

"Er, the drawing room, I mean," Viola said.

Tabitha gave a quick nod.

The Countess spun toward Viola. "Well, where was it? The library or drawing room?"

"The drawing room! They were in there when you gave us time to speak with our parents, you see. And they were also in the . . . second parlor?"

Tabitha grinned. The drawing room and second parlor were perfect. Far enough away that nobody would hear children meeting in the library.

Or slipping out of it.

"The second parlor," Viola repeated, with more confidence.

The Countess released Oliver and began pacing. "Why, that little *devil* child! And to think I believed she might be related to me. Well, all that matters is that I clearly did nothing wrong. I didn't lock her in my room. Phillips! Agnes! Come with me. We'll be doing a thorough search of Frances's room, the gallery, the drawing room, and the second parlor. Note anything unusual, or anything that appears to have been taken."

They swept out of the room, leaving the children behind.

"What's going on, Tabitha?" Oliver asked. "Do you really believe what you just said?"

Without stopping to think about being odd or inappropriate, Tabitha latched onto Viola with a vigorous embrace. "You *brilliant* girl! You are altogether marvelous!" She released her hold, reddening. "Sorry. It's, um, that was very well done."

Viola fairly glowed at the compliment. "It was nothing."

Tabitha beckoned the rest of them into a huddle. "And no, I don't believe everything I said about Frances. That was a distraction."

"But what about Frances disappearing?" Viola asked. "Aren't we very worried about her and Barnaby, even horrible as they are? And the Countess is *mad*. If she turns out to be my grandmother, I'll run away, I swear it!"

"We should all run away." Tabitha told them what she had seen in the study, ending with her theory that Mary Pettigrew had discovered her employer's secret and had a stroke as a result.

"Murder files?" Viola asked, her chin quivering. "Maybe she's looking into the funding of wrongly charged prisoners. It's possible," she snapped at Edward, who was sadly shaking his head.

"And it's also possible she's been stacking bodies in those locked rooms," he said. "Don't you all think it's rather interesting that she waited until after our parents were gone to divulge her plans to keep one of us *permanently*? Any bodies in your bedroom closet, Tabitha?"

"No, it's a very normal room, Edward. Neatly organized, no bodies. But yes, her breakdown has been conveniently timed. Your parents would never have left you behind if they suspected anything like this." *Unlike my parents,* Tabitha thought, *who have already left me forever.*

"No, they wouldn't have," Oliver said, opening and closing his pocket tool attachments. "So, the murder dates were all before she purchased Hollingsworth Hall? Do you think she's probably"—he swallowed uncomfortably—"stopped killing people?"

Tabitha considered. She wasn't ready to fully make that deduction yet. "I couldn't say."

"Sounds right to me." Edward clucked his tongue. "And now she's gone off the wagon and wants a grandchild to kill. Clever of her to lure us in with money. Mother and Father would hand me right over, thinking they were doing me a kindness, poor sots. Meanwhile I'd be chopped to pieces."

Viola shivered and wrapped both arms around herself. "To think that my entire philosophy on charitable giving revolves around the Countess of Windermere's donations . . . and now it turns out she's a filthy murderer. But maybe she wants the grandchild to live with her because she's trying desperately *not* to go on another killing spree, and she thinks the influence of a family member will halt her urges. Maybe she's—" Her nose wiggled up, up, up, in preparation for another sneeze, then sank. She managed a half grin before her eyes widened and she released an explosive sneeze. "Oh, blast, you're right, she's a raving lunatic. Why would she even give money away in the first place?"

"Perhaps she gave all that money out of a sense of guilt," Tabitha suggested. "As a penance."

"It disgusts me, the entire business." Viola nibbled her nails. "Think of all those thank-you letters."

Oliver snapped his fingers. "The letters! The letters 'MPS'!"

All eyes turned to him with uncertainty.

He nodded at Tabitha. "You said the files were all marked 'MPS' along with the victim's name. The same letters were on the pocket watches of those chaps hanging in the foyer. Their portraits are hanging, that is, not their deceased selves," he added. "I saw that they were engraved and looked closer to . . . check on something." He took out his multi-tool and began opening and closing attachments again. "Perhaps they're relations of the Countess's."

"Did she have two dead husbands?" Viola asked.

"No, but she had a sister who lived with her in the manor," Tabitha remembered. "Perhaps one of them is *her* husband. *M* and *P* and *S* . . . what might they stand for?"

"A family name, perhaps?" Edward suggested. "From before she halted her murderous ways?"

Tabitha cleared her throat. "Evidence speculation aside, we ought to find a way to leave, and we're running out of time to talk," she said grimly. "Between these murder files and the disappearances, I think it wise to leave Hollingsworth Hall before we've no longer the choice. I'm afraid that this manor house isn't as pleasant as it first seemed, and that's even without the ghosts."

"I'd forgotten about the ghosts," Edward said. "Pity you brought them up again. But Oliver's right. What's worse, do you think, staying near the Countess, who may go on a killing rampage any moment, or facing whatever's snatched Barnaby and Frances?"

At that moment, the electricity went out once again. As it was early afternoon, the windows still provided a bit of light. The children's eyes were drawn to the glass. Last night's snowstorm was back, very much in full force.

"We're going out in that?" Oliver asked, squinting and peering into the powdery downpour of snow.

"We are," said Tabitha resolutely. "Best get on with escaping. I'm certain the ghosts will keep to themselves and not bother us a bit." She, of course, was not certain of any such thing, but Pensive was always spouting off speculation with authority and ended up being right a good 60 percent of the time. *I call it bolstering the team, Tibbs,* he'd say. *"Lying" is such an ugly word.*

"It's time we stopped waiting around to be saved," she told the others. Saying it out loud felt right. Pensive-like. A surge of rallying and satisfaction arose deep inside her, scouring the fear from Tabitha's veins and replacing it with something that felt like a rush of high-quality ink, the kind that might be used in the printing of exceptional mystery novels.

Her pulse quickened. She had wasted years doing nothing about her mistreatment, confronting no one, simply accepting her life. Simply waiting for some sort of miraculous change. The time had come for her to take action. "Do you want to do nothing?" she asked the children.

They shook their heads, and Tabitha realized with surprise that they were listening to her. They were *truly* listening. "Do you want to just sit here while people treat you like mindless objects to be used?"

"Nope," said Edward.

"No, thank you," whispered Viola, rubbing at her eyes.

"No, I don't," Oliver said.

Tabitha thought of the "Dish Duty" sign. She thought of her attic space, and of her parents telling her that an invisible child was the very easiest kind to tolerate. She thought of the word *ingrate*. "While you're made to feel like an inconvenience, until you very nearly believe that you are one? Like you're cursed and can never, ever do anything about it? Do you want to feel that way forever?"

Though Tabitha saw that they were slightly taken aback by her sudden passion, the trio shook their heads again.

An unexpected wetness began to soak her eyelashes, and Tabitha sponged it away with a firm wipe of her sweater sleeve, nodding. "Good. Neither do I. Oliver, do you think you might be able to fix the motorcar? Phillips said there was one left."

"But I told you—the snow—"

Tabitha held a hand up. "We must try. The stable isn't too far, and there's no telling what she'll do with us if we stay here. She's only planning on keeping one of us as her grandchild, and she said the rest of us could just disappear for all she cares."

"Disappear?" asked Edward.

"Disappear," breathed Oliver.

"I don't want to disappear," Viola said. "I've got things to do and people to find sources of financial assistance for. If I can ever stop this blasted sneezing," she added, sneezing once again.

Tabitha didn't want to disappear either, not when she was just starting to feel a bit as though she existed in the world.

She placed both hands on Viola's shoulders and squeezed. "Viola. Wonderful, brilliant, confident Viola."

Viola eyed her suspiciously. "Yes?"

"Do you think that you and Edward might find a way to distract the Countess while Oliver and I are out tinkering with the remaining motorcar? Edward, you play a bit of doctor and come up with a plausible sickness for Viola. Or an injury that wouldn't have noticeable signs on the body. Viola, do you think you're up for a bit of acting?"

Viola squirmed. "My voice got all shaky at the charity play we put on for the local orphanage."

"But you were amazing just now, telling the Countess where the Wellingtons went! Trust me, you're a natural."

"It was quite good," Oliver agreed.

"Much better than the mess you made onstage," Edward agreed, tapping his nose. He shifted his gaze to Tabitha. "We will both be brilliant," he said seriously, switching the tapping finger to his temple. "I've got four or five things rolling around up here that could be drastically wrong with her."

"Excellent. There's not much time, but—"

A voice sounded down the hall. "Phillips, get upstairs! I can't have another rotted child disappearing. Come and lock them in their rooms. You'll have to jam a chair under Tabitha's door, as I can't find the rotted key."

Tabitha couldn't hear the reply. "Edward, use all five of the possible ailments if you have to. We'll just do a quick check to see if the car is fixable. We'll need an hour, maybe two. If it's something Oliver can fix, we'll all break out tonight." The alternative was hiding in the passages, and Tabitha, while logical in the most logical of ways, couldn't help but think about the mysterious rush of air that had passed behind her while she had observed the second parlor. Perhaps she would come up with a suitable explanation for the creaks and noises and air currents of Hollingsworth Hall in the next hour or so, but until then, it seemed best not to dwell in the passages longer than necessary.

"Oh, this itching is *ridiculous!*" Viola said, scratching madly at her neck and head and clothing.

"A bit much, Viola," Edward said with concern. "Best tone it down a mite."

"Quick, take these!" Tabitha picked up four hairpins from the dresser and pressed them into Oliver's hand. "Can you use them to unlock your door? You said you were handy."

He summoned a brave smile. "In fact, I can, and I don't need hairpins. I only need this." He held up his pocket tool, then frowned for a moment and looked sheepishly at Edward. "I *do* have a personality, you know. . . ."

"Of course you do!" Edward said. "You're a lock-picking car thief now. Wish I could say the same. Brimming with personality, you are."

"Good," Tabitha said. "Oliver, wait a few minutes after we're locked in, then go get Viola and Edward out. Viola and Edward, go find the adults and keep them busy in a far room. A room *away* from the library. If asked, say that Phillips didn't lock either of your doors properly. Oliver, I'll meet you in the library. I'll wait behind the long curtains."

"But how will you get out of your room? Don't you need me to fetch you as well?"

Tabitha shook her head and raised her eyebrows in a manner that would have made Inspector Pensive proud. "I've got a plan."

18

"A man needs but two things: a reliable moral compass to guide him and a strong dose of integrity to see him through all manner of troubles," Pensive said, raising his utensil with a wink. Tibbs stared doubtfully at the fork and said, "That's not integrity. That's boiled potato with cream sauce." Pensive paused before answering, taking a delicate bite and dabbing his mouth with a napkin. "Nary a whit of difference, Tibbs," he said decidedly. "Nary a whit."

—Inspector Percival Pensive,
The Case of the Faithful Footman

Once locked in her room, Tabitha refilled Pemberley's water dish and placed a cookie, half a savory pastry, and a cheese cube next to it. "I'm sorry I can't give you a more balanced diet at the moment, Pemberley. You'd best stay here. No telling how chilly it will be outside."

With that in mind, she pulled on a second sweater. The children's coats were still in the front hall closet, and it wouldn't be worth the risk to fetch one. She gave Pemberley a kiss on his fur. "You're an excellent Tibbs, Pemberley, and I shan't ever think of replacing you as my go-to man-mouse, but would you mind *very* much if I consulted our most excellent colleague, Oliver Appleby, while determining the best course of action to take in solving this peculiar circumstance and getting us out alive?"

Squeak.

"Thank you. You may feel free to play with your fancy collar." She nudged the jeweled ring toward him. "Now, to find the passage." Tabitha patted the key and blew a kiss to the painted child. "Where to, please?" she asked him. A moment of silence passed. "No response? How very rude. What's that? I'm the rude one?"

Squeakity-squeak.

"Very well, Pemberley. You're right, that's quite enough nonsense."

The oil lamp flickered in her hand, lending life to the room's nooks and crannies. She gazed along the wall, looking for a keyhole at a similar level as the one in the Countess's room. There was no paneling here, only wallpaper with intricate images of grasses and trees, meadows and lakes, rabbits and birds. The effect was rather dizzying.

Crouching, she reached a hand out, feeling the smooth paper up and down, skipping the spots behind the bed and wardrobe and dressing table, slowly making her way around the room until . . .

There.

Tucked snugly into a corner, right in the middle of a group of rabbits nibbling sweetgrass, she found it. Holding her breath, Tabitha placed the key inside. It was an exact fit, and for the briefest of moments, she had the odd wish that she could be key-shaped and could find a space where she fit so perfectly.

"Good-bye, Pemberley. With any luck, I'll be back soon with a way for us to flee." And laying another kiss on his mousy back, she opened the secret door and dipped into the passage with a lit lamp, hoping very much that it led to the stairwell that led to the library.

One set of winding narrow stairs and several twists later, Tabitha peered into the library to see a very nervous boy poking around the curtains. Popping the shelf open, Tabitha gave a low whistle and watched as Oliver jumped nearly out of his skin. "It's only me," she assured him.

"Oh, a hidden passage! What a neat trick! How'd you find it?" With a final glance through the cracked library double doors, Oliver slipped behind the bookshelf and handed her something. "I risked getting your coat, madam." He grinned, bowing awkwardly in the space. "Didn't want you to think I was too dull to give it a try."

"I found the passage earlier today, by chance." She took the coat. "And you could never be dull, Oliver. You are an exceptional escapee."

He blushed. "Go on, then. Which way?"

Tabitha eyed the passage behind her. "If we follow the main path around, it'll take us to the kitchen."

"I thought we were going for the motorcar, not to get food. Do you fancy a snack first?"

"Excellent question," Tabitha said, patting his shoulder and thinking that Oliver was doing a bang-up job as a Tibbs/Pemberley replacement thus far. "And no, I'm not hungry. Agnes mentioned a garden entrance off the kitchen. Follow me."

Oliver took the oil lamp and trod lightly behind her. He paused by the winding staircase.

"That goes to the second floor," Tabitha told him. "And the third. The nursery, Phillips called it."

"Tabitha," Oliver whispered as they wound their way to the kitchen. "What do you think is in the locked rooms? Other than the one you're in, of course."

I'd rather not think about it right now, thank you very much. "Hopefully nothing more than memories," she said.

Whatever sense of adventure the two had been feeling was quickly extinguished at the very real realization that kidnappers or ghosts or whatever had been making children disappear might presently be somewhere along the passage. It had crossed her mind that the remaining children might just squat in hidden wall spaces until their parents arrived on Sunday, but that no longer seemed wise.

Tabitha had lost the wherewithal to falsely suggest that the disappearances were innocent in nature. A sinister unease had crept onto her shoulders like a creeping spider that refused to be shaken off. Using the passages to escape was a risk that was best taken in a hasty manner. Still, she pointed out eyeholes along the way, trying to make things *interesting* rather than *frightening*. As the Pensive of this excursion, she owed it to her Tibbs to be calm and confident.

A single peephole gave her a view of the kitchen, which appeared empty.

Oliver sniffed twice. "Does something smell queer? I would swear there's been a familiar smell in the passage . . . almost like—"

"Barnaby Trundle," Tabitha confirmed. "It's his cologne and hair crème, still lingering from last night."

"Maybe he and Frances found the passages on their own?" Oliver said hopefully.

Recalling Barnaby's night scream and the struggle in the Countess's room, Tabitha thought not. "Maybe. If that's the case, let's be doubly quick and hope they haven't already fixed and taken the motorcar themselves."

Unlatching the lock and being careful to shut and secure the passage door behind them (it was cleverly masked by a carved block made to hold ladles), the two children crept to the garden entrance off the kitchen. Through a window, they watched the snow blow violently. Oliver insisted that Tabitha wear his gloves.

"At least our footprints will be quickly covered. Ready?" Tabitha put her hand on the doorknob. "'Into the fray, together we go.'"

"'Out of the warmth and into the snow,'" he agreed.

The wind slammed the door behind them, and Tabitha was flung onto Oliver's back by a strong gust. His knees buckled and they both tumbled into a drift. The oil lamp buried itself in a bundle of white beside them.

"Oh! I'm sorry! Get up, get up." Tabitha yanked Oliver with all her strength, which was difficult in the thigh-high drifts that had formed against the back of Hollingsworth Hall.

Wind whistled around the outer corners of the house and the high gables, catching on stone, rushing down through branch and bush, swirling and moaning a haunted tune.

Oliver jerked his head toward the manor. "What's that noise?"

Tabitha shielded her eyes to look toward the top of the Hall. "Just the wind. But it almost sounds like children's cries, doesn't it?" She saw three diamond-shaped windows, along the back side of the highest point, which matched the ones she'd seen on the front of the manor. The nursery, Phillips had said. One of the locked rooms.

Squinting, she thought for the briefest of brief moments that she saw an image appear in the center window. *All this talk of ghosts has me seeing spirits,* she thought, wishing Pemberley was closer. "Let's go."

Through the snow they waded and stumbled, past a garden shed, past the stables, and over to the barn, which housed motor-cars instead of horses. There was more snow than Tabitha had ever seen, with more on the way. But now that they were outside, it was evident that a good deal of the "blizzard" was really just drifts being blown about.

When they arrived at the right structure, Oliver reached for Tabitha's gloved hand. His eyes were bright, and he pointed to the road leading away from the estate. "The drifts are in our favor, do you see?"

Tabitha did see. Very faint but discernible tire tracks traced parallel lines in the snow. "I'm surprised they aren't completely covered by now." She followed the lines back to their origin, but instead of leading back to the barn, the lines seemed to go down a short hill toward Lake Windermere. "Do you think that's even the road?" She blinked and tried following the tracks again, losing the slight indentations as a fresh blast of wind shot snow into her eyes.

Oliver yanked open the barn door and ushered Tabitha inside, smiling at the remaining car parked at the rear of the building. The car's hood was popped and perched open, as though someone had been tinkering. Shutting the barn door behind them, Tabitha reveled in the silence and lack of wind and slight scent of motor oil. They both shook themselves like dogs, bits of snow flying onto the floor and melting immediately.

"This is the brand new Daimler model. She'll get us through." Oliver rolled up his sleeves and peered around. "Best light a few of those lamps." He squatted beside an open box of curious metal instruments, appearing to recognize some. "Tools, excellent!"

Tabitha dodged boxes to fetch the lamps. Even having worn gloves, her hands ached with cold, and she did finger-bending exercises for a moment before lighting a match.

Oliver scooted a wooden crate over to the car and stood on it.

He was soon making clacking sounds and grunting like a happy pig. Tabitha almost warned him to be quiet, but there seemed little danger of being caught. She highly doubted the Countess would venture into the outdoors.

"That's it!" Hopping down, Oliver took both of her cheeks in his oily hands. "I found the problem. It was jammed." He held up a tiny hammer. "This was stuck down deep in the thingamajig," he said, then blushed slightly. "I haven't quite learned all the proper names for parts yet."

Tabitha grinned and squirmed away from his dirty grip, wiping at her face. "Oliver Appleby, I have a hard time seeing you running a top jewelry company."

"As do I." He sighed. "There's not much of a chance they'll let me be a car doctor, though, is there? It's as though they've got my future already planned for me. Sometimes I feel like they'd be better off with a completely different child."

Tabitha stared at him. "Oliver, do you think your mother and father love you? Have they ever told you that?"

He looked embarrassed. "Yes, of course."

Wiping a hand on the side of her apron, Tabitha tapped a finger to Oliver's temple so that her words would stick. "Then they are perfect parents, no matter their shortcomings in understanding. And if we get out of this, I'm sure you'll find the courage to tell them that you want to turn your back on the jewelry business and pursue what you're truly interested in: stealing cars." Tabitha smiled. "You're very lucky to have them, you know."

After a brief silence, he snapped his fingers and winked.

"You're absolutely right. And what will you be doing, while I'm a great engine man?"

Tabitha laughed, thinking of the possibilities. "A teacher, maybe . . . but no. Don't want to deal with bad eggs. An Inspector, I think, for the Metropolitan Police. Scotland Yard for me, thank you very much."

Oliver nodded approvingly. "You'd be wonderful." He motioned to the car again. "All the valves are loosened too. I just need a proper wrench and we should be zooming through the snow with ease. Nothing on my multi-tool is the right size." He rummaged through a pile, examining each item before tossing it aside. "Hmm, seems to be missing. Maybe there are extra tools in the boot."

Slipping around the back of the motorcar, he lifted the lid of the attached luggage trunk. Plucking something from the depths, his two hands emerged, clutching a matching pair of Siamese cat statues, their blue-jeweled eyes glittering in the lamplight. "Horrid-looking, aren't they? Bunch of junk in here." He closed the trunk and smiled at Tabitha. "Help me look around for another tool set, will you?"

Though sheltered from the wind, the building was exceedingly cold. Still, Tabitha thought there were *far worse things* than searching for escape tools with a new acquaintance who smiled at you. Worse things included:

- searching for escape tools with Barnaby Trundle
- having been snatched by a ghost

- having been snatched by something other than a ghost
- being a file folder in the Countess's secret drawer labeled "Crum, Tabitha"

Tabitha checked shelves and pulled out drawers but found nothing of use. Piles of blankets, extra furniture, old stalls filled with the lingering scent of horse and straw, stacks of books, bound boxes, ropes, and yard equipment. A large piece of canvas was draped over a dark corner of the barn. Tabitha lifted the heavy cloth and stumbled back.

"Oh my!"

"What is it?" Oliver called.

"It's paintings." Tabitha had missed the gallery tour, but she was certain these belonged with the historical crime paintings in the manor. She sifted through the five frames, quickly wishing that she hadn't. "There's a tavern scene that's quite brutal-looking." The oils depicted a tall figure in the foreground overlooking a setting of overturned tables, broken bottles, a blazing hearth fire, and a set of barmaids, identical in their positions, necks turned unnaturally, blood pooling at their sides.

Oliver grimaced. "That'll be the murders at The Buckled Duck. One of those was hanging in the gallery as well. Edward said that the medical examiners never figured out what killed them first, the broken neck or the stab wounds."

Tabitha covered the paintings, tucking the canvas around the frames as though they might get up and try to sneak into her sleep to cause nightmares. "Well, I'm out of places to look. Shall I run out and check the shed?"

A noise at the back of the barn halted Oliver's reply.

A rather distinct noise.

A rather distinct noise that sounded exactly like a door opening.

On instinct, Tabitha blew out the oil lamps.

"Tabitha," Oliver whispered in the very faintest of whispers. "Did you close the door very firmly behind you?"

"I think so."

Their eyes met in fear, and Tabitha stabbed a finger toward another corner. They hurried behind a set of crates and huddled together. The door creaked open once more . . . and was that a long shadow moving into the stables? It was. The long shadow gave way to a long body with black shoes, a black uniform, and a formidable chin.

"*Phillips*," Tabitha whispered. "What's he doing here?"

A long, taut chain in Phillips's hand indicated that he had Burgess in tow. He looked around the barn slowly. "Could have sworn I saw a glow in here, Burgess. Well, let's just have a quick check of things, old boy, and—" Phillips was jerked off his feet with a muffled thump as the dog ran off. "Burgess!" he called, standing and shouting into the storm. "Get back here!" Phillips waited a half minute before reappearing, cursing his dog and the cold. He lit the lamp that hung next to the entrance and closed the door behind him.

"What's he checking? I thought he was inside, looking for stolen goods," Oliver muttered.

"Shh! He's probably searching for Barnaby and Frances." Indeed, Phillips appeared to be doing just that. He gazed around the entire space, then checked the horse stalls. He poked his head into the motorcar's attached trunk, leaving it wide open as he continued his search.

Walking deliberately over to the canvas, Phillips tore off the cloth. Tabitha waited for his exclamation of shock when he saw the disturbing images. Instead he picked up a painting and studied it, brushing off a rogue piece of hay and tucking the frame under his arm. The frame dropped to the ground at the sound of Burgess, who was frantically barking somewhere in the distance.

"What is it now?" Phillips called. He put the painting back with the others and threw the canvas over them. "Good God, what are you barking about? Probably Her *Ladyship*, ready to order me around more," he grumbled, walking back to the door. "I do believe that being a countess has gone to her head. She's gone mad with power. We don't want to get ourselves killed for talking back, though, do we? A nasty one with knives, that woman is. . . ." The door opened quickly, then slammed shut.

Tabitha and Oliver waited several minutes, but Phillips didn't return.

Oliver tapped her. "Is it all clear, do you think?"

Tabitha shivered but didn't answer. The light outside the barn's windows was growing less white and more gray. Evening was setting in. "Do you think the motorcar can be fixed?"

"Almost certainly." He held up a finger. "But I still need a tool that isn't in that box."

"Tell me about it. I'll check the garden shed while you keep working."

Oliver nodded and described the wrench he needed. "Take a lamp," he told her.

The shed door was quite sticky and Tabitha nearly gave up, finally forcing it open with a tremendous yank. Hoes, rakes, shovels, and other garden implements were stacked neatly in a row, and a series of watering cans lined a wall, just below a charming display of birdhouses. It was a large shed, full of pots and organized seeds and a metallic dresser of sorts. A chair in one corner was lumpy with something, covered with an embroidered picnic blanket.

When she had checked the tools in plain sight, Tabitha turned to the blanket. *Perhaps there's another box under there.*

Instead of finding a box, she let out a short, piercing scream at the sight of something that was very much the opposite of what you might expect to find in a garden shed. She had found Mary Pettigrew's body, slumped with her hands crossed neatly over her frozen lap.

Backing away, Tabitha slammed into the watering cans and fell, her ankle twisting in an awful way. Tears of pain squeezed out, blurring the image of the missing dead maid. Poor Mary was still in the clothes she had worn only one night before.

Of course she's wearing the same clothes. Did you think she would get up and change for the weather?

Tabitha stared at the body. "Nobody should be treated this way. This goes beyond foul."

Avoiding the dead woman's face, Tabitha fixed her attention on the carving on Mary's wooden bracelet. In her haste to remove the brass key at their last meeting, she hadn't taken care to really look at the carved creature. *Even the smallest items can be clues that give an indication of character,* Pensive lectured in her mind. Mary's dress sleeves were exposed enough to see a glimpse, but she would need to get closer.

Calm breath, calm thoughts, calm decisions, she said, repeating Inspector Pensive's mantra for the most intense of discoveries. She took several deep breaths.

"First, a body cannot hurt you, and you've already been close to it once. It's her who's been hurt, so have compassion. Secondly, it's actually quite logical that she's here. She would have started to stink and rot. It's best for the sake of any family members who claim her that she stay frozen." Tabitha wondered about that. Did Mary have any family? What was she doing, sneaking along passages? Had she suspected the Countess of foul play, and had she been in the midst of planning an escape when the first stroke hit?

With trembling fingers, Tabitha reached for the bracelet and turned it over. Staring back at her was something unexpected. The long, intertwined carving ended in two avian heads at the clasp. What she'd thought was a fantastical serpent was, in fact, a duo of swans, just like the wax seal on the invitation. Their heads were exactly the same size. *Friends, not a mated pair,* Tabitha thought, recalling Edward's words.

"Thirdly," she said, grimacing and crying out when she tried to stand on her twisted ankle, "thirdly . . . if our Countess is a murderess and her maid was Mary Pettigrew, how did Mary come to have this bracelet?" Was Mary a thief like Frances?

"Hmm," Tabitha said. A fresh theory was laid in her mind. She concentrated hard on every clue available, and the idea's shell began to crack.

"The Countess of Windermere has decided to take guardianship of her grandchild, having changed her mind about handing over the trust fund to the child's family. She has a drawing room with cigars, but despises smoke. She walks in a clipped manner in her high heels and uses a foot soak and wears gloves over her rough hands and has mean eyes. And she has a library full of the most magnificent books in the world and claims not to read much. As for Mary Pettigrew . . ."

Mary's hands were not those of a maid. Nor had her eyes been fraught with anything other than loneliness, panic, and pain. "Oh, dear God," Tabitha whispered, touching the dead woman's hand. "Are *you* the mysterious, reclusive Countess of Windermere? And you were trying to tell us all along?"

Tabitha felt certain the woman before her was not a murderer. *But then why the horrific files, detailing murders?*

"Think, Tabitha. What sort of person is interested in crime to the point of keeping a gallery of famous assassination paintings and keeping reference books about deviant behavior? To the point of having detailed files on horrendous criminal activity?"

And, she thought, what sort of person signs a letter, *In glorious crime and justice*?

Inspector Pensive floated to the forefront of her mind, and as his imaginary self raised an imaginary pipe in the air and winked, the answer came.

"An investigator? No, that doesn't make any—"

Before any further conclusions could be made, the shed door burst open behind her.

19

"I admire you, Tibbs, do you know that?" The inspector puffed on his pipe thoughtfully inside the weathered walls of the seaside restaurant. He ordered another port for himself, and a third dish of pickled herring for his partner. "Though you, Timothy Tibbs, toil tirelessly beneath my fame, I am intimately acquainted with your worth. And secretly, in the back cupboards of your mind, old chap, I suspect you realize that you are the cleverest of us all. Yes, I daresay, Tibbs, I'd be nothing without you."

—Inspector Percival Pensive,

The Case of the Maudlin Mariner

Oliver rushed into the crowded shed, his breath emerging in bursts of white. "Tabitha! Tabitha, are you all right? We have to go! Phillips came back into the barn and I barely got aw—" His mouth opened at the sight of the frozen body.

Tabitha spoke for him. "Yes, it's Mary. Or maybe not."

Firmly grasping Tabitha's arm, he pulled them both back through the door and into the snow. "Hurry, *please*. Oh!" Shoving her to the ground, Oliver collapsed on top of her and rolled them around the small building. "Shh! He's *there*."

The snowfall was now blessedly thick, and the wind spun it in erratic patterns, but Tabitha could still make out a tall figure standing outside the barn. Though she didn't see a dog or the butler's features through the world of white, she could see the man lift a hand to his brow, as though he was scanning the landscape. Tabitha tried to stand and gasped, sinking down again as the pain in her ankle returned with vigor. "Let's go around by the kitchen, Oliver."

"Wait," he urged. "If we can see *him*, surely he'll see *us* if we stand up."

The two of them waited an impossibly long time until the obscured figure walked around the front of the manor, fully upright, marching as though the storm were nothing but a light breeze.

With effort, Oliver and Tabitha made their way to the kitchen, peeking through a window before pulling the door open to take shelter in the warmth. Rather than dashing blindly into the hallway, they both simply collapsed in what was, by far, the coziest part of the grand manor house. For a magical few seconds, the pain in her ankle lessened, and Tabitha let her senses drift about the place, soaking in the comfort.

Paved in large rust-red tile, the kitchen was swept clean. Shiny copper pans, ladles, and spoons hung from low beams, along with strings of garlic and onions and an abundance of thyme and sage.

Though more modern conveniences were evident, a giant rustic hearth took up much of the west wall. Over a neat blaze hung a cast-iron pot, bubbling away with the gorgeous scent of stew. The lazy haze of pork, fowl, or beef broth wafted alongside a yeasty smell of freshly baked bread, and the odors both revived the children and melted their resolve to do much of anything.

The hypnosis broke, and Tabitha rubbed her foot, sighing deeply and trying very hard not to succumb to a fault of Inspector Pensive's—despite his bravado, Percival was a rather sensitive chap who thought himself above pain, yet couldn't handle a bit of it. *Be like Tibbs for once,* she urged herself. *Hearty and healthy and full of restraint.* "We should leave the kitchen, Oliver. Someone will come in at any moment."

"We can rest for a bit. We're probably as safe here as anywhere else. Smells good too. Maybe there's some—" He frowned, seeing Tabitha's grimace. "Your ankle's twisted. What happened?" He reached out and touched her left foot.

Two small peeps escaped her. "Leave it. Just give it a minute to rest. I'll be fine." She found herself dearly longing for Pemberley. And, strangely enough, she longed for the safety of her attic room. That wouldn't do.

Stop that. You asked for something exciting to come from the envelope. No pouting since it turned out to be a different sort of excitement. Concentrate on that stew smell—lovely, isn't it? Takes your mind right off the searing pain in your ankle and the dead woman who might be the real Countess of Windermere.

While this internal lecture was going on, Oliver had roused

himself enough to find that two fresh loaves sat on a stone cutting board in the center work slab. One of them was cut, so he nipped two pieces and plopped back down. "Here. It's still warm. Didn't see butter about."

Tabitha took the bread gratefully. "Oliver," she said, pressing her lips together. "I have to tell you something. A couple of things, actually. First, I may have imagined it, but I thought I saw someone in the nursery room window when we were outside. An image or a person."

"Oh." Oliver chewed slowly. "Barnaby or Frances?"

Tabitha nodded. "It's possible, isn't it? That they're hiding up there. Or trapped?"

"Why would someone keep them up there? You think it's Phillips or the Countess?"

Tabitha shook her head.

"Cook or Agnes?"

"No. Oliver, do you believe in ghosts?"

He swallowed. "Do you . . . do you suppose a ghost could do that sort of thing?"

"Don't know," she admitted. "It doesn't truly matter. What matters is that we need to find a way out of here. Soon. And if Barnaby and Frances are trapped, we won't leave them behind."

Tabitha had been thinking about the small key in her apron pocket. If it opened a secret file drawer and hidden doors, was it possible that the key opened the locked rooms as well? The Countess herself had accused Agnes of having the key to Tabitha's room, so clearly it wasn't part of the brass ring. If her apron key *did* unlock the manor's off-limits doors, perhaps they could find their way to the third floor without entering the possibly haunted passages again.

"Yes," Oliver said, nearly reading her mind, "but what if the thing that's trapped them is up there on the third floor as well?" He saw her determined expression and nodded. "Right. Must go either way." He sighed and took another bite of bread, chewing deliberately as though it would delay the inevitable. "Do you know, I was rather excited about this whole weekend, and now I can't wait to get home. Feed the cats, write school papers. That sort of thing."

Tabitha said nothing. She had no home to return to.

"Don't you want to go home? That's right, though, you said you would be leaving the country."

"Just my parents are leaving. I'm orphanage bound," Tabitha told him, studying the kitchen tiles. "I'm to be a washer girl at Augustus Home."

"A washer girl?" Oliver blinked, incredulous. "You can't mean it."

Tabitha kept her eyes focused on the red squares, observing how they fit neatly together to form a single unit of floor. Her parents had taken away her ability to fit in anywhere. She felt the boiling sensation in her belly again, and she finally recognized it. It wasn't sadness or fear or guilt. It was anger, and it wanted very badly to be released.

"No, I don't believe you." Oliver shook his head. "Nobody is that horrible."

"They are," Tabitha affirmed quietly. "They are horrible, horrible people and even worse parents." She stared at him in wonder, letting a hot rush course through her. "Do you know that's the first time I've said that aloud?" Her heartbeat quickened. "And I think perhaps they deserve my disfavor. They've earned it, the same way I tried for *years* to earn their love."

Her breath came faster, inhales becoming gasps. Something painful and tight and icy inside her was finally breaking apart and melting. It freed itself from her chest, changing and turning into warm wetness that poured down Tabitha's face like raindrops of relief. She let the tears come, feeling lightened as they left her.

Washed of the acute outrage she'd kept secret even from herself, Tabitha met Oliver's sympathetic gaze. "Some people are just terrible and there's nothing you can do to change them. And it's not your fault." She wiped her eyes and raised her head with resolution. "It's not my fault."

Oliver remained silent for a moment, then reached a hand out and took hers. "No, it's not your fault at all."

Tabitha sniffed and smiled. "I'm so sorry, but you have no idea how good that felt."

He nodded. "Feel free to say it again. The hating your parents part, that is."

"No, I'm done." Tabitha grinned. "You see, they were hoping that I'd turn out to be pretty, so they could marry me to someone rich. That's why they adopted a girl. What a disappointment I turned out to be."

"Nonsense," Oliver said firmly. "You're already very decent-looking." He touched the top of her head. "That haircut will grow out, you know."

Tabitha gave his shoulder a light punch. Yanking her short hair, she remembered what her mother had said. "They wanted to keep me as ragged as possible until the time came to groom me. My twelfth birthday is coming up. I'm sure they were planning to unveil me as a swan any year now," she joked. "They'd have had a time of it, that's for certain."

"Well, you've got a nice friendly face and clever eyes . . . hazel, aren't they?"

She nodded. "Like yours."

"Well," said Oliver. "We'll think of a proper plan to attack the problem of where you'll live after we escape, but first, let's take a look at that ankle. I never should have let you go to the shed alone with ghosts and vile countesses and dead bodies about. You don't do that to a friend."

What had Oliver just called her? *He called me a friend.* But surely he hadn't meant anything by it—it was a slip of the tongue and nothing more. Children like Oliver didn't collect friends, as they were already certain to be full up. Silly Tabitha.

She opened her mouth to respond, but he raised one finger to his lips. "Try to stay quiet, now." He lifted the soaked shoe from Tabitha's ankle, wincing along with her. "I wish Edward was here. He's probably read a book on this sort of thing. Shall I cut off your stocking?"

Tabitha shook her head, taking deep breaths and trying to quell her shivering. The pain had faded for a while but returned fiercely with the jerking motion of her shoe being removed. Now it hurt too much to think, let alone to have Oliver cut her stocking with a knife. "Oliver, I must tell you something. I'm nearly certain that Mary Pettigrew is actually the—"

Footsteps approached. "Under that curtained butcher block," Tabitha hissed, her voice coming out in breathy gasps. She was suddenly feeling a bit feverish. "Quiet. We must remain quiet."

The children scuttled underneath the waist-high wooden counter and squeezed next to a bucket of potato and carrot peelings. There was another bucket, smelling fleshy and foul. They slid the curtain over and tried their utmost not to breathe.

Two sets of stockinged legs entered. Through a tiny break in the fabric, the thick and thin ankle sets were unmistakable, as was the quaver in the thin-ankled woman's voice.

"Oh, do be quick with the chicken broth for Viola," said Agnes. "She looked positively miserable."

"She did at that. Can't rush good broth, though. This will take at least a quarter hour, even with my base. Will you grab some chicken bones from under the corner block? I tossed them in a bucket."

Agnes's light, fast steps advanced toward them. Tabitha wrinkled her nose and tried not to shift, ignoring Oliver's horrified expression. Agnes's hand had just begun parting the curtains when Cook spoke sharply.

"Wait! Fetch me a chicken from the cold storage instead, please. Those bones have been sitting for too long, and the girl deserves better. If it were for the Countess, I'd say old bones were fine, but I'll make the girl something fresh."

The two bustled quietly about the kitchen, distinct sounds

telling a story of chopping and reaching and scooting and stirring. It was several minutes before either of them spoke.

"Cook, are you frightened?" Agnes asked.

"There, there," said Cook. "Chin up, eyes down. As long as we make it out of here without being bodies in the snow, we should count it as a successful weekend, don't you think?"

Oliver raised a finger to his nose. His nostrils were flaring and his eyes watered.

No, no, no! Tabitha shook her head, willing him not to sneeze.

"Even the Countess has heard the ghosts," Agnes insisted. "I heard her telling Phillips about cries and muttering behind the locked doors. She told him that perhaps selling the estate was in order."

"Listen, dear," Cook continued, "ghosts or no ghosts, the truth is, I think it's time for us to—"

The door opened with a terrific bang. "There are no ghosts, you twits," the Countess said icily, "except the future ghosts of your employment, which will be quite deceased after this weekend. Now, what have you done with the Herringbone boy and Dale girl? What have you two been up to?"

Oliver's mouth twisted side to side, desperately trying to hold the sneeze in. Tabitha clapped two hands over his nose, then pinched it tightly, though not too tightly as she didn't want him to cry out. After a moment, Oliver's face relaxed and he nodded. Tabitha held in her sigh of relief.

"I'm making a broth with a specific blend of herbs, like young master Edward instructed."

"I told you to treat them in the high parlor."

"That's where we left them. And we locked the door behind us, just as you instructed."

"They aren't there. Phillips is checking the house."

The door swung open again. "I've checked it," came Phillips's voice, sounding hollow. "There's no sign of them." He walked around to the butcher block, stopping near the Countess. "They're gone."

Tabitha felt her heart drop silently to her toes. It hit the floor with a noiseless bump and lay there, carrying on with its numb thumping. Edward and Viola had been taken. She closed her eyes, imagining the parlor. Had the children been snatched from there? She tried to remember whether there was a painting of a child in the room, but couldn't recall seeing one. No live, physical person could have entered that room secretly without a hidden door. Perhaps . . . perhaps there *were* powerful and vengeful ghosts at Hollingsworth Hall.

"Nonsense," said the Countess. "*NONSENSE! Nobody is gone!* People don't just get whisked away into nothingness! We have the other two—Appleby and Crum. Go get them. *Now!*"

Oliver sneezed.

The Countess bent and shifted the curtain aside. She smiled a wicked smile. "Oh hello, children. Phillips seems to have done a poor job of locking your doors as well. Good butlers are so hard to find these days. Tabitha, you wretched, cursed beast of a child, do *come along*. I'll lock you in myself."

With that, the Countess jerked Tabitha to her feet. Or foot, rather.

Noticing their soaked legs and shoes, the Countess sneered. "Been outside, have you? I wonder if your friends are all out there as well. *Phillips!* Check the back garden and the shed and the stables and the barn."

"I've checked."

"Check again, since you're useless with doors. Cook, you and Agnes watch young Oliver while I deposit Tabitha in her room and see to a matter in my study. I'll be back for you during the dinner hour, Mr. Appleby." Yanking Tabitha out the door, the Countess marched down the hallway. "Hurry up," she ordered. "Why is your shoe off and why are you dragging your leg?"

"It's injured."

"Good. No running away from the Countess for you, then."

Up the staircase they went, the Countess huffing and dragging Tabitha with surprising strength. Tabitha's ankle screamed in protest as it bumped a stair. She tried to hop but was being flung forward in a jerky manner, quite independent of her own power. "You're not the Countess at all. You're an imposter! You're the maid, and the frozen woman in the shed is—"

"Shut up," was the answer. "Shut up, shut up, shut up. Me, a *maid*? Idiot girl! I'm no maid, and you know *nothing* of imposters."

But Tabitha knew plenty about imposters. Entire plots had been dedicated to the detection, unveiling, and punishment of them in at least four Inspector Pensive novels. And imposters, like all criminals, were always after something of value. *One-hundred-thousand-pound trust fund that will be released to the family on the twelfth birthday . . .*

"This is all about the money," Tabitha said, in an Inspectorish voice that came out sounding much more confident than she felt. "You found that note, written by the real Countess, didn't you? And now you're planning on keeping her grandchild under false pretenses, so that when the trust is released, as legal guardian you can snatch it up along with the rest of the Countess's money. Were you planning to dispose of the child immediately or wait a few months to avoid suspicion? Whatever your plan, it'll never work! There are six of us, and the papers will find out what's going on and you'll be ruined and—"

"Enough!" The Countess was wild-eyed and breathing hard. She stopped at the top of the stairs. Removing the butcher knife from her handbag, she began tossing it in the air, neatly catching the handle each time. Seeing Tabitha's expression, she winked. "Learned to do it over the years. It relaxes my wrists for chopping."

Dear God, perhaps this faux Countess did all the murders in those terrible files. And she's invaded the house to get back at the real Countess, who was so shocked by her appearance that she had a stroke. And now there will be a file on me with—

Oh, stop! You're hysterical and making wild claims!

She's going to chop me to pieces.

Well, that one actually seems spot-on.

"Phillips!" Tabitha cried. "Phillips will stop you!"

For the love of Pensive, stop antagonizing her!

I can't help it! I'm a nervous talker.

A nervous thinker, you mean.

Oh, do shut up!

"Phillips will do whatever I tell him to," the faux Countess assured her. But she stopped flipping the blade and seemed content to let Tabitha remain in one piece. "He will hunt the rest of you horrible children down, and you will all stay here until I have what I want. And nobody will be talking to the papers. Now, *move*."

They arrived at the east wing's short hallway, and the Countess halted at the sight of a chair firmly jammed under Tabitha's bedroom door. "The chair's still in place. Put it back after Oliver snuck you out, did you? Clever beasts. Unfortunately for you, I know how to jam a door properly, and nobody's left to fetch you." Her eyes darted up and down the hallway. "Nobody at all." She moved the chair and opened the door, quivering a bit.

No amount of money can save you from fear or madness, Tabitha thought. "She'll haunt you, you know—the ghost of the real Countess. Ghosts always haunt those who wrong them."

The faux Countess's eyes searched the midsize room, narrowing at each corner. "That's poppycock. Vermin plop. Baker's piss-pot pie." She was breathing even harder now, bits of spittle spraying with every word she spoke. "She wasn't humble a day in her life, do you know why?" Her hands gripped Tabitha's sweater, shaking her. "I asked if you knew *why* she wasn't humble?"

Tabitha shook her head.

"Because," the Countess spat, "you can't be humble *and* rich, not when—aaagh! My God, there it is!"

Expecting to see a spirit floating in the air, Tabitha was even more shocked to see a glint of light flashing on the floor.

Pemberley charged at Tabitha's captor, the jeweled ring around his neck once more, courage and loyalty bursting from his tiny eyes as he leaped onto the woman's ankle and sank his teeth in.

The Countess shrieked. Tabitha knew this because of the hideous woman's openmouthed expression, but sound had temporarily stopped. Seconds turned to hours as the Countess kicked her leg out with ferocity. Time came to a near halt as Tabitha watched in slow motion while Pemberley (her *dear, dear* Pemberley) was flung into the air.

Was smacked onto the floor with the Countess's gloved hand.

Was crushed underneath the Countess's awaiting boot.

Was kicked to the wall, where his body lay quite still.

Quite motionless.

Quite dead.

Suddenly eager to leave, the Countess thrust a candle and a set of matches into Tabitha's hands. "Don't get taken," she advised, and slammed the door. A low grunting and scraping noise followed, the sound of the Countess jamming the chair underneath the knob.

The force of the slammed door had sent a shock of cold air into the room. Along with the sound of the door closing and the sight of the room being plunged into darkness, Tabitha felt the blow of that frigid air both outside and within herself.

Not bothering to mentally consult Pensive novels about what action to take, she lit the candle and searched the wardrobe until she found the right handkerchief to fashion into a blanket. "Oh, friend," she whispered to Pemberley. "Oh, my dear friend."

No *squeak* or movement answered, and Tabitha placed the cloth over the mouse, a few tears slipping silently off her cheek and dropping onto the floor. The makeshift blanket was a rich mulberry. A book she'd read said that mice were color-blind, but Tabitha knew that Pemberley preferred mulberry.

She picked up the soap dish he'd used for water, tracing its outline with a finger before blowing out the candle and setting its stand beside the bed. Then Tabitha's own body became stiff and frozen, first by despair, then by anger, then by a thick emptiness, a heavy and draping sadness that enveloped her completely, covering and flattening her to the floor.

An hour later, or perhaps two, something scratched near the wall. Tabitha groaned and lifted herself to a sitting position. "Pemberley?" she whispered, though the sound had come from the wall opposite the one where her friend's lifeless body lay. "Do you hear that scratching?"

The lump of him beneath the mulberry covering looked smaller. Deflated. Almost disappeared, as though his spirit had been such a large part of him that when it was released, his physical form became quite insignificant. Tabitha felt that a piece of her spirit was gone as well.

The sound repeated.

"The house is settling, Pemberley," she said, rising. She wiped at the crusted bits of salt that tears had left on her cheeks. "Don't be frightened. It's not as though it's a . . ."

A ghost.

The shuffling moved farther down the wall, and Tabitha recalled the ghostly stream of invisible air that had whooshed around her in the passage.

Ghost. Ghosty. Ghost, ghosty, ghost, ghost.

"Oh hush, Tabitha, there's no such thing," she scolded herself. "However, Pemberley, if that's *your* ghost, do come over." Hastily, she relit the bedside candle. In the process, she dropped the soap dish that she'd been cradling.

"Blast," Tabitha whimpered as it rolled under the bed.

She bent, bringing the candle as close to the bed frame as she dared before sticking her head underneath. And there, beside Pemberley's overturned dish, was a curious and tiny drawer, built right into the wall. "How funny," she said, and opened it.

Inside were a series of pictures. Drawings. Crude pencil sketches of faces and flowers and birds, and one that appeared to be a pony with a beak. At the bottom of each one, the same names were carefully written in the hand of a child.

For Thomas, from your Elizabeth.

Something happened then. A prickle, but not from the bed or the candle flame or one of Pemberley's tiny claws. It was an instinctual prickle that caused Tabitha to stand up. She studied the wall, following the progress of a fresh shuffling noise.

Slowly, with some dread, she saw exactly what that small prickle had been telling her to look for. The door to the hidden passage began to jiggle.

And then, as though a scene was unfolding in one of her very worst nightmares after reading a particularly suspenseful bit in an Inspector Pensive novel, the hidden door began to move.

Though she jumped up and ran to the bedroom door, freshly twisting her ankle in the process, Tabitha knew very well what she would find. It was, of course, still blocked. There was nowhere to hide. She had no choice but to turn and watch in horror as the hidden door moved again.

As the hidden door pushed open.

As a very ghostly figure entered the room.

20

Stressful situations cause alterations in behavior that reveal true character, Tibbs. If a person gradually begins acting like someone else altogether, you may very well find that they *are* someone else altogether.

—Inspector Percival Pensive,

The Case of the Picklemouthed Priest

Tabitha hadn't even the breath to gasp. Inspector Pensive was mistaken. Ghosts clearly existed, and directly before her was the proof. Ever so slightly thinner in the afterlife, the form of Mary Pettigrew stood dimly in the candlelight. Death had been kind, and the droop of her face and slump of her shoulder were noticeably absent. The ghost seemed shocked to see Tabitha as well, and then looked . . . relieved. And then there was the same heartache, the same desperation in her eyes that had been present when Tabitha met her living counterpart only a day before.

"Oh my, child," the ghost whispered. It set down the lamp it was holding, placing it neatly on the dressing table. Its eyes looked misty, but that might have been a trick of the light.

Having never dealt with spirits before, Tabitha thought it wise to address intentions, even while trembling uncontrollably. "Are you here to harm or haunt me?"

"Harm you? Haunt you? Of course not. Neither."

"Oh. Well, good then." Tabitha stayed close to the door, turning the knob back and forth. Filling her chest with air twice, all the while aware of the specter's eyes upon her, she drew courage from a small reserve that had hidden itself somewhere so as not to be noticed until such an occasion arose. "Well, since you are not here to harm me, what can I do for you? I might add, I was awfully sorry that you died. You seemed a kind woman."

The figure's eyes turned watery, and a single tear fell down each cheek as she nodded.

"Oh my, that's interesting and somewhat odd," Tabitha chattered nervously, standing on her toes and drumming her heels alternately to the floor. "Your tears look quite real. I'll have to tell Oliver, assuming he doesn't get a visit from you. Will you go see him next, do you think?"

Through her fear, Tabitha realized it was the first time she'd thought of needing to tell anything to anyone, other than Pemberley. Oliver, who had raised a glass to toast with her. Who had squeezed her hand in a darkened foyer for comfort. Oliver, who had called her a friend. And he had meant it. He had. *Does Viola feel the same? And perhaps even Edward?* The flicker of hope that still burned within her, that Tabitha had guarded with care her entire life, said, *Yes. Yes, I think perhaps they do.*

Infused with the thought that she had a friend to report to

and friends needing to be found, Tabitha gave herself a mental slap for clarity and gathered her wits. Although the ghost seemed emotional, there was a logic and an authority to its speech thus far. She must respond in a similar manner.

Summoning the assurance of Inspector Pensive, she composed a short speech. "I am Tabitha Crum. If I'm to believe the current lady of the house, you are the spirit of Mary Pettigrew."

The spirit shook her head, waiting.

"No," Tabitha said, "You are the spirit of . . ."

The spirit gave an encouraging nod.

"Camilla Lenore DeMoss," Tabitha said. "Countess of Windermere."

"That's right." The spirit frowned. "Well, no, it's not, as I'm not technically a spirit. Or at all deceased. But I am half of the Countess of Windermere."

"Half?" Tabitha stepped sideways. "How can a person be half of a Countess? I don't understand."

"Please." The figure stepped forward, reaching for Tabitha's hand. "Tabitha, please."

The voice had a soothing effect. And the woman's face was so very gentle and open and kind. And there was something else as well. A weariness and sadness and desire for connection. A quiet desperation and heartache. In a way, it was like looking in a mirror.

Instead of recoiling, Tabitha let the hand touch her own. It was the same kind of soft skin that the dead maid had been graced with. She thought hard. Her eyes drifted to the woman's face, where she found a familiar nose and high cheekbones. The same blue eyes. Each of the woman's ears held a delicate silver bird with ruby jewels dotting the wing. *Red jewels, not blue ones.* Tabitha's gaze sank to a very familiar wooden bracelet.

"Half of the Countess." With her free hand, she reached for the woman's bracelet and twisted until she was staring at the duo of swans. "Two swans. There are two of you. I thought you looked rather too solid for a spirit, but I've never encountered one and . . ." Tabitha tried to clear her mind. *Be like Pensive, get your facts.* "So you're not a frozen block in the garden?"

"No. I never was."

"So," she said slowly, "the dead woman is—"

"Is my sister, Millicent. I am Henrietta—Hattie Darling. We're twins, you see."

"Twins." Tabitha nodded. "It was there all along, and I simply didn't think of it. I'm terribly sorry if this is rude, but before you tell me who exactly *is* the Countess, by half or otherwise, you haven't happened to see four missing children, have you?"

Hattie smiled. "They're all quite safe on the third floor, my dear. And we are both the Countess of Windermere. We take turns, you see."

Tabitha relaxed, then stiffened again. She eyed the area between her and Hattie Darling. Only after devising a clever way of jumping onto the bed and around the woman to access the passage did she ask her next question. "The files, madam. Can you explain the files in your study?" Tabitha tightened her muscles, prepared to spring at the slightest sign that the woman was guilty of the deaths. "The *murder* files."

Hattie burst out laughing, then stopped suddenly, seeing Tabitha's petrified eyes. "Oh my, dear, those are *work* files. It's what we do—my sister and I. We look at old cases that—well, never mind all that. But rest assured, those violent acts happened without my involvement whatsoever. The worst Millie and I could be accused of is fanning the ghostly rumor flames that surround Hollingsworth Hall."

Deductions flooded Tabitha's brain. "The noises. It was *you*, frightening the servants."

Hattie's eyes twinkled. "Sometimes Millie, depending on the month. Or the royalty—they've been known to get loose in the passages." She sighed. "Terribly mischievous, the royalty are."

"Royalty?"

"Millie's cats, all named majestically and deferentially for the royals of England. You should see Henry VIII—spitting image of the lumpy king. But yes, I suspect wandering cats contributed to the ghost rumor. They sometimes slip into the passages, and their howling can be quite haunting. And a few have dreadful hairballs. We were looking for Anne and George and Victoria for nearly a week once. Albert kitten was inconsolable. Albert's our calico, and he dotes on Victoria."

"Cats! Why didn't I think of that?" Tabitha felt much better having assigned the whirling air in the passage to a member of the feline royal family. "This room does have a faint odor like Mr. Tickles."

"Who dear?"

"My parents' cat."

"Ah. We mostly restrict them to the nursery, but they like it in this room as well. And in our own bedroom."

"Of course. Viola's been sneezing all over the place, and she had a terrible fit when I sat next to her at breakfast. I must have collected some stray hair on my clothing. And she had another fit when we went into the Countess's, er, *your* room."

"Oh dear. And Viola's just been left in a room with several cats. Do come join your friends, and I'll shoo them all away. I must decide how best to handle Miss Pettigrew." She picked up *The Case of the Duplicitous Duke's Doorway* and peered at Tabitha for a long moment. "You enjoy Pensive novels, do you?"

Tabitha blushed. "Yes, but I'm hardly an Inspector. I seem to have gotten everything muddled up. So, the woman posing as the Countess is Mary Pettigrew?"

Hattie nodded grimly. "Yes," she said, ducking into the wall. "Mary was our cook. She and Phillips have been with us for two years. We got weary of having to personally orient all the staff every six months, so we chose those two to stay on and do the kitchen and house training themselves.

"I should have known something was amiss when I went to fetch food for myself earlier this week and she'd ordered enough delicacies for a king's feast. Though Millie did love to indulge in sweets and rich food, she would certainly never have the cook order a dozen lobsters and fairy cakes beyond count. No, that cheeky Mary was always wanting to try out the most expensive things possible, and I suppose she got her chance. Now, I need to quickly fetch a letter from my manor room's jewelry case. Follow me, dear."

Stepping lightly into the passage, Tabitha favored her right foot and held the two walls to help keep pressure off her injury. Hattie moved slowly, trying to make her footfalls as noiseless as possible. She slid open a wall panel and continued along the second floor toward the west wing.

"You were talking about Mary," Tabitha whispered as they crept.

"Yes, I never liked her much and threatened to fire her all the time. Millie was a more trusting soul. Loved the woman's cooking. She was too trusting, as it turned out."

Hattie bit her wrinkled lip and shook her head. "I was preoccupied in the nursery with paperwork from a recent trip to London that ended several days earlier than expected. On Wednesday when the new staff arrived. Millie didn't even know I was back at the manor, and I didn't realize she'd had a stroke. Not until I heard all of you booming about in the house yesterday evening and came down from the nursery to investigate."

"But how did you get on the property without notice?"

"I wore a driver's uniform. We keep disguises in a locked closet in the barn and in the bedroom you were given. We have the cars serviced often and make a point to have deliveries made as an excuse for vehicles to be coming in and out. Then we can slip in as kitchen workers or maids. The staff always report sightings of an unfamiliar person to whomever of us is playing Countess—that's often how we know that we're both in the manor. We normally meet at least once a week for tea and work meetings, but depending on the switching calendar, sometimes we go a month without seeing each other, so I wasn't in any particular hurry to check in. We sometimes leave each other notes in the study and catch up that way. Again, I had no idea all you children were here. Millie must have discovered a new lead and arranged the whole weekend, bless her heart."

The "crime and justice" note. "She did," said Tabitha. "I saw a letter she wrote, telling you about it. Mary Pettigrew must have found it along with your file trunk." She considered the letter's contents. "It sounded like she was terribly sick."

Hattie nodded sadly. "The doctors said she was due for a stroke with that heart and diet of hers, but she always said it was nonsense." Her voice broke and her eyes brimmed once more. She stopped at the outline of a passage door. "Oh dear. I do suppose I'm quite alone now that Millie's gone."

Tabitha thought of Pemberley's absence and knew just how Hattie felt. She supposed that the shock of losing everyone you hold dear and being left behind was no easier for an adult than it was for a child. Maybe it was even harder, adults being less inclined to form relationships with mice, who were lovely substitutes for human attachments. "I'm so sorry. But you're quite certain it was a second stroke that killed your sister?" There had, after all, been other people around.

"Oh, yes. Anne and Victoria were with me. I was watching Millie before the electricity went out, and the second stroke had already begun. The light went out of her eyes completely." Hattie's face hardened. "Mary Pettigrew may not be a killer, but I feel certain that she didn't rush to get a doctor in either case.

Speaking of light going out, this candlestick is growing short. We should hurry."

Candlestick. "Miss Hattie," Tabitha said. "You say Mary isn't a killer, but I'm fairly certain that she took a swipe at your sister. She broke a vase that was directly next to Miss Millie's head. She may not have done the deed, but she could be capable of murder after all."

The light from the candle flame dipped with Hattie's lowered hand. "If that's the case, I am more determined than ever to see her punished. I'm so sorry I didn't fetch you all from her clutches sooner, but by the time I knew what was happening, the phones were out from the storm. I didn't know how dangerous she was at that point and didn't want to risk causing damage by startling Mary. She's awfully quick with those knives." Hattie peeked through the peephole. "Come along, dear. The room is empty for now."

They stepped into the Countess's grand bedroom, and Hattie immediately strode to the dresser and began rifling through a jewelry case. "Wretched Mary," she mumbled, lifting her head and glancing about the room. "It appears that she's stolen my things and tried on every shoe and dress Millie and I own. Shouldn't have kept that bundle of money in with the letter, I suppose. She's stashed the envelope somewhere, no doubt. Well, it's useless to waste time searching for a memory while we've still got one more child to save. Come along."

Tabitha halted as they passed the door to the bedroom she'd stayed in. "Wait, please! I'd like to . . . I'd like to get something from here." She peeked into the room. "The door's still closed, and nobody's in there."

"Fine, but hurry, dear."

Tabitha stepped into the room and walked over to Pemberley's body, picking up the mulberry handkerchief to see only floor. "He's gone," she said.

"Who's gone, dear?"

"My pet mouse. The Countess, Mary Pettigrew rather, stomped on him. But he was right here."

"Oh, my. Well, King George has gone missing again. Mad cat, that one, but quite nimble and shifty, sneaking into rooms with me on occasion. He's probably hiding in here right now. I'm not looking for you, George," she said in a singsong voice, "so come out or starve eventually." She sighed. "Mad creature. I'm terribly sorry, Tabitha."

So Pemberley had become a feast for a cat.

"Trust that his spirit had already left him, Tabitha," Hattie said, pulling her into an awkward half embrace. "I felt the same way when Millie was put into the cold, but the best part of her was already watching over us at that point."

Tabitha nodded, but she would have liked to give Pemberley a proper good-bye.

They stood in respectful silence for a moment. Hattie picked up the framed photograph and looked at the smiling couple next to the bassinet.

Tabitha grazed the black-and-white image with her fingers. "So, this is you and your husband and Thomas? You looked very happy." She peered between the woman's face and Hattie's. "Different, but happy."

"Me?" Hattie stared at Tabitha in astonishment. "My dear girl, I'm not in that photograph." She nodded to herself and placed the small frame into her skirt pocket. "The letter would have helped explain. Now we'd best get back, and then I've got to see about the last child. Oliver, is it? Simmons may have some ideas there. Do you know where Oliver is, Tabitha?"

"Who is Simmons? Oh, and Oliver is in the kitchen, being watched by Cook and Agnes until the dinner hour."

"Good, the kitchen is convenient to access. Simmons is a bit of help who arrived just hours ago. He's checking the grounds now. Apparently the papers seem to have whipped London into a frenzy about this little gathering, and our employer was concerned enough to have him telephone. When he couldn't get in touch with me or Millie, he was dispatched to investigate. We'll launch a rescue for Oliver once he reports back."

Dispatched? What sort of employer did a countess need to have *dispatched*?

"Come," Hattie said. "There's more to tell. So much more. Up the staircase we go." And with that mysterious sentiment, Hattie returned to the hidden passage.

More to tell. Well, if there was one part of a Pensive mystery that Tabitha would never skip over, it was the solving of them. Besides, had dear Pemberley been alive at that moment, Tabitha felt certain he would have uttered a squeak of excitement.

"Let the revelations and final deductions commence, dear

friend," she whispered. A murmur in the back of her mind was the only thing that dampened her spirit a bit. That particular voice reminded Tabitha of Mary Pettigrew's increasingly volatile behavior. The voice tugged at her with another disturbing development. "Miss Hattie," she called softly.

"Yes?"

"You should know that Mary has a revolver."

21

Twins are a particularly interesting type of phenomenon, Tibbs. They are able to act undeniably well as a single unit, despite differences. For instance, this curiosity on my plate came with two completely individual yolks, and one even has that funny red spot, but if I close my eyes, I'd swear it was one extra-large breakfast egg. Pass the salt, please, and stop staring at me like that.

—Inspector Percival Pensive,
The Case of the Tempestuous Twins

Ferocious sneezing greeted Hattie and Tabitha as they climbed out of the wall and into the third floor. What had been a young boy's nursery was now a comfortable living area with a small kitchen and pantry and a rather thrown-together but elegant parlor. One corner of the room held desks, one scattered with papers and the other neatly organized. In the opposite corner, twin beds were pushed matter-of-factly against the walls, one of which held a cowering, snuffly, blotchy-faced Viola.

At least six cats roamed the open space, winding around table legs or plopping themselves on various pieces of furniture. "Out with you all!" Hattie cried, plucking up three and herding the rest down the staircase. "I'm so sorry, Viola. Tabitha told me about your allergy. We'll get you out of here as soon as possible."

Viola lifted her watery eyes and blinked at the doorway. "Oh, Tabitha! Hello! Yes, and sorry, Miss Hattie, but Edward and I were a bit too wound up to say anything after we were snatched—I mean, rescued." She rubbed her eyes. "He's cracked a window and I feel better already."

Edward crunched on something and swallowed, pointing to three steaming mugs on the table. "We made cocoa, Miss Hattie. I hope you don't mind. Found some crisps as well." He handed a mug to Tabitha and tilted his head toward a nearly catatonic Barnaby and a suspicious-faced, rigid-backed Frances. "Weren't good enough for those two, apparently. All the more for me, I say."

Hattie pulled a pocket watch from the depths of her dress and checked it. "Of course. Help yourself to anything, dear."

"Where is Oliver?" came a hollow voice. "Is he all right, do you think?"

Tabitha stared at her school nemesis, Barnaby Trundle. To think he would be the first to inquire about the only missing child. The boy was full of layers. In fact, if there was one thing

Tabitha had learned from the weekend thus far, it was that people had all sorts of facades about them, covering tucked-away bits of badness and goodness. Fear and courage. Helplessness and hope.

Hattie reached over to pat Barnaby's hand, ignoring his momentary flinching. "Yes, I'm certain Oliver will be fine. Now, I don't want to panic any of you further, but Simmons will be here shortly, and he and I will need to gather our wits into some semblance of a plan to address the situation downstairs. In the meantime, please try to settle yourselves while I do a bit of explaining." She gestured for Tabitha and the children to seat themselves on less fancy versions of the main house's furniture.

"What's to explain?" Frances spat. "This place is like a failed sanatorium for idiots and crazies. All those lies the Countess told us about inheriting one hundred thousand pounds. And I was sure I was the grandchild." She sniffed at Tabitha. "God knows *you're* not. I wonder what she even invited us for." She pointed rudely to Hattie. "This version of that dead maid has told us nothing. Who knows what her st—"

"Frances, do try to keep up," Tabitha said. "She's not a maid, you mean thing. She and the maid are the real Countess, the fake Countess is Mary Pettigrew, and Mary Pettigrew was the cook." She gave a small smile to Hattie.

"The Countess? Mary was who?" Frances frowned but put her nails quietly in her lap and sat up straight.

Hattie smiled in a nearly patient sort of way. "I believe you were pouting in the bathroom when I mentioned those things,

Frances. Rest assured, the inheritance is quite real, as is my status as a grandmother. Now pay attention."

Viola and Edward took winged armchairs next to Hattie, both of them smiling at her nervously. Frances and Barnaby took up a rouge-colored salon sofa with twin pillows, sitting as far from each other as the cushion length would permit. Tabitha picked a delicate carved bench near the fire, stretching out one foot so that her sore ankle soaked up the warmth of the flames.

"You see, once upon a time, I was a happily married woman. My husband and my sister Millie's husband were agency men with the Yard. Their portraits are in the foyer."

Tabitha inhaled so quickly and deeply that she certainly would have choked had the chocolate drink already been sipped. "Scotland Yard? *The* Scotland Yard?" She slapped her forehead. "The murder files," she said, knocking a fist against her brain for not giving her the information sooner. "They were marked 'MPS' for Metropolitan Police Service—also known as Scotland Yard. I can't *believe* I didn't think of it before. And the watches in the portraits were marked 'MPS' as well," she added. "Oliver noticed the engraving."

Hattie clapped thrice and held up the watch she'd just checked, tapping the engraved letters. "That's exactly right. My husband Reginald was brutally killed in 1879, along with Millie's husband. Our son Thomas was only three years old.

"The double murder is true then?" Edward asked. He whistled. "That's terrible. I suppose that lovely batch of crime paintings belonged to them?

Hattie paused a moment before answering. "Yes and yes. That gallery was their pride and joy. They were both collectors and historians, you see. They requested that Millie and I keep it up and donate it upon our passing, hence the more current Whitechapel paintings. They both agreed that contemporary crimes could often be solved by looking to the past."

"Inspector Pensive says that!" Tabitha cried, rising from her seat, then slowly returning, embarrassed.

"He does." Hattie winked. "Reginald and Humphrey were both fond of those novels as well. Anyway, Millie and I devised a way to keep from being witless old widows by taking on secretary work for the Yard men. Very soon, with a little insistence on our part, we were given the murder cases that had run into dead ends. We reviewed old case files and found ways of interviewing people who didn't even know they were being interviewed. After all, who would suspect an aging female to be doing detective work? We were quite good at it, as it turns out. And very well paid for our silence and willingness to give the Yard credit."

A delicious chill stole up Tabitha's back and neck. "The Yard allowed you to work actual cases?"

"Yes, but neighbors notice things, and our activity level began to attract attention. A series of newspaper articles were written about violent acts against the Metropolitan Police Service and our names came up time and time again as widows of high-profile victims. So in 1880 we claimed we were moving to the Continent, and we disappeared. I became Camilla

DeMoss, a recent widow with a young child. And Millie posed as my sister, equally grieving from the recent loss of her husband. She had quite a bit more bulk about her in those days, and nobody suspected we were identical. We had more inheritance money than we could spend, even after buying Hollingsworth Hall. Hence my charitable donation record."

The small hearth flickered, and the crackling wood and comfortable room made Tabitha feel as though she were wrapped up in the warm pages of a just-about-to-be-read novel. *Don't relax too much,* she warned herself. Each Pensive novel she'd read had a confrontation scene with the criminal in question, and Tabitha felt as though her rushed accusation in the hallway hadn't been quite dramatic enough to qualify.

Yes, there was still a menacing confrontation with Mary Pettigrew to be had, Tabitha was certain. She patted her empty apron, aching for the wise and whiskery consultant it once held.

Hattie pressed her lips together. "One year later, Thomas left us in 1894. The king gave me that blasted title to impress a woman friend who was babbling about how charitable I was. With the title, people started paying more attention to the household and my and Millie's travel. The title complicated everything. No longer were we able to travel freely to conduct investigative work. And at home, even our staff started snooping about for something Countess-related to sell to the press. Sad as it is, with women's rights finally starting to gain some attention, had someone found out that Scotland Yard was employing women to investigate murders, it would have caused a terrible scandal. Well, we had to do *something*, or our investigative days would be over. We didn't want to pick up and disappear again. So we killed off Millie that year."

"I knew it!" Barnaby said. "I knew you were a killer." He ran to the door and started shaking the handle.

"They didn't *really* kill her, Barnaby," Tabitha said. "She was sitting with us at dinner one night ago."

"Oh. Right." He came back to the parlor area and chewed nervously at his lips. "Go on, please."

Please? I didn't know Barnaby even knew the word "please." Tabitha wondered if the weekend would change him. Not that she'd be around to notice. She was still bound for Augustus Home. *Quiet, now,* she told herself. *Just enjoy the story, as it's more real than any Pensive novel you'll ever read.*

"After her unfortunate demise, Millie began a weight-loss regimen until the two of us looked exactly alike. One of us could be out investigating in disguise and the other could play a proper countess. That way, there was no chance of anyone discovering our connection with MPS. We had two specialty keys made for the rooms we chose to lock, the passages Thomas had found as a boy, and our work files.

We were so diligent about keeping our secret. Really, it was the only thing we had left to live for. The only thing giving our lives purpose." She looked at Tabitha. "Though Millie appears to have slipped up and left Thomas's old bedroom unlocked going to and fro. My sweet, forgetful girl. The cruelest joke," Hattie said, "is that—"

An impressive-looking gentleman dressed in a dark suit blasted through the passage door, soaked with melted snow. He looked very much like a man who got things done. Even his freshly trimmed hair looked efficient.

"Murderer!" yelled Barnaby, rushing to grab a fire poker and cower in a corner.

Hattie gave him a queer look. "Points to you for securing a weapon, Barnaby, as you were no doubt prepared to defend us all, but there's no need. This is Simmons."

"Simmons?"

"Yes, he's with Scotland Yard. Simmons, the last boy is in the kitchen being watched by Cook and the maid, Agnes. Fetch him, won't you, and have the ladies stall while we think of the best way to restrain Mary Pettigrew. She's armed, and I want all the children safe in the nursery before we go after her."

"As you wish. And more Yard men are on the way, both to Hollingsworth Hall and Clavendor Cottage as you suggested."

"Excellent work, Simmons."

"Are our parents in danger too, then?" Barnaby asked, eyes still darting around the room for threats. "Does that place have a deranged maid or cook as well?"

Simmons placed a hand on Barnaby's shoulder, taking it abruptly away when Barnaby let out a startled cry. "I stopped by the cottage on the way here and they're all fine, though the Crums seemed quite shaken up by my visit. I assured them that more Yard men would be coming to check on them."

"Children, children." Hattie waved both hands. "I'm all for

unexpected reunions and joyous revelations, but we've got a rather nasty woman to deal with before I chatter on."

"Miss Hattie?"

"Yes, Tabitha?"

"I fear that having Simmons enter the kitchen through a hidden passage to demand Oliver might not be the best of ideas. I rather think that Cook might arm herself with a cast-iron pot."

"I believe I can handle a lady chef," Simmons said with an amused smirk.

Edward laughed. "Clearly you're not acquainted with Cook. I imagine she could get quite beastly. Has a temper and a fore-arm thick as a tree. I'm a bit shocked she hasn't brained the fake Countess like a cow already."

"Hmm." Hattie looked thoughtful. "That's true, a strange man would give them a fright. And then there's the issue of Mary having large knives and my revolver. I assume she's quite skittish at this point, and we don't want any messy accidents."

Tabitha wished her own Tibbs were available for collaboration. *Collaboration*. What they needed was a team effort with solid distractions. "I think I may have an idea," she said. "You're certain Mary Pettigrew doesn't know there were two of you?"

"I hardly think she'd be impersonating me otherwise."

Tabitha nodded. "Good." Drawing on techniques from *The Duplicitous Duke's Doorway* and neatly accounting for the altered environment and available materials, she outlined her plan.

"Well done!" Hattie clapped her hands again, a hint of rosy

life coming to her cheeks. "Tabitha, follow me down the hidden passage with Simmons, please. The rest of you stay here."

"But why does *she* get to go with you?" Frances griped.

Hattie walked over and patted Frances's hand sympathetically. "Because, dear," she said, "you've been a frightful annoyance thus far, and I can't imagine that will be cured anytime soon. And because Tabitha thought of it"—Hattie winked at Tabitha—"with the help of Inspector Pensive. I do favor children who read rather than prattle on."

"I read! I read in *French!* But what about your heir? When are you going to tell us who is the—"

"All in good time. I do think you're all in for a bit of a shock where that's concerned. Come along, Tabitha. Into the passage, dear. Simmons, bring King Richard the Lionheart along. He's hiding under Millie's bed—see his tail there? And Millie's cigars are hidden under her desk." Her eyes became glassy before she shook herself free of some memory.

Simmons found the cigar box, plucked a large tawny cat from beneath one of the twin beds, and followed them into the wall.

22

A ghost is a ridiculous excuse for a poorly executed boat party, Tibbs. The "disturbances" can more likely be attributed to resident rats than angry spirits. Though I daresay I'd be angry too if I had to haunt this odorous nightmare. Smells like bad tuna and feet. Do take my extra hanky for your nose.

—Inspector Percival Pensive,
The Case of the Galley Ghost's Gumption

Agnes was audible through the wall long before they reached the secret entrance to the kitchen. Leaning down to the peephole, Tabitha solidified her bearings. The hidden door would come out right between the cold storage and pantry. Cook was directly opposite her, chopping onions as though she were punishing them. Agnes lingered by the door to the hallway. Oliver was seated in front of a large wooden support beam that ran from floor to ceiling, his arms disappearing behind him.

"I'm terribly sorry, but can't one of you loosen these?" he called.

"Oh, is it very awful?" Agnes cried, rushing over to him. "She's tied them so tightly, I can't loosen them a bit. I'm so very sorry!" She tugged at his wrists. "Cook, can't you simply cut through them?"

Cook shrugged. "I could, but the Countess has gone mad. You saw her, raving about wretched children disappearing and who she'll be ransoming once they're found. She won't kill the boy, though. He's the only one left at the moment, and she seems very intent on this grandchild business. She's got a revolver and she's taken over Phillips's hound, who'll track us down if we go anywhere. I don't care to die by either means this weekend. I'd rather be taken by ghosts."

Tabitha took a steadying breath and opened the passage door. "Nobody will have to die, and you needn't fear ghosts. Not even this one." She stepped aside for Hattie and Simmons, ignoring Agnes's gasp of delight, knowing what would follow. "Now, Agnes, let me explain about—"

But Agnes had caught sight of Hattie, as evidenced by a low moan and a spasm that swept her entire body. She muttered noiseless words while her eyes traced every contour of the twin. Her eyes then moved to Tabitha and widened in sorrow. "Oh, dead! All of them must be dead!"

"Tabitha!" Oliver exclaimed.

"Oliver." She nodded back.

"Aggie?" Cook said, then followed her friend's eyes. Cook

clutched the butcher knife in her hand, moving between Tabitha's trio and Agnes. "Don't move, Aggie. Spirit or not, I'll put up a fight."

"Cook, it's fine!" Tabitha insisted. "She's the Countess's *sister*."

"Whose sister?" asked Oliver.

Cook glared, her frown wrinkles deepening. "Then why's she the spitting image of Mary Pettigrew? And who's he? And where are the children?"

"The children are all fine, Simmons is with Scotland Yard, and the mad woman you *think* is the Countess is the former household cook." Tabitha walked to Agnes and took her hand. "I'm quite fine, you see. And look." Tabitha hefted Richard the Lionheart, who'd been weaving between her legs, into the air. "Your wall ghost—well, one of them, anyway."

With considerable effort, Agnes held off fainting.

Hattie set a grim look on her face and approached. "Hello, Cook. Agnes. Let me explain. I'll keep this brief. My sister and I have been sharing the role of Countess for years, one of us in disguise while traveling on business or living in quarters in the nursery while the other ran the household. My poor sister had a stroke, and I'm afraid that Mary, who was one of two trusted servants who stayed with us always, took advantage, declaring herself to be Countess and my poor sister to be a maid."

"So I've been working for a *cook*?" Cook asked. "No wonder she was so bleeding picky."

"We need to subdue her quickly," Hattie said. "Where is she?"

Agnes looked quite ill. "She's in her, erm, *your* study. She's just asked for soup."

Tabitha smiled at the bit of serendipity. "Excellent. Cook, can you prepare the foulest bowl of soup possible?"

Cook grinned and bowed. "My dear, I thought you'd never ask. You'd be amazed at what floor sweepings and an excess of salt can do to a dish." Reaching for a clean bowl, she busied herself, humming a low, cheerful tune.

"Where's Phillips?" Tabitha asked, handing Agnes a kitchen towel.

Agnes smiled gratefully and blew her nose into the plaid pattern. "He said he's been sent to search the grounds again with that hound of his for signs of the children. The poor man's been following her orders like a trained automaton. She's been horrible to him."

Tabitha wasted no time explaining the plan.

Only Simmons seemed dubious. "Are you absolutely certain you want *me* in the wall?" he asked. "I'll tell you again that I rather think you and the boy should be protected."

"She has a revolver," Tabitha reminded him. "She might shoot you, and that wouldn't do. And you're the strongest physically, which will be imperative. And Mary's far less likely to shoot a future investment like a grandchild. True, she only needs one of us, but for all she knows, the parents will produce some sort of unexpected proof and she'll be ruined if she shoots the wrong child. This way, nobody gets hurt. Agnes, deliver the soup, please."

With an obedient bob, Agnes picked up the soup, eyes focused on the very shaky bowl she carried. She backed through the swinging door, muttering, "If I don't come back, I suspect she's done away with . . . but no, oh please, oh no, oh . . ."

Tabitha hoped Agnes would hold her tongue and spill only soup in front of their target, and not plans. "Cook, cut Oliver's bindings, and Oliver, stay put until Hattie frees you." Feeling flushed with excitement and nervous about the impending brush with danger, Tabitha directed Hattie to the pantry. "Wait for my cue."

"I will," Hattie said, closing the door behind her.

Tabitha turned back to the Yard man. "Mr. Simmons, don't light the cigar until I say the word 'fire.' We must wait until Mary is in position."

Simmons frowned, but nodded and disappeared into the passage.

"Places, everyone! The order will be soup, cat, me, Hattie, Oliver, then smoke. Got it?"

Oliver saluted enthusiastically, then tucked his hands behind him with a wink. Tabitha hid herself behind the butcher block just as the faux Countess blasted into the room in a fit of anger.

"Fired!" Mary Pettigrew shouted, a wild look in her eyes. "You'll never work again!" One hand pointed the small revolver at Cook. The other held a barely touched bowl of soup, which she flung into a corner where it splattered, landed, and shattered.

Agnes scuttled in behind her, eyes locked in genuine fear and panic.

Distraction number one, Tibbs, Tabitha thought.

"I should *kill* you for that texture. And the salt! It was like drinking the ocean, you idiotic, pestilent, plague-ridden excuse for a—" Mary Pettigrew froze, her gaze shifting to the large feline resting on the side counter. "Is that a *cat*? You brought a filthy cat into my manor! Shoo!"

Distraction number two.

Richard the Lionheart recognized hatred for his species and rose to the occasion. He hissed and snarled, lifting a paw in the air with a terrific meow that was silenced as Mary smacked him off the counter.

"The cat isn't hers," Tabitha said in a clear voice, popping up from behind the butcher block.

Distraction three.

Mary stared in bewilderment from the cat to Tabitha, her expression quickly changing from confusion to anger. "I knew it! The children have been hiding this whole time. Get over to that pole, you little beast. I should have tied you up to start with. I should have tied you all up! Against the wall, Cook. You too, Agnes. Phillips! Where are you? Fetch a rope!"

"You sent Phillips outside to search for us," Tabitha reminded her, "and the cat belongs to the *real* Countess."

Mary smiled and let out a maniacal peal of laughter. "Oh? Well, the real Countess is *dead!* Dead, dead, dead!"

"She might be dead," Tabitha said, "but I think *she wants her cat back* anyway." She pointed toward the pantry.

Hattie slowly walked forward. "Been looking in my file trunk, have you, Mary?"

Distraction four.

"But you're dead," Mary whispered to Hattie, her voice wavering. To her credit, Mary only shook very hard but did not drop the revolver. "You're . . . you're a figment of my imagination," she whispered to herself. "I've been under duress."

"You do *not* run this manor, Mary Pettigrew," Hattie bellowed. She lifted a long arm in Oliver's direction. "You are free, Oliver Appleby."

Distraction five.

Oliver's eyes filled with surprise, and he jumped up and wiggled his arms. "I'm free! The spirit has powers!"

As Tabitha predicted, Mary was disoriented, looking in horror between her freed prisoner and the ghost of the woman she was impersonating. Scooping up Richard, Tabitha held the cat outward so that he could see his adversary. He hissed and snarled, causing Mary to spin in a circle.

"Keep that cat away," she shouted at Tabitha, then spun again to face the ghost. "Stay away, spirit!" She caught sight of Cook, who had reached into a cabinet. "Put that frying pan down, you stupid wench! Don't even think about whacking me with it. You'll be dead so fast you'll taste worms."

"Worms?" Agnes asked.

"She means I'll be dead and in the ground, dearie," Cook said, not lowering the skillet. "Which isn't likely."

Hattie slowly advanced. Tabitha and Richard created a

barrier on one side, and Cook wielded the pan across the room. Mary's revolver shook as she pointed it in various directions.

"I didn't kill you!" she cried to Hattie. "You just died! It's not my fault!"

"It *is* your fault. As punishment, I will burn down the manor. I shall set the house on *fire*!" She stepped forward again, forcing Mary another three steps backward.

"What? No! No, don't! You'll ruin my plan! I was going to live here or sell the place for a fortune! I was—" Mary stopped and sniffed. "It doesn't smell like fire. It smells like . . . cigar?" Crazed with fear and anger and confusion, Mary Pettigrew was further disturbed to see a thin line of smoke floating into the room, seemingly from nowhere.

Distraction six.

"What's going on?" she blubbered. Gazing at the air in front of her, Mary lifted a finger to trace the line of floating smoke back to the peephole. Stepping closer to examine the phenomenon, her face came within inches of the smoke's source. "It's almost as though the walls were smoking ciga—"

With a swift and sickening thud, the hidden door swung open, knocking Mary Pettigrew straight between the eyes. As she fell to the floor, the door to the back garden opened and Phillips entered, his hands red and mouth open to speak.

"I've found a motorca—" His face drained of color as he stared at Mary on the floor, the passage door leading into the wall, and the imposing figure of Simmons. A squeak of shock exited his lips, followed by an audible clearing of the throat. He caught sight of Hattie and sank to the tiles, openmouthed and twitchy-lipped.

It was Simmons who spoke, while gazing appraisingly at the butler. "I'm with Scotland Yard, and I imagine it's my motorcar you've found. And this," he said, gesturing to Hattie, "is the real Countess, as you know. Half of her anyway. The other half is in the garden shed, where you left her on orders from Mary Pettigrew. The children have told us everything that's been going on here. You must be under considerable strain."

Phillips stared between Simmons and Hattie. "I d-don't understand," he stammered.

"There were two of us, Phillips," Hattie said, an apologetic tone to her voice. "We're twins. We trusted you and Mary enough to stay on a bit longer than the other servants because it was so frustrating having to retrain the entire staff each six months. I personally found Mary to be rotten from the start. It seems even I underestimated her. You've done a lovely job as butler, but I'm afraid my sister and I had a rather large secret that we had to keep from you. I'm so sorry, Phillips, this must be a terrible shock."

"Oh!" Phillips said, his voice an octave higher than usual. "Two of you, yes, of course," he said. He stared around the room, rather dazed. Seeing Mary Pettigrew on the floor again, he stood, lips twisting as though he were trying very hard not to cry with relief, as it would be a very unbutlerlike thing to do.

Hattie patted his shoulder. "The children have informed me

that the Countess has been awful to you. That said, do you care to explain why you did nothing to remedy this situation? Otherwise, I'm left to assume either pure cowardice or direct involvement."

"Thank God this nightmare is over," he blubbered. "Mary went completely mad. The threats she made on my life were rather . . . gruesome. She's quite good with knives, you see. I swear, I only went along with it because I feared she would hurt the children. Is she . . ." He twiddled his fingers over his mouth. "Is she dead?"

"Miss Pettigrew's only knocked out for a bit," Simmons said, scooping the revolver into one capable hand. "She'll come around shortly enough."

"Too bad," Cook said with a snort. She leaned over Mary, large bosom heaving menacingly. "Not everyone cooks things your way, you mean thing."

"Simmons," said Hattie, "can you see Mary and these others to another room? Someplace rather less full of knives, perhaps? Tabitha and I will fetch the rest of the children from the nursery and meet you in the library. Poor Viola must be scratching herself to pieces up there."

Simmons nodded and eyed Mary's body, gauging the best way to heave her into his arms.

Agnes seemed to have recovered herself and was sneaking glances at Simmons. "We'll do just as you say, madam."

"It would be a pleasure to help secure Miss Pettigrew," said

Cook, smiling at Mary as though she were a particularly nasty chicken whose time at the chopping block had finally come. "Well done, Tabitha!"

"Hear! Hear!" Oliver said with a grin.

"And well done knocking her out, Mr. Simmons!" Agnes said with a blush as the Yard man picked up Mary's limp form.

"Yes, well done, Simmons," Hattie agreed.

"Yes, quite well done," Phillips said.

"Wish I'd gotten to do it," Cook grumbled.

23

When making final deductions, one must
have a solid grasp on all the fine details.
Having a solid grasp on a fine glass of
sherry is a nice touch as well.
—Inspector Percival Pensive,
The Case of the Dastardly Double Cross

Cook leaned against a bookshelf and smiled triumphantly as Tabitha, Hattie, and the rest of the children emerged from the hidden passage. She waved a hand toward Mary Pettigrew, who looked terribly uncomfortable. Mary was bound and gagged, seated in an armchair that was scooted so close to the library's fireplace that it was uncertain whether Cook meant to restrain or roast her.

Hattie gestured for the children to sit once again. This time, Tabitha joined Oliver on the sofa with Viola and Edward, leaving Barnaby and Frances to squabble over the one available armchair. Barnaby soon lost and stood awkwardly and miserably for a moment before sinking to the floor, cross-legged.

Tabitha was surprised he didn't begin to suck his thumb.

"Look and see what we've caught," Cook said. "Finally shut her up, didn't we? We've tied her up like a suckling pig, my sweet Agnes. Oh, Aggie, do lighten your load. The witch will get her due course, and that bump on her head is nothing compared to the blackness of her heart."

Mary Pettigrew struggled toward Cook, her eyeballs nearly popping out. Her head shook back and forth and she tried to scoot the chair forward, succeeding only in nearly knocking herself to the floor.

"Let me finish my story, dears," Hattie said, ignoring Mary and taking a seat next to Oliver on the sofa. "Where was I?"

"You were saying something about a cruel joke," Tabitha told her.

"Ah, yes. The cruelest joke is that Millie and I, investigators by trade, could not even track down our most important case. Not for years."

"And yet you set up a trust fund for the child," Viola said, "not even knowing if you'd find him or her. One hundred thousand pounds," she mused. "I wouldn't even begin to know who to donate all of that to." She reddened. "If I turn out to be your grandchild, of course."

"Well." Hattie smiled. "It would really only be fifty thousand, wouldn't it?" She reached into her pocket for the framed photograph from Tabitha's bedroom and raised it for general view. "I was sent this picture just over twelve years ago. I kept it in Thomas's old bedroom to remind me that an unforgiving heart becomes a lonely one. It's my Thomas and his Elizabeth and—"

"Hang on," Frances demanded. "What do you mean, only fifty thousand pounds?"

"This is what I mean." Hattie pointed to a spot on the image. The bassinet.

Tabitha looked closer and saw only the feet spread apart, peeking out of the blanket's edge. And then she saw it and inhaled sharply. It was barely noticeable if you weren't paying very close attention. "Two left feet," she whispered. There must have been another child nestled inside. She stared at Hattie in wonder. "Two babies?"

Hattie nodded and perched the photograph on the mantel. "So the six-month-old twins were given away. A boy and a girl. I knew their approximate birth date, and Millie finally discovered that they'd been adopted from Basil House. I found correspondence in Millie's desk between her and the orphanage head. The woman said she was terribly sorry that she couldn't identify the specific children left by the attendant or even tell Millie which ones were siblings. When babies are left, she said, they're simply logged as male or female and given an approximate age, if one is not indicated by a note.

"She had to go through old records to find out who the children were given to, but said that she remembered May of 1895 because it was so unusual to have three sets of twins dropped off within a matter of weeks. Few people want to adopt a pair of children so you were all given away individually." She clasped her hands to her heart. "I'm so pleased that Millie sent for you all. And just so you know, the intention was never to keep you here. Only . . . only to meet you. To know you."

Even Frances looked properly gobsmacked. "Wait, do you mean that—"

"Oh quiet, Frances," Tabitha said. "Let Miss Hattie finish." Her mind spun with the unraveling chain of mysteries. She stared at her fellow invitees, doing a quick mental calculation.

Hattie smiled. "I think you all can guess the rest."

Barnaby and Frances still looked puzzled, their heads tilted at a similar angle.

Viola smiled enormously. "Oh, Edward! Can you imagine, we've known each other our whole lives and never knew!" She rushed to him and threw her arms about his thick frame. "Won't our parents be absolutely thrilled? We're twins!"

"Are we?" Edward asked, pulling away from the embrace, his lips shifting until a studious grin appeared. He straightened his glasses and nodded. "Makes sense, we're very compatible. I couldn't have picked a better sibling if I tried, dear Viola. But I feel like the older twin, just so you know." He winked at Tabitha. "That'll mean I'm in charge."

"Oh, what an awfully nice surprise," Viola continued. "And Barnaby and Frances being redheads," she said. "I expect they're a set as well."

"*Me?* Sister to *that*?" Frances, horrified, drew herself farther into the armchair, as though those precious inches would make the truth false.

Hattie nodded. "It would seem so, dear. You two do look awfully similar."

Edward nodded sagely. "*Awful* indeed. Now that you mention it, those two make even more sense than Viola and me. Franny and Barney are two rotten peas in a spoiled pod."

"B-but I'm a Wellington," Frances sputtered.

Barnaby perked up. "I'm a Wellington too?"

"And she's a Trundle," said Edward pleasantly.

"I most certainly am *not* a Trundle," Frances said. "I refuse to be associated with him. It's simply not true. The only person I could possibly be twins with is myself."

"Bit dim, those two," Edward informed Miss Hattie. "Nasty tempers as well."

But if Barnaby and Frances are truly a pair, and Edward and Viola are a pair, then that means . . .

"So Oliver is my *brother*." Tabitha looked to Hattie for confirmation.

Hattie looked them over, and Tabitha tried to see herself and Oliver from an outsider's perspective. Both tall, gangly, dark-haired children. One well-dressed, one not. One from a loving family, the other . . . not.

Siblings.

Family.

Tabitha felt emotion build behind her eyes at the thought of the word she'd held so dear for so long. It had taken the awfulness of being abandoned for her true family to become clear. Family, it seemed, was not always a matter of who one was born to, or even who one's parents were. A person's *family*, Tabitha realized, was the thing that held them up, so that life could still be illuminated in the darkest of times. A family member could be a mouse. A family member could be an Inspector that nobody would ever meet outside the pages of a novel. Depending on the circumstance, a family member might even be discovered in a person you just met.

"Oliver is my brother." Tabitha let the realization wash over her like a warm bath. *I am not alone.*

With moist eyes, Hattie smiled. "Yes, you two are similar as well."

"Nearly the same haircut," Oliver joked shyly.

"But which pair of us is related to you?" Frances demanded. "Who are your grandchildren? Who gets the money?"

Hattie fixed each of the children with a solid stare, pausing at one face, going back to study another, her brow furrowed in concentration and effort.

All breaths were held.

"Oh dear." She sighed. "I'm afraid I can't be sure."

"You *what?*" Frances shrieked. "Now, you listen here, whatever your real name is, I'll have—"

Simmons entered the library and straightened his coat. "The motorcars have made it through and will be ready to escort Miss Pettigrew to the police station when you're ready. I'll just see to the butler. He appears to be quite shaken but is briefing the other Yard men as best he can. Apparently the imposter woman has stolen a few things. He mentioned missing gallery paintings and a few household items that he suspected she'd taken. The other inspectors have been to the cottage. I'm afraid the Trundles and Crums are gone. They stole one of the motorcars together."

"Gone?" exclaimed Barnaby. "But where?"

Tabitha raised a finger. "You might try Spain."

"Gone," repeated Barnaby, bewildered.

"We'll be after them, never fear," Simmons said. "An inquiry has been placed with the head London constabulary regarding their financial activities. Mr. Trundle was fond of gambling with other people's money, it seems. Spain, you say, Tabitha? I don't suppose you have any other information or documents?"

Tabitha hesitated. The mention of Spain had been a poor slip of the tongue, but she supposed an entire country was roomy enough to keep the Crums at large. Lawfully, she had more information to share, but it seemed wrong to mention documents that were certain to send her parents to jail, were they ever found. After all, Mr. and Mrs. Crum *had* raised her. Surely, a logical and moral person like her beloved Inspector Pensive would not act out of spite.

Because spite could be a slow poison to the heart. If there was a lesson to be learned from Hattie, it was that forgiveness was a blessing. It would be a hard, stubborn thing to harbor ill feelings forever, even toward those who deserved it. . . .

Then again, Tabitha suspected that her parents might logically and morally benefit from being punished. So she nodded. "Bank statements and more. In my carpetbag in the bedroom."

Perhaps the authorities would allow her parents to keep Mr. Tickles in jail with them. After all, the Crums were very fond of him.

"Good for you, Tabitha," Oliver said, patting her arm. "Any parents who plan to send their child to an orphanage belong in jail anyway."

Miss Hattie looked sharply at Tabitha. "What? Is that true?"

"Please, it doesn't matter." But, of course, it did matter, and Tabitha felt her shoulders sink beneath the weight of Hattie's concern. She inclined her head and spoke softly to the floor. "Yes, it's true."

"Well," Agnes said, breaking an awkward silence, "I'll just show Mr. Simmons to Tabitha's room." She smiled shyly at the Scotland Yard man. "If that's quite all right, sir." She gave a little curtsy while Cook frowned at the space between the two of them.

Oliver coughed. "And mine? My parents?" He glanced at Hattie and Tabitha.

"The Applebys and Herringbones and Dales are cooperating fully."

"My parents as well, I'm sure," Frances stated confidently, tossing her hair.

Simmons shifted uncomfortably. "Actually . . ."

Frances stomped her foot. "Actually *what*? Out with it!"

Simmons grimaced. "The Wellington woman got a little agitated while the investigative conversation was taking place. She let it slip that the only crime that's occurred is that someone's stolen the large emerald they were in possession of. She described the stone in detail."

Miss Hattie raised an eyebrow. "You aren't talking about the Lady Envy stone that was stolen from the British Museum recently? That's all over the papers."

Simmons nodded. "The very same."

"You might ask Frances about the missing piece," Viola said jovially. "A big green sparkler, right? I think she might have some answers for you, Mr. Simmons."

"Jail?" Frances's head shot back and forth between Hattie and Simmons. "You're putting my parents in *jail* for a stupid jewel?"

Well. It seemed that Frances wasn't the only thief in her family, and either by coincidence or pure subconscious instinct, Tabitha had suggested that very thing to the false Countess just hours before. *Points to Inspector Crum.*

The library door opened again. The moment Phillips came into the room, a brown dress coat draped over his arm, Mary Pettigrew began flailing and fussing as best she could, wound up in her cocoon.

Still jarred by the presence of his former employer's twin, Phillips did a double take at the sight of Hattie, then bowed. "Madam, the authorities have informed me of the whole situation. I'm so sorry about your sister. Believe me, I was only going along with Mary's ruse under penalty of murder." He looked at Mary Pettigrew and gave a distinct shudder. "You can see that she has no respect for life."

Tabitha thought mournfully of Pemberley.

"Oh, for goodness' sake," Hattie said, looking at Mary Pettigrew. "Simmons, please remove the gag. Let's see what the traitor has to say for herself."

But Mary Pettigrew had no words for Hattie. The first thing she did was work up an impressive amount of saliva and spit it across the floor at Phillips. "She died of a second stroke, you imbecile! I didn't even care by then if the right child was identified, and that smug, rich vulture had it coming, but someone bumped me before I could properly strangle her and then I missed with the candlestick and hit the vase, not her head, didn't I? So nobody killed her."

Phillips shrugged. "Nevertheless, you intended to kill her, and you were the only one in the room who didn't feel a smidgen bad about the death." He glanced at Frances. "Well, perhaps her as well. The children are very lucky," he added to Simmons. "She was planning to off the one who stayed at the manor after getting the inheritance money released."

Mary's voice grew even more shrill and nasty. "You told me you *loved* me, you worthless piece of gristle! This whole thing was your idea! You're the one who found her with that crumpled letter. And yes, maybe I was the one playing a role, but you went along with it. You told the new staff I was the Countess and . . . and you said I looked nice in her dresses."

"Self-preservation, Mary. You threatened me with knives during the day and tied me up at night." He rubbed his wrists, winced, and nodded at Simmons. "It's true."

"Liar!" Mary struggled against her binding. "We'll be rich, you said! Bloody rich enough to have . . . to have . . ." Her voice had developed a quaver, and her angered posture had lost some of its feeling. She collapsed, as much as a woman tied to a chair can collapse. "To have a life together."

It's just like Pensive said in The Gilded Guardian, Tabitha thought. *Money, power, and love, all muddled together.*

"Mary, dear," said Phillips. "Stop lying. I would never have wanted a life with you, even less so after you tried to suck me down into your, how should I phrase it"—he sniffed—"'vortex of filth.' And to think, you told me my accent was charming. Said it was a pity I had to hide it for work. I'd rather have come from a hard place in the East End of London and turn out to be just a butler than be born into the Lake District cooking scene and wind up a would-be murderer. It's you who turned out filthy, Mary."

Mary wept loudly.

East End of London, Tabitha thought. *The posh one isn't his real accent.*

And what is it about that dress coat . . . ?

"Oh, for goodness' sake, I'm putting the gag back in," Cook said, flexing the cloth. She paused only very slightly before bending to the hearth to rub the gag with dirty floor ash.

"Well, I'll just be off now," Phillips said, tipping his brown hat and swinging his suitcase with a certain amount of effort. "Haven't had a proper holiday in fifteen years. No need to drive me, I'll just take the last motorcar."

Haven't had a proper holiday in years . . . why did that sound familiar?

"You'll need to be available for questions over the next day or two," Simmons warned him.

"Oh?" Phillips paused, though his feet continued to alternately shuffle up and back as though he were dancing in place. "Of course, of course. Whatever the investigation calls for, sir. You'll be able to find me at the Hotel McAvoy, glad that I'm no longer having my life threatened. I'm surprised I haven't already fainted from stress." His steps echoed down the hall.

And fainting . . . what of fainting . . .

"Wait!" Tabitha shouted, rushing to Simmons's side. "If Phillips's life was being threatened, why didn't he do something when the Countess fainted—after Millie died?" She turned toward the retreating butler. "As Edward pointed out, he could have easily taken away her knives and tied her up in that moment."

And the Hotel McAvoy, Tabitha thought. *What was it about the Hotel McAvoy?*

"And Phillips doesn't *have* a suitcase here," she said. The Jacket & Hat fellow's telephone voice from the Hotel McAvoy had clicked fully into place. "He left his behind just in case."

"In case of what?" asked Viola.

"Yes, in case of what?" echoed Hattie.

A bitter but anguished cry broke from Mary's throat as she jerked her head back and forth, dodging Cook's gag-filled hands. "Yes, yes, in case of what, Phillips? Phillips, you weren't going to *leave* me, were you?"

Simmons took three steps toward the library's entrance. "Come back for a moment," he called to Phillips, who obediently paused at the doorway. "Where's this suitcase, Tabitha?"

"At the Hotel McAvoy. Waiting to be picked up on the chance that things didn't work out. So he could make an escape, I presume. He was there spying on us the day we all arrived." She looked pointedly at the butler, who had hesitantly stepped back into the library. "You were wearing fancy brown dress shoes when we came to Hollingsworth Hall, Phillips. They matched the jacket and hat you have on right now. At the time, your shoes were all squelchy because you'd been out in the weather. You changed your clothes when you returned to the Hall but neglected to put on your butler shoes when you greeted us, because Mary Pettigrew had shined them up for you and you couldn't find your proper ones. You're wearing them now." She pointed to the simple black pair on his feet.

Hattie frowned. "Whose suitcase is that in his hand, then?"

"That would be my extra one," Frances said. "Cheeky of him."

Oliver let out a cry. "And the motorcar! Phillips must have jammed it—he's already stashed stolen goods in the trunk."

Tabitha clapped him on the back. "That's the way, Tibbs!"

Oliver looked at her. "Tibbs?"

"Never mind, brother. Go on."

He nodded and held up a deducing finger. "He stashed the gallery paintings behind that length of canvas—it's him that's going to steal them."

Barnaby gave a triumphant whoop of glee. "I told you the butler did it! I said it from the start, didn't I?"

"For God's sake, shut up, Barnaby," Frances said. "Somebody stop Phillips. He's nearly out the door with my suitcase!"

For a moment, the only response was an increase in the pace of Phillips's retreating heels. Simmons sprinted to the library door, but before he reached it a decidedly unmanly scream echoed in the foyer, followed by a crash of armor, followed by a cry of pain.

Everyone rushed out to see Phillips flopped on the floor among the scattered metal, his suitcase knocked open, jewelry and small works of art scattered across the floor. The butler rose to his feet, moaning in agony, hands grasping at a glint of metal lodged firmly in his cheek.

"Get him!" shouted Viola.

"Knock him flat," called Edward, wearing a huge grin.

"Death to the butler!" Barnaby joined in, blushing when the others frowned at him.

"Idiot," Frances scoffed, possibly referring to every individual in the manor house.

Simmons tackled him easily. "Got you, naughty fellow. I must say, an escape is no time to be clumsy." Simmons blanched at the sight of Phillips's right cheek. "My God, man. What in the world . . ."

"Rat!" Phillips barked, shivering as his gaze flitted across the floor.

"Rat!" cried Frances, clutching Barnaby's shoulder.

"*Rat?*" said Tabitha, puzzled.

"Rat," Phillips affirmed ruefully. "I was startled by a nasty, filthy rat. And then I was stabbed by *this*. Give me one of my hands back or yank it out yourself." With considerable whimpering, the butler remained still while Simmons pulled the offending object out and held in the air.

The bittern pin.

Tabitha gasped at the sight of it and watched as Hattie pushed through the throng of excitable children to stare at the brass bird. The old woman's mouth dropped open slightly, and her breath made a small rushing noise, not unlike the sound heard when wind changes direction.

"Oh dear," said Hattie, raising a hand to her mouth.

"Oh dear," said Tabitha. Before she could take responsibility for the pin's presence and apologize for the pin-lodged-in-butler's-cheek incident having shocked the poor woman, her stockings caught on the fallen knight's armor. Bending down to free herself, she came nose to nose with an enormous diamond ring. And jammed snugly into the ring was a rather happy-looking mouse.

"Pemberley! You're alive!" Forgetting herself, Tabitha scooped him into her hands, cradling him into her neck as she twirled and cooed and kissed. "Oh, I cannot *believe* it! You weren't crushed after all! You were just knocked out! But how?"

Oliver came over, tickling Pemberley on the back. "Must have been the ring. Nobody could crush his head with a diamond that big sticking up around his neck. Lovely to meet you, Pemberley."

"Oh, you gorgeous, marvelous little mouse! I love you so!"

Tabitha brought him close to her lips and whispered soft promises of happy endings and cheese.

"Rat girl," Barnaby said to his sister Frances, pointing at Tabitha. He snorted. "Tabitha Crum is a rat girl."

Frances snorted back to her brother. "And Oliver Appleby is a rat boy," she agreed. "What a nasty pair they make."

While Simmons tied Phillips up with some kitchen twine fetched by a delighted Agnes ("Can I get you anything else, Inspector?" "I do hope you're staying for the evening meal, Inspector"), the children shuffled back to the library.

Two suited men came in, deftly picking up the chair with Mary Pettigrew and carrying it out as though it weighed no more than a cup of tea.

"What excitement," Viola said, cheeks flushed. "Mummy and Daddy will be thrilled with the whole story!"

"You played quite a role," Tabitha noted, pleased to see her friend turn even more pink. "Tell them everything."

"We'll have to discuss a few things before anybody shares anything about this weekend," Hattie said.

"Oh?" Frances asked. "And what are you going to do to stop me? You received a title from the *King of England* under false pretenses, and you expect us to keep our mouths shut?"

"That's right, shut tight. Just like the bad clam that you are," Cook said. "You know, Miss Wellington, I believe I rather hate you more than the false Countess."

"So do I," Viola blurted out with a mixture of nervousness and delight. "I hate you too!"

"Hear! Hear!" Edward cheered. "Well said, Viola."

Hattie nodded at Simmons, who had appeared in the foyer with Agnes. "Thank you, Cook and Viola, that's much appreciated, but nobody will believe any of this madness, and the Yard will take care of any isolated problems. Cook, would it be awfully troublesome to set up a meal in the dining room?"

Edward leaped up. "I'll help."

Cook gave him a rare smile. "I hope you know how to chop and read a recipe as well as you eat, young man."

"I'll come too," Viola offered.

Cook eyed the remaining children. "Best bring the trouble twins as well. Come along, Frances and Barnaby."

The children followed Cook out of the library, leaving Oliver and Tabitha alone with Hattie. Tabitha eyed Frances Wellington as she left. "I've been thinking, Miss Hattie. And I believe I know where your missing envelope is."

"Where?"

"Behind your Wordsworth. Frances stashed something there."

"Oh? Let's fetch it, then."

Stepping lightly on the ladder, Tabitha pushed herself over to the poetry shelf. There, behind the poetry of William Wordsworth, she found the envelope, which contained a thick stack of paper money.

"There's a letter in there. Why don't you read it?" Hattie suggested, watching Tabitha carefully.

Folded and placed at the end of the bundle was a sheet of paper, yellowed with age. It could almost be mistaken for another bill, and Tabitha guessed that Frances hadn't even noticed it. Unfolding the paper, she read the words aloud, hands and voice having a hard time remaining steady.

Dear Mrs. Darling,

I know that you disapproved of your son choosing to marry me, but you see, when we grew up together and fell in love, we weren't aware of the challenges of class structure. Thomas never meant to hurt you by running away with me, and I never meant to hurt or disrespect you by loving him. We only wanted to start a family of our own. Knowing what I do of your disapproval of the match, I don't wish to burden you with further contact.

Not that it is any of your concern, but the babies are lovely. A boy and a girl who would very much enjoy the company of a grandparent. Perhaps you will meet them one day, if your heart can look beyond your feelings toward Thomas and me. They need a grandmother who can love them as dearly as they deserve, which is an infinite amount.

The post came yesterday, and with it came the

enclosed photograph we sat for just one month ago. Please accept it as a remembrance of me, Thomas, and your grandchildren. I wish you and Aunt Millie the very best. Also, Thomas and I wish to return the complete sum of my wages, in hopes that it will help your disappointment to fade.

—Elizabeth

Tabitha felt the weight of the words. "Forgiveness," she said softly. "They only wanted forgiveness. For wanting a family."

A gentle hand touched Tabitha's shoulder. "I never gave it. Elizabeth acted with such grace, and I never responded to the letter," Hattie said. "I acted so shamefully. And Millie knew how guilty I felt about the whole thing. That's why she didn't consult me before inviting you children. I once told her that if we found my grandchildren, I would have mailed the inheritance rather than face my shame." She shook her head, hands rising to wipe her eyes. "And to think the bittern was here all along. Perhaps she sent it back and Millie never told me. . . ."

Tabitha stiffened. "Do you mean the pin?"

"Yes, I had it sent to Elizabeth when Thomas came to me with his decision to marry her." Hattie shook her head. "It was . . . a symbol of the fact that something beautiful was no more. That she'd taken my son from me forever. I suppose I thought it terribly, fittingly poetic at the time. I thought it would make her rethink the marriage. I can't imagine how it came to be here."

Tabitha's heart quickened. "My mother gave it to me. She couldn't remember where it came from." Her mouth opened. "Miss Hattie . . . might it be my token?"

The color left Hattie's cheeks, and she squeezed Tabitha's hand very tightly. She swallowed twice before speaking. "The bittern belongs to you?"

"No." Tabitha shook her head. "It belongs to *you*. And I brought it back, so you see, the bittern isn't a sign of leaving at all. We were both wrong about that. Elizabeth proved us wrong."

"Pardon, Miss Hattie, but is this yours too?" Oliver slipped a hand in his trouser pocket and took out the small multi-tool, the outside carved with the initials *TSD*. "It was with me at the orphanage. My parents told me it belonged to my father." He squirmed a bit under Tabitha's curious stare. "My parents and I agreed that I shouldn't tell the Countess, in case it was a revealing token. They weren't sure they could trust her." He grimaced. "Seems they were right."

"I don't blame you one bit," Hattie said, reaching for the tool and turning it over in her hands. "Yes. Thomas Sebastian Darling." The smile turned her face into a mass of bittersweet wrinkles, a furrowed garden of regret and delight. "This belonged to my son. The Yard had them made for all the field men. Reginald had one specially made for Thomas the same year that he was killed."

She walked to the fireplace mantel, where she'd set the framed photograph. "And there you two are," she said, placing a finger next to the bassinet. "There is no doubt in my mind now. Tabitha, you are the spitting image of a twelve-year-old Elizabeth. I thought maybe I was just hopeful before. I didn't want to show favoritism. But with the bittern, I feel certain. You are my granddaughter and Oliver is my grandson."

Tabitha's breath caught in her throat as she thought back to dinner the evening they'd arrived. *El . . . beh.* Millie hadn't been telling Tabitha to get her elbows off the dining table, she'd been saying the name *Elizabeth*.

Hattie leaned down until her old tears touched the young cheek. "And I am most glad to finally meet you," she whispered. "And you, Oliver," she said, taking his hand. "You are a fine young man, indeed. You have your father's eyes, my dear boy." She wiped Tabitha's face. "So sorry, dear. There seems to be an extraordinary amount of dust in this room. You may still call me Miss Hattie as we're getting to know each other. All right?"

Tabitha nodded, her own eyes suddenly feeling itchy and moist. "An extraordinary amount of dust," she echoed. Looking at the photograph again, her heartbeat fluttered like a bird.

Like a bittern come back to life.

"Tabitha? Sweetheart, are you well? Is it your ankle? You've been limping."

"My ankle's fine." Tabitha took her grandmother's hand and gave it a squeeze. "I think that perhaps this is what happiness feels like." She looked at her brother's eyes for confirmation, finding it in the flecks of amber and mahogany and grass and honey. "You see," she said softly, "I was very much hoping there would be someone like you both and that we'd find each other one day. I knew it was an impossible hope, but I couldn't seem to give it up."

"Stubbornness," Hattie nodded. "A trait you picked up from your father and grandfather, no doubt."

"What now?" Oliver asked.

"Now? Well, Tabitha will be with me, and Oliver, you will stay with your parents, but I do hope you'll visit. I really don't deserve it, but if you can find it in your hearts to forgive me, I would be eternally grateful. Are you two ready to be a family of sorts once more?"

Tabitha smiled. "I am."

Oliver nodded, relief flooding his cheeks. "I am."

"Good. Because I need help. I've got a most beloved sister to put to rest and a funeral to plan for Camilla Lenore DeMoss, Countess of Windermere. I find that I've grown weary of having this false identity. It's dreadfully tiresome to keep one's true self hidden."

"And we might think of what story we'll be telling to the papers," Tabitha said.

Hattie frowned. "The papers?"

Oliver nodded. "Oh yes, the *Times* wrote a story about the invitations. No doubt they're chomping at the bit to see what's happened. You'd never had visitors, you see, and everyone wants an explanation."

"Ah, yes. Well I suppose I should be grateful, since the Yard wouldn't have sent Simmons if there hadn't been some sort of public fanfare." With a sigh, Hattie tapped at her chin. "I suppose we'll have to write up a statement. I'm not feeling very creative at the moment. Tabitha, you've read enough Pensive to come up with something plausible. I don't suppose you'd do it?"

Tabitha paused, then smiled a very large smile. "I'd be delighted."

24

All's well that ends in a good meal, eh, Tibbs?
Or in your case, a few good meals and a tankard
of milk. Honestly, Tibbs, what kind of fully
grown inspector drinks milk from a tankard?
—Inspector Percival Pensive,
The Case of the Fresh-Faced Foundling

Two weeks later another snowstorm blanketed the Lake District. Green and red Christmas decorations adorned Hollingsworth Hall's interior, pine scent from endless garlands filled the air, and the drawing room Victrola was turned up to its highest volume, carrying holiday cheer throughout the manor. Tabitha's grandmother sat beside her on the library's sofa, reading the newspaper, taking care not to lose the place in the overturned Inspector Pensive novels scattered along the cushions.

"What are you knitting, Tabitha?" Hattie asked. "Oliver and Viola and Edward will be over for the weekend soon. Cook said the luncheon is nearly ready, so you can go wash up. She

21

made an enormous cake, just like the one she made for your birthday. Oh! Hello, Pemberley," she said, stroking the head of the mouse who was seated on an end table, nibbling from his very own dish.

"Will they be here soon? I've lost track of the time."

Frances and Barnaby would be unable to attend the small reunion, to the delight of the others. Barnaby had been taken in by an uncle who'd promptly sent him to boarding school, and Frances had only one distant relative, a missionary who was overjoyed to learn that fresh help would be sent to live with her in a remote South American village.

Tabitha lifted the length of blue scarf. "And this is for Oliver—a late birthday present." She turned at the creaking of the library's double doors. "Oh, hello, Cook. Hello, Agnes. I'm just coming."

"We're just checking to see that you weren't lost in a book again," said Agnes. "You've missed five meals in the last fortnight."

"Sorry about that. What's the cake for, Cook? Are we celebrating something?"

"We're celebrating the demise of Camilla DeMoss, of course. Nasty woman, at least the one I knew." Cook blushed. "Begging your pardon, ma'am. You and your sister would have been quite different, I'm sure."

"Thank you, Cook," said Hattie with a smile. "And I *do* hope you and Agnes will join us wherever we end up. I'll pay you generously, and we can discuss any benefits you have in mind. Tabitha was quite right in telling me that your cooking is divine."

The blush deepened, and Cook exchanged glances with Agnes, who was nodding an emphatic *yes*. "We'll certainly discuss it, ma'am."

"Wisely done," Tabitha said after the two left the room. "They seem an awfully close pair."

"Yes, and I thought it prudent to keep them nearby for a bit. Don't want any secrets getting out. Tell me, Tabitha, what do you think of their natures? Your grandfather had wonderful instincts for reading people."

Tabitha sighed and frowned a little. "I suppose I'm not good at reading people at all. I had all sorts of things running through my head two weeks ago. I would have let Phillips off the hook, though I suppose he gave me a funny feeling right from the beginning. A tingle of some sort. And the Countess—Mary Pettigrew—as well. She seemed off, but I got the whole business dreadfully mixed up."

"First cases are meant to be bumbled a bit." Hattie leaned over her, reaching for a small handle attached to the side table. "Just a moment." She pulled a blank envelope from the drawer and waved it in the air. "For you, Miss Tabitha. A late birthday present."

"What is it?"

Hattie winked. "Could be anything. But before you open it, read this." She handed Tabitha the newspaper. "They've run your statement in the *Times* again with another article."

"Have they?" Tabitha took the paper and smiled at the headline.

BRITAIN STILL BAFFLED OVER COUNTESS'S STATEMENT, LACK OF HEIR, GIFTED INHERITANCE, DEATH

In what can only be described as the most anticipated news story of 1906, Camilla DeMoss, Countess of Windermere, invited six young children to her manor last month. Rumors have abounded as to the cause, with speculation ranging from Countess DeMoss naming an heir to her fortune, to an obscure form of lunacy, to a failed mass murder plot.

The attendees have been sworn to silence, and eyewitness accounts by those who have broken the Countess's request have been deemed false and inadmissible by the Metropolitan Police Service. The only thing the *Times* can report with certainty is that the weekend has resulted in the Countess's death, the jailing of six citizens, and a very large sum of money being given to the Dale family of London.

In a fateful and bizarre turn of events, the Countess of Windermere wrote the following formal statement only hours before her unfortunate demise:

I, Camilla Lenore DeMoss, have invited several children and parents to Hollingsworth Hall, and I'm certain that the whole of England is wondering what such an eccentric old woman could be up to. In the event of my untimely demise, I shall set it down on paper so that the truth may eventually be known about me.

The truth is that I am a lonely soul. Since the death of my husband, sister, and son, I have felt anger and fear at times. I have no heirs, and my solitary place in life is my own creation. My only solace is in giving money away to charities, in hopes that the pounds will do the good that I have failed to do myself over the years.

I find myself nearing the end of my days, and I question what it is that I find important. The answer is family. Though I am rich and titled, the one thing I long for cannot be bought or earned. I invited the children because I missed witnessing life. I missed my family and I hoped to catch a glimpse of them in others.

I write this note on Sunday morning, after a highly successful weekend. In a world beset by crimes committed in the name of money and power and love, it can be tempting to trade hope for seclusion. This weekend I've been lucky enough to mingle with the better side of human nature. I have seen compassion, loyalty, courage, and friendship. Most importantly, I've found peace and release in the most difficult of acts: forgiveness.

Do follow my lead, dear Britain, and forgive me my reclusive ways. In the name of family and forgiveness, I have earmarked the bulk of my remaining monies, one hundred thousand pounds, to begin a progressive foundation that people can apply to for help, servicing a variety of organizational and individual needs. I hereby name Miss Viola Dale as chief executor of the funds.

Camilla Lenore DeMoss

Countess of Windermere

The Countess of Windermere was found dead of natural causes on Sunday afternoon by the children, who have no doubt been scarred into the realm of making up fantastic stories.

"Fantastic stories," Hattie said, leaning over Tabitha's shoulder. "That, my dear, is true enough."

Tabitha gave a final glance to the article. "It's a shame about my parents, isn't it? Pity they were both assigned to work in the prison kitchen. Mum and Daddy hate dish duty."

The Crums had been caught boarding a ship to Spain and were charged with years of petty theft and bank fraud. There had been a riotous chase scene up the gangplank and Mrs. Crum had toppled overboard, breaking her nose and shoulder when she belly flopped into the ocean. Mr. Crum had left her and made it aboard the *Lady of Spain*, where he collided with a shoe-shine boy, resulting in a most unfortunate lodging of the boy's polishing brush in a most unfortunate place on Mr. Crum's person.

"It was very lucky, though, that the lead policeman's daughter wanted a cat. They'll take comfort in knowing that Mr. Tickles is well cared for. And the Trundles are only a few cells over. Surely they'll have meals together now and then."

"Well, sometimes fair is fair, Tabitha," Hattie said. "And now, for your envelope. Several weeks ago you received one from my sister, because she knew that I might not have the courage to send it myself. So here's one that I've put together on my own."

Tabitha smelled the paper, just as she had done with the first envelope. What was it she had wished for?

A summons from Scotland Yard to become an Inspector-In-Training.

An invitation from King Edward to attend and gamble on a horse race.

Notification from a long-lost relative who actually wants me and wouldn't view me as an imposition.

One wish fulfilled out of three wasn't bad at all. She held her breath a moment before tearing the seal open. At the sight of the envelope's contents, her mouth dropped fully open.

"Let me guess," Hattie said. "It's a written declaration from me, saying that you can be my Inspector-in-Training."

"Please tell me that you're being perfectly serious," Tabitha whispered.

Her grandmother smiled. "Well, it's a bit unofficial for now," Hattie allowed. "Just you and me. But since, in addition to devising a successful plan to disable Miss Pettigrew, you were instrumental in bringing in the Lady Envy thieves, I think you're ready to learn a few tricks of the trade."

Tabitha nodded happily.

Hattie patted her hand. "Now, I want it to be perfectly clear that I'm not forcing you into the family business. A proper guardian wants only health and happiness for their child, even if that means they stray from the paths we try to set for them. A lesson learned too late for me, due to a mistake I don't intend to repeat. Some parents try to create small version of themselves—a ploy at an extended life, I suppose. But"—she held up a finger—"a child is ultimately and always their own person with their own choices, and I would never presume to—"

"Rest assured, Grandmother, I *choose* to be an Inspector," Tabitha said, hugging the note to her chest. *That's two of the three. Hmm.* "Grandmother, just how well do you know King Edward?"

"Why do you ask?"

"I just thought maybe you might fancy a horse race and a little gambl—"

A door knocker sounded, and Tabitha jumped up. "They're here!"

"So." Hattie clapped her hands. "Quickly, one more piece of business before you young ones tear up my secret passages and mess about with the disguises in Thomas's bedroom. The paperwork has come through, and the will of Camilla DeMoss sends our remaining funds to a numbered account in Switzerland. I caught word of their splendidly quiet banking and chose a small outfit in Zurich. That shall be our first stop. We'll sell Hollingsworth Hall and all of its contents during our absence. Millie was always fond of buying nonsense for the house, including that dreadful front door knocker, but I'll be glad to leave it all behind. Having done away with my alias, I think it's best to make a fresh beginning somewhere else. After all, there are far worse things than starting over."

"*Far worse things*," Tabitha murmured. "Do you know something? I actually think it's not a very good use of my time to think of *far worse things*. From now on, I shall keep a list of *few better things*."

"Sorry?" Hattie turned in her couch seat.

"Yes," Tabitha continued. She placed a pen in her mouth as a pipe and paced back and forth. "For instance, there are *few better things* than:

- unexpectedly receiving an envelope on a foggy day
- being thrust into a genuine mystery
- finding out that the people you've been spending time with are *friends* . . ."

"Any others?" Hattie asked, a bemused look upon her face.

Tabitha took a puff of her pen and nodded decidedly. "Yes," she said, marching within inches of Hattie. "Finding a grandmother. There are *few better things* than finding out that you have a grandmother. Especially one who's not a reformed or current murderess." She darted forward and placed a playful kiss on Hattie's forehead.

"Well," Hattie said, a delighted flush making its way to her cheeks. "Well."

"Can Pemberley come to Zurich?"

"Of course! We shall have to get him a friend. Perhaps a lady mouse. You're certain Pemberley is a he?"

Tabitha blushed. "I really wouldn't know anything about it. He always seemed like a he."

Her grandmother winked. "We'll have someone find out. If that appears to be the case, perhaps we'll get Pemberley a companion and see if we can't breed a new generation. Yes, Tabitha Darling, I'm awfully fond of new generations, and I'm far more fond of mice than cats. Cats were always Millie's preference. I'm so glad the Herringbones and Dales thought of giving the royalty to orphanage children."

"Sorry, what did you call me?"

"Tabitha Darling. Do you mind very much taking on your original last name?"

Tabitha shook her head. "Not at all." It was hard to believe that she was no longer an unloved Crum. But really, she had never been unloved. Just misplaced for a bit. "Though once I make it as a Scotland Yard inspector, I may have to change it to Tabitha Mysterioso or Tabitha Clevertop."

"Tabitha Clevertop?" Hattie frowned.

"Only joking." Tabitha leaned into her grandmother, curling into the welcoming warm body like a child who was making up for lost years. Which she was. "I know names aren't important. It's the person behind them."

"That's right, love."

"But just so you know," Tabitha clarified, "it feels awfully nice to be a Darling."

And with that, Tabitha Darling pecked her grandmother's cheek and dashed away to join her friends. If everything went according to plans made via vigorous letter writing the week before, they would spend a glorious weekend eating splendid food, pelting one another with snowballs, exploring passages, and perhaps, if Oliver was still up for it, sneaking a motorcar out for a drive.

Acknowledgments

Thanks to a case of overwhelming gratitude, I am pleased to share a nonexclusive list of the dear people who helped mold an idea into a manuscript, then signed on to transform that manuscript into this book. They are, in no particular order:

TINA WEXLER

Heir to a jumble of innumerable, yet-unsent, messages asking for advice on everything from story ideas to pizza suggestions, this literary agent is exceptionally quick-witted, good-natured, and wise. She is known to have vast reserves of patience that she keeps in a secret vault somewhere in New York City.

KRISTIN OSTBY

A Michigander and selective hoarder of authors and illustrators, this fiercely intelligent editor spends her time poring over pages and finding magical ways of improving them with a keen eye and open heart. She is a literary detective whose ability to boldly untangle stories, discovering their essential threads, is admired and coveted by many. She is also very kind and very funny and very fond of animals.

LUCY RUTH CUMMINS

This book designer is known for taking marvelous amounts of care with stories and artists, combing over pages, sketches, photographs, and layouts to create unique reading experiences. Her savvy and style impact an incredible breadth of books. It is a gift to have her expertise touch these pages.

NATALIE ANDREWSON

An artist of many talents, this woman has an uncanny ability to read about characters and bring them to life on the page. Her eye for color and line is unparalleled, and her depiction of a rather motley young girl and a beloved mouse has brought the author of this book countless grins of delight.

JUSTIN CHANDA AND EVERYONE AT SIMON & SCHUSTER BOOKS FOR YOUNG READERS

Innovative and adventurous, here is a group of people who dedicate themselves daily to both readers and writers. The book lovers of the world (and the author of this novel in particular) are fortunate to have them in the publishing business.

JOY MCCULLOUGH-CARRANZA, TARA DAIRMAN, BECKY WALLACE, ANN BEDICHEK, MELODIE WRIGHT

These cheeky, brilliant, lovely, honest, story-loving ladies were early readers of this tale and are well known throughout the author's household for their ability to induce giggles, admiration, and much revision. They are, in no uncertain terms, the very best sort of society.

The author will continue to offer her appreciation for the above list of people with all due fortitude. As Inspector Percival Pensive might say, they are "the sort of company that one invites to dinner, splurging ridiculously on the food and drink in hopes that they'll tell stories long into the evening, perhaps staying on through breakfast. Ah, breakfast; a lovely sort of meal, don't you think?"

Turn the page for a sneak peek
at Jessica Lawson's next novel,
Waiting for Augusta,
available now.

The Lump

Last month Mama caught me rubbing my neck. Even though I told her what I guessed was wrong, she snatched me over to Dr. Landry, Daddy's tumor doctor before he died, who said there wasn't a thing the matter with me. When I told *him* what I thought the problem was, he gave me a funny look and told Mama maybe I should "go see a different kind of doctor."

Next Mama took me to Dr. Temple, who I'd been going to my whole life for checkups. He was Daddy's and Uncle Luke's doctor when they were young and said maybe it was that awful Adam's apple of the Putter boys, gurgling around before it got ready to spring itself on the world during puberty. "Putter boys might end up small," he told me, "but they've got overzealous larynxes to make up for it." Then he snatched my drawing pad away and said I needed to get outside more.

Then Mama took me to Dr. Bartelle, a head doctor who

goes to our church, who said with a whole bunch of head nodding and chin stroking that my neck rubbing was a cry for help. "You're too quiet for an eleven-year old boy, living in your head too much. You better work through whatever feelings are rattling around up there or you're liable to go crazy like my sister Bernice did over her no-good boyfriends." Then he told me that I wouldn't be able to let Daddy go until I'd had a good cry about it.

"Yes, sir," I'd answered. I didn't have the heart to tell Dr. Bartelle that when it came to Daddy, it was like me holding a golf club. I'd never really gotten the grip down, and it was hard to know the proper way of letting go of something when you were never holding it right in the first place.

After the appointments, I didn't tell a soul about the lump in my neck, even though I knew by then exactly what it was. Nobody would have believed me anyway. In the month after Daddy passed, everyone except Mama seemed to be going about their business, sucking down the sky like it was a glass of strained lemonade. Nice big lump-free gulps. Sure, every now and then I'd get a pat on the head and someone saying "You poor, poor thing" or "You poor, poor boy," but that wasn't gonna help a thing. Plus, it didn't seem too nice to rub in the fact that Daddy never made much money and any extra he had mostly went toward hitting balls at the driving range and walking rounds of eighteen holes.

So I didn't say another word about the lump, but there

was no doubt in my mind that I had a golf ball trapped in my throat. Maybe it didn't show up on any X-ray, but I knew it was in there. Hiding inside me like it was waiting for something.

And you know what?

I was right.

Honey Air and Lightning

Alabama's heat started waking up and stretching around the same time Daddy died, and by the first full week of April it'd gotten good and dressed. Overdressed, I'd say, with the golf club thermometer stuck to the hog shed filled up just past the ninety line. A record high, the radio had declared, the afternoon announcer saying that if he were still a boy, he'd have ditched school for the pool on this steaming pot roast of a Tuesday, and thank goodness a battalion of storm clouds was heading our way to cool things down. Between the heat and the thunder grumbling and the lightning flashing on the horizon, it wasn't the best of evenings for running away, if a person was thinking about doing that sort of thing. Which maybe I was.

With a heave, I hauled open the iron lid of the backyard smoker and caught a blast of fiery air and sizzling pork scent. Eyes stinging, I turned and shook my left arm's day-old burn, trying to ignore the way the raw spot flared and shouted *Hey, you! Watch it this time!* when it neared the burning coals. Grabbing the metal grabbers, I loaded up our double-deep pan with good hunks of pig and waded down the side yard through air thick as honey, careful so I'd spill nothing more than a little of the juice. House rent was on that tray—might as well have been bundles of money instead of meat.

Even though our barbecue didn't compare to when Daddy manned the big pit, and even though we had to set up business in the front yard when we were short on a café payment after he died, we still got a steady set of regulars and word-of-mouthers right at our house between noon and seven or so at night. The bank may have taken back the café property, but it couldn't take away our barbecue. Sauce and sympathy were keeping us afloat.

I plopped the pan on the wooden saucing table tucked off the front porch near the side hose, where we'd taken to finishing the meat before putting it in the public eye, and swiped my arm across my forehead. Salty sweat got into my burn, but I held off hollering. Mama was already worried that she left me alone with the smoker too much, and she was close by on the porch, cutting pieces of sheet cake while she minded the cash box and her long table of side dishes.

"Benjamin, you hurry up now and slather those good!"

"Yes, Mama." Dipping a paintbrush into a bucket of ketchup, chili powder, vinegar, paprika, crushed mustard seed, little bit of cayenne, chicory, and brown sugar, I slathered those ribs up and down like I was painting a fence, which was the only kind of art Daddy ever approved of. He was a golf and barbecue man through and through. Both took plenty of time and focus, he said.

"Get 'em nice and red," someone called from one of the four picnic tables set up in the front yard. "Sure is fine, your mama's sauce."

"Sauce was Daddy's," I muttered to the ribs, even though they knew it already. We were almost through his supply and he'd never bothered to write down his exact recipe, so the Putter flavor was bound to change. I dipped two more brushfuls and took my time making the color nice and even.

Poking into my eye corners were the orange and yellow from our neighbor's tulip poplars and white from her magnolia trees that hung over into our yard. Flower colors in Mrs. Grady's yard were always better and brighter than anything in my art box, but I wasn't much impressed by flowers lately. Didn't even care about the ones that smelled like Erin Courtney, who sat in front of me in class and had the nicest hair I'd ever seen.

No, today those petals and leaves whispered together in the hot wind, saying *There's Ben Putter, he's got a golf ball right in his throat, see him rubbing at it with his free hand, do you see him, he's got no friends, no he doesn't, yes, I see him, how about you, why yes, I see him, too . . .*

"You all hush," I told those leaves and petals, picking up the pan and walking past the tables to Mama. The ribs were heavy, and I was glad to set them down next to bowls of Mama's beans and potato salad. I wondered who'd help her with everything if I went running. I rubbed the lump in my throat and wondered who'd help me get back to normal if I didn't.

"Lemonade, Benny," Mama told me, her elbow digging into my side and her head jerking toward the road. "Get a glass for Mr. Talbot and May when you're done filling at the tables, won't you?" She pointed to the brown truck coming down our dirt street. "And tell Mr. Talbot that I've got a big package of pork made up for his family." Her eyes drifted to the top of the house. "It was beyond kind of Rudolph to fix that roof leak."

When I saw the distant, approaching outline of May Talbot sitting beside her daddy in the passenger seat, I swallowed hard and felt the golf ball lump rotate in my throat. I wondered if she'd asked to come along. My chest went tight and the banging inside it sped up, from nerves or hope. Both maybe. "Yes, ma'am."

"I put your paint pad and drawing book on the kitchen table, in case you were looking, sweetheart," Mama said, lowering her voice, though the twelve or so customers were out of earshot, scattered among the tables down in the yard, eating and talking and fanning themselves with hats or whatever was handy. "You know you don't need to hide them in the sofa cushions." *Anymore*, she didn't add, but I still heard it. "And that art teacher of yours called again. Miss Stone, right? You really need to call her back, okay?"

Clearing her throat, she called out, "I declare, it's hot as Georgia out here. Who wants more lemonade? Quarter a cup with a refill, good and fresh, coming right up." She waved and smiled at Mr. Talbot as he drove up our long driveway that circled around back to the hog shed, hauling the pig we'd ordered. A few customers turned toward the vehicle, and I watched their faces, saw eyes narrow or drift back to plates, saw lips get tight while they stared or looked away fast, saw within moments what kind of difference, if any, it made to them that the Talbots were colored.

By the time I looked at the truck, my hand ready to jump up in a careful wave, May's eyes were aimed straight ahead. They'd been aimed straight ahead for the last four months. I didn't know what I could do to get my friend back. I just knew that things weren't the same, and a glass of lemonade wasn't gonna change that.

After I'd mixed two new batches, I walked the picnic tables and tipped the lemonade pitcher for two men I knew from town and four dusty-clothed workers who looked to be from the railroad yard. Hobo workers, Grandma Clay had called them, back when she was alive, though Mama always hushed her and said traveling railroad hobos died out long ago.

"Hey, son."

"You sure are looking like your daddy."

"Thank you, kindly, boy."

People knew I hadn't said much at all since Daddy passed, so I felt fine letting one nod do for answering all their chatter. All those men loved him. He'd always been there at the end of their work days, handing them good food to make the body aches fade, listening to their talk and then cracking enough jokes to make their troubles disappear just a little.

My eyes wandered around the side yard to see Mr. Talbot heaving the pig off his truck bed, then I refilled the paper cups of two men, a woman with tired eyes, and a dirty-looking kid who didn't appear to be with anyone in particular. Maybe she was one of the railmen's daughters.

The girl was around my age, maybe a little younger. She looked up at me with sauce all over and big mean eyes like I'd spit in her drink. I refilled it anyway.

Pouring two fresh cups, I kept my feet moving, my gaze grazing the fence that separated our front yard from Mrs. Grady's. The same kind of fences were just about everywhere in Hilltop, lining the roads and splitting yards, but they weren't proper barriers. They were nothing more than a post every twelve feet with two lengths of raw wood between and didn't keep a thing in or out.

The Talbots were both waiting outside the shed. Looking in the open doors, I saw the hog had been placed on the three-foot-high cutting station that had catch drains all around it. "Thanks, Mr. Talbot." I handed him the lemonade.

He took the glass and squinted sweat out of his eyes. "You're welcome. You need help cutting him up?"

It was the same question he'd asked since Daddy died. "No, thank you. Mama has a package of pork for you." I looked at May's shining shoes and passed her the second cup, feeling her fingers brush against mine as she took it and thanked me. It was a polite but faraway kind of thank-you—the kind I'd heard her use with the teachers at school who'd made it clear they didn't want her there.

"That's fine. You and May catch up for a minute."

Mr. Talbot's tall form walked around the side of the house, and May and I were alone. She was dressed real nice, like she always was, and I was suddenly shy of my ash-stained clothes. Don't know why I felt that way. She'd seen me like that about a million times. "Hot today," I said.

"Mm-hm."

"You draw anything lately?"

"Maybe," she said, tugging at one ear.

May was good at art. The first time we'd met was when we were both five years old and Mr. Talbot had brought a hog over to the café. I was around back, trying to make watercolors from a load of Popsicles that hadn't made it to our freezer in time and were too melted to sell. She sat right beside me, and I handed her a stick brush and a piece of paper. She took them, and that was that.

Since then, we'd seen each other at least twice a month during deliveries. As her daddy and my daddy had gotten to know each other, the deliveries had turned into short visits, and May and I had worked our way up from making Popsicle paintings to taking walks and tossing rocks in the nearby streambed. We even made plans to meet at a spot at the creek on some Saturdays.

We'd sit and draw. We'd talk or not talk. Sometimes she'd write words beside her sketches and paintings, cross some out, leaving just a few to make the picture into a story. *Water, rock, hand, splash. Pecans, trees, basket, pie. Crane, frog, dive, dinner.* She was the best friend I had in the world, and the day I told her that, she'd said I was hers, too.

But all that had changed over the last year. I wished there was a way of going back to before.

"I'm thinking about running away for a time," I told her, the words spilling out before I could remind them that May and me weren't the same anymore.

A hint of light hit her eyes, and they flashed. "What problems could you have to run away from?" Her tight mouth burst open and formed a delicate O. One of her hands lifted to cover it. "I mean . . . well, other than your daddy passing. Never mind. I'm sorry about your daddy."

I shrugged. The truth was, I felt squeezed. Hilltop felt a

whole lot smaller with Daddy gone. Seems like some space should've cleared up with one less person, but I felt tight all over. That darn lump needed to bust outta my throat, darn toes wanted to bust outta my shoes. Seemed like my whole self wanted to bust out of my insides altogether. I didn't want to run away forever. Just for now. Something had been pulling on me since Daddy died, and whatever it was, it wasn't in Hilltop.

She frowned at my neck. "Why do you keep scratching at your throat like that?"

I dropped my hand as Mr. Talbot came around the house corner. We had maybe a few more seconds when it was just us. Sweat was dripping down my forehead and back, and whatever pressure was bubbling inside me couldn't hold back any longer. It had to come out somehow, and it came out with—

"I don't know what I'm supposed to do. It's like everything's changing and I . . . I just don't know what to do." The ground was a comfortable place to look, so I shoved what felt like my whole self in that direction. I raised my head a couple of feet to meet the answer halfway.

"Well," she said, arms wrapping around her waist as her father approached. "Maybe you changed, too."

My ears got hot first, then my cheeks and neck.

Mr. Talbot's hand squeezed my shoulder on the way to his truck. "'Bye, now, Ben. May, let's go, honey."

She stared me in the eyes while Mr. Talbot opened the driver's door and motioned her around the other side. Then she walked away.

I lifted my chin and blinked at the gray-whites and dark blues smeared rough across the sky like brushstrokes being blown straight into Hilltop. Straight into me.

"'Bye," I finally said, staring at the side of May's face as the truck passed by me. She turned in her seat and watched me, her brown eyes soft and wanting, mad and sad and disappointed, and I think that maybe she looked through my body and saw my insides as the Talbots drove away. She was the only one who'd always seen me, and she was leaving.

I decided right then, for certain, that it was time for me to leave, too.

Join Megan, Cassidy, Emma, and Jess as they experience the ups and downs of middle school along with their favorite classic literary characters!